THE
LINES
OF
HAPPINESS

About the Author

Venetia Di Pierro grew up in the city of Melbourne in Victoria, Australia. She belongs to writers' groups and book clubs and has a writing and publishing degree. She currently works in the corporate world and wrote *The Lines of Happiness* in the car on her lunch breaks. She laughs easily, especially at herself, and believes what you set your mind to you can achieve. She can usually be found reading, writing, running, or spending time with friends and family. She thinks the most important thing in the world is love and living every day to the fullest. She lives with her son and daughter, overflowing bookshelves and a few too many pot plants.

THE
LINES
OF
HAPPINESS

VENETIA DI PIERRO

BELLA
BOOKS
2022

Bella Books, Inc.
P.O. Box 10543
Tallahassee, FL 32302

Printed in the United States of America on acid-free paper.

First Edition - 2022

Editor: Heather Flournoy
Cover Designer: Kayla Mancuso
Photo credit: Nick Walters (www.nickwalters.com.au)

ISBN: 978-1-64247-355-1

For Anita

CHAPTER ONE

Wyoming
1998

Only that morning Gloria had been folded over a donut and gritty coffee in the airport lounge, waiting for her flight departing Melbourne to be called for boarding. She had spent the long-haul flight and every stopover with herself and she was getting sick of her own company. By Jackson Hole Airport, she was trying to use this as evidence to convince herself that everyone she'd run away from would also be relieved, but it was a tenuous line she was drawing. The more distance she put between her future and her past, the better. Being on the road was easier, the bus—so different from the buses back home—full of locals with their TV-like accents and the foreign scenery a distraction from the on-again, off-again love affair she was having with herself. She was strong and independent. No, she was weak and cowardly. It continued beneath the dirty plastic of the bus depot shelter as she waited for the taxi to take her to her destination, a place she could only imagine based on films and books she had read as a child. The thought made her heart skitter and sent her longing back across oceans toward a home she couldn't go back to. She jerked her head as the bus officer leaned out of his building to wave and point toward a cab. Gloria picked up her suitcase and made her way to what she hoped would be the final journey into a new life.

It was just her luck to get a chatty driver, a thin nervous man who kept restlessly flicking radio stations and stopping midsentence to change topic, then double back to his original subject. He was still going as they left suburbia behind, making Gloria long for the anonymity of the bus with its sooty language of squeals and hisses. Again, there was an abrupt turn of conversation, and the driver craned around to look at her, his milky brown eyes finding hers for long enough that Gloria was nervous he would swerve off the road. "You heard about it, I guess? I mean, if you're going there you know. Quite a while ago now, but it's still fresh. You never really get over something like that." She didn't confirm that she knew, but he continued anyway, glancing at the road ahead then back at her in the rearview mirror. "The family, my father went to school with Peter's father. A good family, even though I don't really know them personally—well, just a bit—you hear things, you know? It's a shame what happened to the little one."

"The little one?" Gloria echoed.

"Dolores used to be so…robust, that's it. A good-looking lady, too, but I don't think she's left the ranch since. What I heard is they ain't opening up the guesthouses this spring. A real shame, because it brought a lot of tourism to the area too, see? Now, I shouldn't pry, but makes me wonder if they might open them up again. That why you headed there?"

"Not exactly." Gloria's straight eyebrows pulled together and she looked back out the window at the green stretch of land. She'd forgotten how small towns worked, the way gossip scorched the ground like wildfire. She was curious about the family she would soon be living among, but she knew the value of privacy so she didn't provoke further dialogue on the matter.

"If you look up ahead to the left you should see it. Something, isn't it? Look at all that corn! Do you know how many products contain corn syrup? Much more than you'd think."

The car carried them down a hill, and there in the expanse of blue-green was a house, set back behind long fields, the mountains glowering shadowy in the background. Along one side of a hill was a row of evenly spaced wooden cabins of varying sizes, and beyond them impossibly neat rows of green maize leaves curling their way toward the sun.

Gloria's stomach pulled tighter on the knot it had been forming. The house in the distance was becoming a reality. She felt in her pocket for the dog-eared letter that had kept her company since she'd left Melbourne. Although it didn't say much, it provided tangible reassurance that there would be something to catch her on the other side of her journey.

"You're not here for a vacation then?" the driver asked.

"No."

"Friends?"

"Work."

The driver's eyes found Gloria's, but she looked out the window at the black pines against the skyline. He drew a breath, but something stopped him and he left the rest of his thought unsaid. The road continued to roll away, bearing them closer to the ranch. The driver—he'd said his name was Sam or Steve but she couldn't remember—burst into conversation again, the way someone might burst into song, something about a hot air balloon shaped like a hotdog. Outside, horses grazing in the fields flicked their ears at the passing car but didn't stir, and overhead the sky arched a thoughtful blue, pulling the land in close and dappling the ground in cloud shadow. The car's indicator clicked despite the emptiness around them, and they turned onto a dirt road. Above, a large wooden sign hanging on rusty chains from two towering poles declared the property *Heaven's End*.

Gloria rolled the window down, the smell of wild grass and cold mountain air rushing at her, searing her nostrils and catching in her lungs as though they'd never breathed before. She felt lost under the vastness of it all, and it was terrifying and exactly what she wanted. It felt good to let someone else do the driving, and she didn't even mind as the car sped a little too fast down the dirt road, slowing abruptly as the brown house that had seemed like a wooden toy from the road loomed over them. It had arrived at her so fast that she hadn't gathered her thoughts, so she hastily opened the letter and scanned the top lines again. A rangy, spotted dog wandered out to investigate and Gloria pitched forward as the car halted to allow it passage. Rather than traveling the next few yards toward the wooden porch, the driver pulled on the handbrake and turned expectantly toward Gloria.

"That'll be forty-two dollars, miss."

"Oh, they said…" She looked toward the entrance to the house. "I hope someone's home." She'd been puzzling over the cab fare on and off since before she'd even left the bus. She still hadn't drawn a conclusion other than the letter said they would take care of all her expenses, including travel, a big draw when she was traveling all this way. Forty-two dollars was a lot of money, close to all that she had.

Beside the house was a beautiful oak tree, and hanging from one of its outstretched arms was a tire knotted to a long rope. Gloria suddenly wanted to know about the "little one," but before she could ask, the screen door flapped open and a thin woman appeared clutching a long knitted cardigan around herself. She slipped into leather boots by the door and clipped down the pine steps to greet them. Gloria opened the car door and stepped out, her legs feeling weak on firm ground. She smiled and kept it pasted to her face even though the woman didn't return the gesture. A flash of déjà vu gripped her, pulling her back through her memories to place the woman's face. She drew a blank, but the feeling persisted.

"Sorry, we're not taking guests this spring." The woman's hazel eyes were guarded and she placed a soothing hand on the dog's neck as he came to stand beside her. Her voice was like a slurp of treacle, full and slow, but her face had a sharp look which belied her gentle tone. Her skin had the yellow undertone of a suntan left to fade, fine freckles dusting the bridge of her straight nose, and her messy hair was a mixture of reds and golds that reminded Gloria of autumn. Disheveled as she was, her movements carried an unselfconscious grace that instantly made Gloria conscious of her own gawkish actions.

"No…I'm Gloria Grant." Gloria hoped the words would be the magic salve to soothe the confusion, but she could see by the woman's expression that it only added to it.

The woman blinked at Gloria for a moment, then looked out toward the road, then back at Gloria. Her long fingers stroked the dog's neck thoughtfully. Behind them the driver opened the door and came around to retrieve Gloria's suitcase from the trunk. The seconds stretched before she addressed Gloria. "Did Peter tell you to come?"

Gloria reached into her jacket pocket to retrieve the worn piece of paper. Her hands shook as she unfolded it. "Here." She held it toward the woman, but the woman glanced at it without taking it.

"Oh, Jesus." She took a deep breath and looked out over the fields as though searching for the fortitude to help her deal with what she had to say. "I'm sorry to tell you that you've come out here under false pretenses." Her gaze returned, falling to Gloria's suitcase with its airline tags still clutched in the driver's hand. She sighed. "But I think I can see what's happened and I guess you'd better come inside."

Sam, or Steve, glanced anxiously between the two of them, quieter than he had been the whole drive, one hand scratching his forearm although Gloria was sure nothing was itching him except the awkwardness of the moment. The woman's eyes flashed with understanding. "Give me a moment and I'll find payment. Steven, how much do we owe you?" Steve mumbled a figure and the woman shook her head to herself as she turned and resolutely clomped back up the stairs.

Gloria stood by the car, watching the wind rippling through the long grass and feeling as though her heart might be swept away with it. Helpless humiliation was a feeling from childhood that she avoided visiting but which stubbornly seemed to find her. She turned to the driver. "It's okay, I'll fix you up." She put her hand into her pocket and pulled out the last wad of notes she had.

The screen door banged again. "No, here. If Peter caused this mess, he can damn well clean it up." The woman was holding a fistful of notes. "Steven, how is your mother?"

"Doing good since the treatment, thanks for remembering, Dolores."

The woman nodded. "Glad to hear it." She looked up at Gloria and said curtly, "I'm Dolores, but please call me Lo." She pronounced it "Low." Despite her messy hair and odd arrangement of clothing, her voice had a steady authority.

"Pleased to meet you. I'm Gloria." She realized she'd already said that but didn't add that she was also called Lo, sometimes Glo, by some of her friends. She felt she was occupying enough of this woman's territory.

As the taxi drove away, Gloria felt as though she would disappear like vapor into the clouds above. Instead, she followed Lo up the steps and into the shade of the veranda. Lo kicked the boots from her feet. "You surprised me so much I didn't even check for critters in my boots."

Critters, Gloria thought. If she hadn't known she was in wild country, she did now.

Inside the house was the creaking stillness of a tall ship set adrift on mild waters. There was pine everywhere—the floorboards, the walls, the rafters. It was a living thing lying dormant, just like its mistress. Lo looked to be in her mid to late thirties but her measured gestures suggested someone who was tired. Gloria thought of what the driver had said about the little one—a child—and felt like an intruder into her sleeping world. The thought depressed her. *Lo*.

In a surprisingly cheery kitchen with paintings of cowboys and cowponies streaking across yellow pastures, the light falling in creamy slabs through the expansive windows that called in the wild fields, Lo let go of the handful of cardigan she had been clutching to her chest and folded herself down onto a stool at the long peninsula. She was all loose limbs and angles beneath baggy clothes. She indicated to the seat closest to her. The last thing Gloria wanted to do was sit down again but she did anyway. Despite Lo's languid pose, her eyes were heavy on

Gloria, letting her shift uncomfortably as she glanced at Lo then away again, finding things to land on like a buzzing fly, the jar of wilting chives on the counter, the newspaper folded neatly at one end of the long wooden table, the window with its generous view. She was about to comment on the beauty surrounding them, just to break the silence, when Lo spoke.

"So, Gloria, you can tell me…what's Peter at now? Are you a shrink?"

Gloria let out a huff of nervous laughter. "I guess you could say that."

Lo's brown brows shot up to meet the strands of coppery hair that had fallen across her forehead. "An accent. And from which continent have you appeared? One with caches of legal sedatives? Or are you going to pry open my skull and peer into my mind? I'm an unwilling patient you know."

Gloria smiled. Despite Lo's hostile greeting, she could sense a warmth and generosity of spirit lurking underneath. "You're safe with me. I only treat horses."

Lo smiled, just for a second. A flash of teeth across bloodless lips. "Australian. Well, I see my husband has had to cast his net across the Pacific Ocean to catch a willing fish. What has he told you?"

"That he's prepared to do what it takes to repair the damage. Two horses, both in need of rehabilitation and Grand Prix training. I was under the impression you had dressage horses. I really wouldn't know what to do with Western horses. Training-wise, I mean."

Lo raised her eyebrows again. "Western horses?"

Gloria gestured out toward the fields. "What you have here. They're beautiful, but you may as well get a local to train your horses for you. No point flying me in." To Gloria's ears her accent sounded flat, pedestrian.

"I don't know what Peter told you, but I'm done with dressage. The horses he's talking about, they are down the back end of the property. Kip looks in on them, but I don't want to see them. Peter has never been interested in the horses and he doesn't need to start feigning interest now." The lilting twang had taken on an edge. "It's a shame you've come all this way because Peter can't help but intervene in what is becoming increasingly less his business. He's barely here, so it seems you and I have been thrust together in a most uncomfortable way. I don't covet company, and I don't want to think about the horses, much less have someone here handling them."

Gloria rubbed her eyes with her fingertips. She felt incredibly tired all of a sudden. "Okay then, what do we do?" She remembered how her mother used to say the best way to handle a big problem was to break it down into manageable tasks. What they would be in this situation, she couldn't begin to imagine.

Lo studied Gloria's face for a moment. "You've come all this way. I guess Peter has offered you a decent wage?"

Gloria had to admit that he had, even though she didn't reveal how she had been banking on that first paycheck coming in soon. She had been relying on a place to stay and a regular income. After the breakup with Mike, home as she'd known it didn't exist anymore. She'd walked away with nothing but a suitcase and her dignity.

"Dammit, I really hate it when he does this!" Lo's chin dropped to her chest and there was a long pause where Gloria could almost hear the debate going on inside Lo's head. She finally looked up. "He knows what I'm like, see, that's what makes it worse." She scrutinized Gloria again, this time her eyes casting all over her in a clear assessment of aspect and character, making Gloria conscious of her travel-staled appearance. "I can tell you're not a bad type, it's not about that, but you can't stay on here."

Gloria had been squeezing her hands together and they flung open, releasing a butterfly of anxiety. "Can I at least speak to Peter? Sorry, but this was not what I was expecting. I've left everything I have—had—behind to come here because I thought there was a job."

"Cry me a river, darlin'." Lo folded her arms.

Gloria could hear the blood rushing through her own ears. She stared a second longer, her mouth almost hanging open in disbelief, before standing and taking the handle of her suitcase. There were a million thoughts churning mud in her stomach. How to get home being the loudest, and what a rash idiot she was coming in a close second. "Can you at least take me back to the airport?" She was loath to admit she'd arrived with about $60 in her pocket, but she managed to trip the fat, furry words from her mouth. "I don't have any money." She'd thought back home, scurrying through the house in her underwear, throwing clothes into a suitcase in the half light of a new strange day, she'd slumped to the bottom of what her character would allow, but the slimy depths were only beginning to reveal themselves.

Lo's arms dropped from their defensive pose and she looked toward the back door as though a helpful volunteer might materialize to drive Gloria to the airport. "I don't...I can't. Jesus, I can't believe I am even having this conversation. Peter!" His name flew from her mouth like a curse, and she stared angrily through the window at the swaying grass. "After last time when that stupid woman from Arizona came with her herbal remedies, he swore he was done with this shit."

Gloria was pretty sure she was "this shit," and she shifted the suitcase to her other hand. "Well, looks like there's not much to be done. Perhaps we can call Peter and let him know I've arrived and he might be able to give us an explanation."

Lo's laugh was bitter. "He won't answer when he's deep in a case. Look, you're right. Sue-Anne will be here at some stage. Maybe you can stay until you can get a flight back. Who am I to care anyway?"

Gloria wasn't sure whether Lo's last remark was sarcasm or not, but she wouldn't turn down a few days' grace to get sorted. "Thank you. If I can just speak to Peter, then maybe we can sort out this miscommunication."

Lo looked skeptical. "Miscommunication, hmm...My husband, Peter, he's an attorney, one of only two in this town."

"Who's the other? Maybe I can stay with him," Gloria said, a smile lifting one side of her mouth.

Lo looked at her evenly. "Me."

Gloria wasn't sure why, most likely overtired delirium, but a laugh bubbled up inside her, and she had to bite back on it. It wasn't the thought of Lo as a lawyer that made her want to giggle, it was the release of tension the unexpected information had given her. In fact, now that she knew, she could see that Lo did possess the self-assured posture of someone used to commanding authority.

Lo looked at her incredulously before a half smile pushed at the sides of her mouth. She stood up and turned away. "If you don't mind a bit of dust, there are plenty of cabins to choose from. I'll show you where to find things. And listen, if there's one thing Peter knows how to do, it's communicate directly. The reason he's not here to welcome you is because he's intended it that way. He doesn't want to deal with me. Come on."

Gloria picked up her suitcase and followed Lo back into the dim corridor. They crossed through a large living room with high ceilings, more wood and cowhide and paintings of landscapes and horses. A framed photo of a woman on a horse being presented with a large rosette was hanging on the wall above a brown leather sofa. Without craning her neck, Gloria recognized the lines of Lo's long limbs. It was a well-bred horse, she could tell at a glance. She longed to linger over the photo and study his lines, but she didn't dare. The slightest provocation could buffet Lo's resolve back the way it had come. Across the expansive living room was a staircase that went up toward the bedrooms.

"Living room, obviously, bedrooms upstairs." Lo pointed toward the landing above then turned around again and led Gloria past a bathroom and then back out by a washhouse which smelled like washing powder and looked old but well looked after, a basket of pegs sitting on top of the outdated white machine. "That's all there is to know about the main house. There'll be no guests, so you can pick whichever guesthouse you like apart from the cottage over by the barn where Kip lives." Lo opened the door from the washhouse and they went down the wooden steps to where a clothesline was strung from a lemon tree across the lawn. "Just go along and pick one, it won't matter which."

Gloria walked hesitantly down the stairs and felt as though she might burst into tears. In all the daydreams she'd had about her new job, in none of them had she imagined she'd be unwelcome. She stood, feeling like an orphan at a train stop, looking out at the swaying grass, trying not to be enveloped by panic. She heard Lo sigh then mutter something behind her. "Gloria, just come inside. You'd better stay in one of the bedrooms for now. Those cabins have been closed up all winter." It seemed Lo had neither the heart nor the patience to turn her back on the problem that had arrived at her door.

Gloria wasn't sure what would be worse: being isolated, or being inside with people who didn't want her. They went back into the house and Lo took her through the living room and up the wide staircase to the landing with its rocking chairs that looked down onto the living room below. "This house was built in stages, so it has an odd layout, but it works if you're used to it." There were four closed doors on the landing. Lo stopped at the first door, which was ajar, and nudged it with the heel of her hand then walked in and looked around. Gloria faced her in the doorway, clutching her case with both hands.

"You can stay here until we sort this mess out," Lo said. "If Peter asked you here, then he can pay what he likes and don't you feel bad about it. This isn't a guest ranch any longer, and I keep to myself. Feel free to look around, but leave me and my horses alone." She scrunched her cardigan closed with a fist again and turned on her heel. As she walked across the landing, she pulled one of the doors firmly shut then disappeared up a steep staircase cut into the wall between the middle two rooms, presumably into the peaked attic room with its single window that Gloria had seen from the road.

Gloria waited but there was no further discernible noise, so she turned and looked at the room. In one corner, a single bed covered in a pale blue quilt with a plump pillow sat against the wall, beside it a little chest of drawers with a brass clock and a lamp with a lopsided shade on top. In one other corner was a chair with a stack of books on top and on one wall hung a mirror, reflecting the world outside. The large window was framed by cream curtains covered in a pattern of blue sprigs of flowers. It was a plain, wholesome room, but the view out onto the mountains was breathtaking. Gloria placed her suitcase on the bed and sat down beside it. She was longing for a shower and a drink of water. Instead, she sat limply staring out of the window at the shifting clouds. When her bodily needs became stronger than her pride, she stood, feeling one hundred years old, and went to find a towel and a bathroom. She thought Lo might appear at the sound of her footsteps, but even as she opened the linen closet and sought out a towel, turned the shuddering faucet on in the pink-tiled bathroom and flushed the toilet, all else was quiet.

By the time she was standing in the bedroom again, her dark hair dripping onto her collarbones, dampening her pale yellow T-shirt and making her aware of the fresh air coming in through the opened window, her stomach felt hollow. Her jeans were loose around her waist, reminding her that it had been almost twenty-four hours since she last ate a proper meal. She wondered about the elusive Peter, with his promises that had set her at ease. Was he stuck at the office, tending to the whole town's legal needs? She pictured an alternate reality where Lo was in a district court, dressed in a somber suit, imparting droll intellection. Gloria pulled a comb through her hair and regarded herself in the mirror, a stark contrast to the image in her mind. Purple circles had set in below her dark eyes and her straight nose with its upward inflection was stung pink by the recent sun through the bus window. Even her lips were chapped. Her physical state seemed to reflect her mental well-being. She was beyond caring, and it gave her the courage to pull on a sweater and go exploring. It was a brave new world and change was what she desired.

The out-of-control feeling stayed with her outside. It was in the piled haystacks and the rustic wooden fences, the density of the pines beyond the barn and the hare that stopped and stared with bright alarmed eyes before disappearing into the grass. She was disoriented, and rather than feel anxious, it calmed the clawing thing that was always at her to be doing something, fixing things. There was nothing here that wasn't perfect at this moment. She was a baby, new in this strange world.

There was a dirty white pickup truck parked by the front yard, but no sign of its driver. It was oddly quiet, only the wind whistling over the land. Even the dog had slunk off somewhere. Gloria felt well-warmed by her adventure, poking around in the large barn and the sheds containing a gooseneck horse trailer parked behind some farm machinery. Off the side of the barn was a smaller building accommodating two rows of stables, a tack room, feed room, and a wash bay. Despite the sparseness of the house, the stables were modern and well cared for, with high beams overhead and ventilation under the roofing. All around was the sweet smell of straw and manure and the clean scent of cut chaff. It was a soothing scent that Gloria associated with the contentment of honest labor and the quiet joy born of predictability. She walked along the row of stalls but there was no sound of hooves stamping or tails whisking, no equine heads peeking out with curiosity. She wandered into the tack room and looked around at the saddlery sitting expectantly on wooden pegs, the woolen rugs folded neatly in the corner, the rows of rosettes on the wall. Gloria ran her fingers along the smooth brown leather of a bridle on a hook and noticed one of the saddles, a child's saddle, sitting on a peg beside its larger counterpart. The quick-release stirrups made for tiny feet. Something about that little object lying dormant on its wooden peg filled her with an emptiness as wide as the flat land beyond.

CHAPTER TWO

The sun was beginning to dip behind the mountain as Gloria headed for the warmth and comfort of indoors. She left her boots on the rack by the back entrance that was already populated by various shoes, most caked with dust or mud. Gloria wondered whose feet had left gray impressions on their insoles. The house still rang with silence. Gloria ventured forward anyway, washing her hands with dish soap at the stainless-steel sink and opening the cupboards until she'd found a dubious-looking loaf of bread. The kettle had just begun to whistle when she felt rather than heard someone behind her. She flicked the flame from the gas burner to still the disturbance and saw Lo standing there. Despite the laugh lines etched around her eyes, she looked like a small girl, her hands stuffed into the pockets of her cardigan, pulling it taut around her neck. Her eyes were puffy.

"Sorry, did I wake you?"

Lo shook her head slightly. "I don't sleep."

Despite her assertion, Lo had pillow marks on one cheek and the fine hair had grown messier in its low bun. Tendrils of strawberry-blond hair had escaped around her face and shoulders.

"Sleep is only for the old and the very young."

Lo looked at her for a long moment. "Forgive me," she said eventually. "I am far from a gracious host. I'm a guest in my own home."

"In that case, can I get you a tea?"

Lo's mouth creaked up toward a smile. "Let me know if you find any. Apart from iced tea, it's strictly coffee or bourbon on the ranch. I may not be too hot at hosting, but I can find my way to the liquor cabinet."

"On an empty stomach?" Gloria wasn't convinced.

"Isn't that the best way to do it? Fresh air and bourbon?" Lo paused, but when Gloria didn't have anything to add, she said, "Usually Sue-Anne is here by now, cooking for everyone, but I sent her home. Actually, I've sent everyone home." She shrugged and pulled her pockets down farther.

"Everyone?"

"Kip, the ranch hands, Sue-Anne…I like the quiet."

Gloria wasn't sure if that statement was pointed at her. It didn't matter anyway; she was intruding and she had little choice. She picked up the wizened bread loaf. "Any idea where I might find a knife?"

"Knife's in the first drawer, butter's in the pantry."

Gloria was conscious of Lo watching her as she sawed through the loaf with a butter knife, rewarded with a lumpy uneven slab and a pile of crumbs. She looked up hopelessly and blew a strand of hair from her mouth.

"Oh, for goodness' sake. There are about thirty well-intended casseroles in the deep freeze. Go and sit on the sofa, I'm about to outdo myself as hostess."

"I don't eat meat," Gloria said apologetically. She had been a vegetarian for five years and still felt the need to apologize for it.

Lo blinked at her as though she was thinking about saying something but eventually thought better of it and pursed her lips instead.

While Lo was gone, Gloria cleaned up the bread crumb explosion and after some contemplation threw the whole loaf into the trash. Lo returned holding a white casserole dish in her hands as though carrying a live explosive.

"Open the oven door, will you?" Lo wrestled the dish into the oven. "Let's get this damn thing on so you can eat before midnight."

"I can't eat all of that and I don't eat meat!"

"Yes, you already said. It's okay, it's a cauliflower cheese thing that no one else wanted." Her eyes gleamed wickedly. "But Wilbur will finish what you won't. He's a garbage guts."

"Wilbur?"

"The dog. Now, surely it's drinks time."

Gloria could see the duality of Lo's mental states; the desire to be alone and the need for company. It was written in the changing weather of her face, the clutching hands and expansive arms. Gloria sat on the leather sofa and waited while Lo took two crystal glasses from a dry bar in the corner of the living room and poured out two stiff drinks.

"Now, this I can do." Lo passed Gloria a glass and eased herself down beside her.

Gloria noticed the hand with its delicate smattering of freckles shaking as she lifted the glass to her lips. Lo took a slug and leaned back against the sofa, the long sweeps of dark brown lashes drawing down over the translucent skin like a fan.

Gloria's eyes strayed to the photograph hanging on the wall. "How long ago was that?"

Lo's lids stayed lowered. "Six years ago, summer of ninety-two. Hamlet. He's a big boy but he sure can move."

"He's lovely. Is he here, at the ranch?"

Lo sighed and dragged her eyes wearily toward Gloria's. "If you knew the supreme effort it has taken me just to swing my legs over the side of my bed in the morning, you'd know to drop it."

Gloria took a sip and almost choked. "Okay, I apologize. This bourbon is penance enough."

"Penance? You Aussies sure are strange. That's a local bourbon you're drinking there. Made right here in Wyoming, other side of that hill. Even the barrel it was distilled in was made out of wood from these parts. You won't taste better."

Gloria took another sip. "Do you own shares in the company?"

Lo didn't smile. "All right then, hotshot. What's your deal? What do you do when you're not flying around on a hope and a prayer?"

"You just summed up my life in that last question." Gloria stared down into the gleaming brown liquid and gave it a little shake, sending it rolling around.

"You running from something, honey?"

Gloria grimaced. "From nothing…nothing left to run from."

"Man troubles?"

Gloria felt a little like she was under the cross. "I guess you could say that, although the problem was probably more me. Are you sure you want to hear it?"

Lo nodded once. "Go ahead."

Gloria had lifted every one of these thoughts to her mind's eye and examined them from every angle for months, so it almost felt like reciting a story she'd told herself. She spoke them aloud anyhow. "At first glance he—Mike—seemed right for me. He's a vet, he likes the outdoors, great with animals and children, looks all right on a horse…tough but sensitive, a really lovely guy actually. I was rapt for a while. We got along with each other's families—my mum loves him—we even bought a place together. It's a lovely house on seven acres, nothing compared to this, though. I thought we were in love. Well, maybe we were in love, I don't even know anymore."

"A cheater?" Lo pursed her lips and dimples sprang up.

"No," Gloria said almost sadly. "He's great. I guess I just fell out of love, or perhaps I needed more space for the love to thrive. Is that a contradictory notion?" She took another sip; either the bourbon was growing on her or she was growing tipsy. "I panicked and left…just walked out. I treated him awfully and he deserved better. Everyone is so angry at me now, even my mother, and I don't blame them. It was cowardly." Her eyes dropped to her glass again. "I'd just gotten in so deep I didn't know what else to do. It made it worse that he was always so supportive. It still wasn't enough, as terrible as that makes me feel. It should have been, right?" It felt good to finally let it all out. It was hard to articulate it to her family, and her closest friends were friends with Mike too.

"It can't have been easy to walk away like that. Too many people stay in bad relationships because they're scared to leave. You did him a service even though he can't see it yet. Love is strange. Sometimes I think love is painted as such a beautiful thing but it's mostly just pain."

Gloria sighed. "Maybe we're just not doing it right?"

"You don't do love, it just happens."

They lapsed into silence until Gloria raised her glass. "Well, here's to love."

"And pain."

Gloria winced and they clinked glasses.

Lo pulled her legs up under herself. "Are you cold? I can light the fire?"

"No, not unless you want to." When Lo didn't shift, not even her direct gaze, Gloria continued, "I felt so guilty that I even left the cat behind. We've had him since he was a kitten."

Lo reached for the bottle and Gloria extended her glass to be filled. The stag's head on the wall eyed her reproachfully. "Don't worry, you're a pretty gal, I'm sure your dance card will be full. There are plenty of boys out here who would love to show you around. How old are you anyway?"

"Twenty-eight. Too old for love and pain." She smiled. "Thanks for the offer, but the last thing I want right now is another man to disappoint."

"Honey, I'm thirty-eight and I'm still loving and hurting. It's a lifelong process. Who and when we love is out of our hands. You can no more stop yourself from falling in love than you can force yourself to love, and it's a lifelong project."

"I'm tired just thinking about it."

"Ah, you've had a bad experience." Lo patted Gloria's knee. Gloria could feel the cold fingers through her jeans. "But here you are, sitting in a stranger's living room on the other side of the world, keeping her from her insomnia. Funny how life's roads are always full of unexpected turns."

"And some cliffs."

"Don't I know it." Lo refilled her own glass and took a gulp. "Do as I say, not as I do. I should practice what I preach, shouldn't I? I'm sequestered away at the ranch, scared of my inner world, scared of the world outside. I should just shut my mouth and let people get on with their lives."

"It takes time to heal from things. I've healed plenty of horses, and it's basically the same thing, learning to trust again. Do you know the show jumper, Double Wonder?" Lo shook her head. "She won silver at the Olympics. Anyway, not long after, she fell at a fence and pulled a tendon. It was traumatic, she got stuck in the wing. Mike treated her, he did a fabulous job, and she was able to recommence her career, however she was so fence-shy, you couldn't get her into the arena let alone over a jump. It was slow going, but she had to learn to trust again. She jumped another year or so and won a lot of championships until she eventually became unsound and they retired her. Mike delivered her first foal last year, a chestnut filly with a star and front socks, very cute."

"People are more complex than horses," Lo said, a note of warning creeping into her voice. "As a criminal attorney I've met a lot of people who are absolute puzzles. Sometimes they are solvable, sometimes they remain a mystery."

"Isn't it your job to solve them?"

"Not really, just to represent them. That means piecing together the evidence so we have all the facts, however, the person may always remain a mystery. Not everyone has such pure intentions." She looked at Gloria over her glass. "It's hard to let go of that sometimes. Not everyone can be saved from themselves."

"Do you still practice?"

"No."

"Do you miss it?"

"Some elements, but not the stress or the pressure of putting together and presenting a case. I have no stomach for it anymore. I've seen things that can't be unseen. Peter still asks my advice on his cases, which keeps me sharp, but I've lost the drive. I've made a life from exploring the psyche and helping people with their problems. It came easily to me, that stuff, even being in a courtroom never daunted me. You might think that it takes a sharp mind to study law, but a lot of it is a good memory and sweat—my mom used to call me every Tuesday evening in college and her first question was always, 'Are you eating your protein for brain function?' Which of course I wasn't. Black coffee or waffles in the dining hall if I'd managed to get out of bed in time…It's quiet out here, a lot of contract work. Litigation is demanding of every resource you have, even your health sometimes. The reward can be great, but so can the disappointment. I don't have the headspace or emotional capability anymore. My young, hungry days are gone."

"I bet you're good at it." Despite Lo's fragile state, a steely intelligence was evident. Her face was astute and interesting, regular features at slightly irregular angles that gave her a clever look. It was like an old-fashioned painting, and the more Gloria looked at it, the more she wanted to keep looking.

"Yes," Lo said blankly. "I was. After…after things changed here, I threw myself back into work but a sea had opened up. I found I couldn't swim. Perhaps I'd never had many problems of my own to solve and they were drowning me. An ocean of my own ego." She ran her finger around the rim of her tumbler, stopping to press her finger into a chip in the glass. "It's easy to skim the surface of life in a blandly happy daze when you've never been sunk into the cold depths of the ocean. I mean, sometimes a case would depress the hell out of me, but it was in a sort of indulgent way. A temporary symptom of a fleeting pain, not something that's grown and mutated within your very cells. I'm heavy with it now, it's spread throughout my organs. A terminal case of grief." She looked down at the vibrant well of blood that had sprung up on her index finger as though it was nothing to do with her. Gloria found herself entranced as Lo pressed the pad of her finger with her thumb.

"Sorry!" Lo said, looking up sharply. "I forget myself too easily." She put her glass down and stood, her hand curled into a loose fist, and went to the bar to fetch a square of paper towel. She stared at her finger for a long second, and Gloria got the impression that if she wasn't there, Lo would have lost herself in abject fascination. Eventually she pressed the paper towel to the cut and returned to her spot on the couch, a dreamy look in her eyes.

"Are you okay? Do you want to put something on it?"

Lo shook her head. "It's nothing, just a nick and I—" Her mouth clapped shut and she looked off toward the side. "It makes me feel."

Gloria waited to see if there was more to the sentence, but apparently there wasn't. She felt sadness tugging at her but was reminded of Lo's words only moments ago about being carried on the wave of someone else's grief. She tried to examine how she felt about it but didn't consider herself enough of an expert to know whether it was a derivative of empathy, or empathy in its truest form. It was a constant question she applied to her emotions: was it better to hold them under the microscope and assess them before presenting them to the world, or was that a false way of living? A life on the other side of the mirror. Self-reflection in a hall of mirrors. She knew if she held herself back from everything as she had with Mike, with others before him, she would never live. In that moment she envied Lo the reassurance of vitality saturating a paper towel with evidence. "It doesn't look good," she said anyway.

Lo picked her glass up and leaned back into the chair, a mildly satisfied look on her face. "Daddy used to call me The Tank when I was little because I used to charge into things, bounce off, and just keep going. He said Mom used to cry when I hurt myself, but I never did. It's nothing to cry over." She returned her gaze to her finger, where she pried open the cut to examine the fleshy doors of skin before blood bubbled up again.

Gloria's eyes strayed back to the photograph on the wall in stark contrast to Living Room Lo with her head bent over her crimson paper towel. In Picture Lo, there was a joyful confidence in the downward tilt of the head as she beamed at a woman fastening a rosette to Hamlet's bridle. Her face, tanned beside the white knotted stock at her throat, reminded Gloria of the carefree girls on television ads for sun lotion and orange juice. That unusual face and unusual coloring. It hadn't been an instant impression, but it was a curious feeling growing upon Gloria that she was sitting beside a unique creature. "Do you have brothers or sisters?" she asked, imagining a clumsier version of Lo, thrown together like the fairy birthday cake she had tried to bake for her niece that only slightly resembled the glossy photo in the book.

"Nope, just me. My parents had trouble conceiving and they were older when they had me." She picked at a hole in the knee of her jeans and Gloria realized she had strayed into dangerous territory: cabbage patches where thoughts of babies and families grew.

"But you grew up here, at the ranch?" she asked hastily.

"My dad and Uncle Bobby did, but Uncle Bobby was the oldest so it went to him and when he went with a heart attack, Daddy took over because Uncle Bobby never married or had kids. It's not a strong suit in my family." Color had crept into Lo's blanched cheeks. "But hang on, how'd we end up talking about me so much? You're a stranger in my home, I want to know about you."

"No ranch back home for me growing up, just a suburban brick house with a concrete drive."

"How'd you end up so handy with the horses then?"

"We were on the outskirts, twenty minutes on a bike and you're out in the paddocks. I guess I've always loved animals and horses seemed extra special because you could ride them. A big, beautiful animal that I could have such an affinity with that it would let me be on its back. I felt stronger, faster, more at peace, on a horse. There's something so gentle about them, don't you think? Anyway, down at the paddocks near the footy field, there was an old pony with one eye, Captain, his name was. A crest like a metal bridge and a mouth like iron. The owners were happy for me to ride him as long as I groomed him and checked on him. I learnt to file hooves myself. He had a wicked buck, too, so I learnt to sit tight." She looked sideways at Lo. "I hurt myself so many times, but I was too scared to tell Mum in case she didn't let me go back. I used to make jumps out of hard rubbish and we'd go around the field. He would approach every jump with his head cocked to the side so he could get a good look, but he was game. He kicked on for a while, old Captain."

Lo squeezed her finger in its paper casing. "Ah, another itty-bitty tank. I think most riders are! Captain sounds like a perfect first pony, you must have learned a lot from him. What about dressage, how did that start? I'm not sure about Australia, but here you need money…It's quite elitist, which is a shame. There's plenty on the circuit who've bought their talent rather than worked for it. It's not so big, the scene here, and it's very cliquey."

"I'm not sure about talent, but I certainly worked hard. I started working for free at a riding school, mucking out stables and tacking up horses. They let me ride as much as I pleased, which was pretty well all the time. They are lovely people, Paul and Judy, they still have the school. They had show jumpers and used to break horses in and eventually they realized I was a tenacious kid who would jump on any horse and point it at any fence. I still get a buzz from it, being lent a pair of wings."

"Being lent a pair of wings, that's a nice way of putting it. I'm not sure I was ever brave enough to jump much, but I liked the technicality of dressage. It's such a challenge, the communication between horse and rider. Dancing on horseback."

"I like that, too, the appearance of subtleness when there's so much communication going on. The invisibility of a rider, just letting the horse express. I was lucky, after the riding school, I moved on to Klaus Hofmann's yard. He trained me well."

Lo let out a whistle. "Klaus Hofmann…Honey, what exactly did he train you in?"

Gloria grimaced.

"Oh, no, honey. So what they say is true, huh? I did always wonder, and there's that cloud of cute girls surrounding him at events. He made a decent play when I met him a few years ago, even though Peter was right there."

Gloria smiled. "That sounds like him. He always had an eye for the ladies."

"How old were you? He's no spring chicken."

"Sixteen when I started with him." Gloria rolled her eyes toward the heavens.

"And how old when *he* started with *you*?"

Gloria huffed the beginning of a laugh. "He waited until I was eighteen, or more to the point, until I knew the correct position. He's very hot on stripping out flaws and starting from the beginning again. He made me work with all the difficult horses before he'd let me near anything worth riding."

"Mm-hmm."

Lo was grinning now, and Gloria thought how much it suited her. Those lips curling up to display creases at the sides of her mouth. A disorienting pull of déjà vu gripped her again. "Oh, stop it. I know, I'm a walking cliché. But hey, I learnt from the best. And I learnt to ride too."

Lo was smiling so hard she clanked her teeth on her glass when she took a sip. "So why aren't you out there now on the circuit?"

"No time, money, or resources. No Grand Prix horse. I've brought on a lot of youngsters but never owned a great horse of my own. It was part of the future plan, with Mike. The carrot he was dangling to coax me down the aisle. It wasn't enough, though. Klaus would help me find a good horse if I really wanted one, but I knew I'd be tied down. It was all too much. So, here I am on your couch, a brief reprieve from my life." Alcohol and pleasant company were giving her memories a remote lens, and she was surprised when Lo's face clouded over.

"Hmm." Lo nodded once and she set her glass down on the table. "I'm sure that casserole must be ready." She stood up, grabbing a fistful of her baggy clothing, her index finger held rigid, and walked quickly out.

Gloria didn't feel so hungry anymore. Her head was spinning from the alcohol and the changing weather sweeping the conversation.

CHAPTER THREE

Gloria awoke the next morning feeling like her head was full of cotton wool. Daybreak was falling across her face in a glug of gold. She pulled the blanket up over her eyes but she was already alert. The clock on the bedside table was ticking insistently, reminding her that he'd been on the job all night even while everyone else was sleeping. The previous night's events swam into focus. She'd eaten a small bowl of dry casserole alone at the kitchen table and put the rest out for the dog, who had probably turned his nose up in disgust. Lo had disappeared unsteadily into the dark staircase and Gloria had washed the dishes and gone to bed.

Now, she rolled onto her stomach and propped herself up on her elbows. Squinting, she stared out through the window at the bristly buttercups and orange butterfly weed dotting the green fields. Off in the distance a red combine harvester chugged lazily along, signaling human life. She wondered if Lo had gone to bed to watch the shadows move and crease her face with sleepless pillow marks. If she didn't volunteer information about the elusive Peter tonight, Gloria would go ahead and ask anyway. She would give it one week and if work didn't materialize, it would be time to go back and confront the situation at home. It was less than a week since she'd crept out of the silent house in Melbourne, a scrap of paper tucked under the small velvet box left on the bedside table. The velvet box, tiny enough to fit in her the palm of her hand, its contents a sparkling grenade. She'd pulled the pin and had to run. The memory made her gut twist uncomfortably. She could picture the darkened room, Mike's docile animal breath as his bare back rose and fell, innocent to the waking world. Only the cat had threatened to give her away, following her to the door to meow insistently for an early breakfast. She'd pushed his furry body away with her foot as she clicked the door shut behind her. The mixture of emotions had been varied, a palette of colors swirled into an unappealing brown. Utter relief that she'd escaped her emotional cell, misery that she was leaving behind a friend in Mike—for he was a friend, had been before they began tentative courtship, and still was despite the sleeping arrangements—and there was guilt, a huge squeeze of it that had become bolder as the other emotions had faded.

She knew from experience that a blanket over the eyes would not stop the thoughts in her head. Even though she didn't want to admit it, she missed him terribly. She understood what Lo meant about love and pain. "Ugh!" she said to no one. After the long journey, she was so sick of her own thoughts. She sat up in bed and flung the covers back, confronted with her bare legs beginning to goose pimple. Out of bed, she took the white towel she had used last night from where she had draped it over the back of the chair and stepped lightly to the bathroom.

Showered and changed, Gloria went to investigate the coffee situation. She felt even stranger creaking along the corridors in her Garfield socks. The spring Wyoming mornings seemed to have a similar crispness to autumnal Melbourne, and her wardrobe hadn't changed much. She'd only thrown jeans, shirts, shorts, and riding clothes into her suitcase. At least Lo hadn't set the fashion bar very high, because what Gloria thought was her white T-shirt in her haste back at home turned out to be Mike's giant one. Depressingly, it smelled like him.

In the kitchen she was so deep in thought as she struggled with the coffee percolator that she didn't notice anyone come up behind her until she heard a voice.

"I've seen boys wrestle a steer to the ground with less effort."

Gloria dropped the packet of filters on the counter and looked up to see a woman of about sixty wearing a yellow floral dress and an apron. In each meaty hand she had a string bag of groceries. Gloria's mouth started to water at the idea of food.

"You gave me a fright."

"And you me."

Gloria stood one foot on top of the other, self-conscious in her rumpled Garfield socks. "Sorry, I'm Gloria Grant. I'm here to, ah, look at the horses."

"Sue-Anne Lewis. You can call me Sue-Anne, we keep it informal at the ranch."

"Pleased to meet you." Gloria smiled because she was too far away to shake hands.

"Just put that down and come and have a seat. I'm here to sort this place out. Sit here, let me fix you something."

Gloria obediently went to take a seat on a stool at the other side, elbows on the counter, and let her chin fall into her hands. Sue-Anne walked with a lumbering side-to-side gait, her large hips swaying in a way that was almost mesmerizing. She heaved the groceries up with a grunt and began pulling wrapped parcels from the bags.

"You know where the chickens are, honey?"

Gloria shook her head, chin still in hands. "I can go find them."

"Round the side there. There's a bucket in the lean-to. Don't let that daddy rooster scare you, he's all bluff. The green bucket!" Sue-Anne called as Gloria stood up and began walking toward the door.

The chicken coop was warm and musty smelling. It was made out of wood and wire, a replica of a gabled house with a little chimney on the peaked roof. Chickens fussily clucked out of the way so Gloria could bend down and retrieve eggs from the straw. Feeling finally productive, she carried the bucket back to the kitchen, its plastic handle bending under the weight.

"So many!" Sue-Anne clucked, rather like a fussy hen herself. "No one has been collecting them. Let me wash them, all that muck everywhere." She ran an appraising eye along the length of Gloria. "You girls these days, what happened to curves? You could use a few good meals. No one was scrambling egg whites in my days!"

Gloria observed that Sue-Anne looked far too stressed by every passing thought. "No fat-free for me thanks, I like the whole egg. I don't eat meat though, I'm a vegetarian."

Sue-Anne looked at her suspiciously, not sure if she was joking or not. "No such thing on the ranch. Why don't you go and wake Dolores up? She could use some routine, not to mention a square meal. Don't be scared of her, she needs a firm hand. That child! And Peter, well, he should be here at home looking after her, not always in town."

"In town?"

"At the office, at the apartment." Sue-Anne slammed a block of butter down onto the counter.

Gloria slid back off the chair.

"And go get Kip!"

"I don't know who that is."

Sue-Anne fixed her with a look. "Tall guy, big hat. Outside. Those ranch hands, no sense of time. I'm not feeding the lot of them if there are any day workers, but get Kip and Samuel. If Clarence is out doing the fences, give him a holler. That's it though."

Gloria didn't dare prompt another slew of vexation, so she quietly excused herself to go and find Lo.

There were two closed doors along the corridor. Gloria tried the first handle. The door swung silently open to reveal a tidy child's room decorated in muted primary colors with a large harlequin-patterned rug on the floor. In one corner was a wooden train set and a miniature farm. The room had a faint sweet smell of a child's talcum-powdered skin, the warm shampooed scalp. A cosseted room, a carpeted tomb. Gloria shut the door and made for the outdoors. There was no way she would rouse Lo from whatever solace she had found.

Gloria marveled at how quickly she was starting to feel at home. The outdoors was her own backyard, the towering clouds and reclusive mountains there just for her. It was utter freedom from the emotional cage at home. An eagle flitted overhead, its gray shadow cutting across the grass. She knew how easy it would be to fall in love with this place, with a new beginning, and it terrified her slightly. She didn't even know why she was there, or where she was at all, in a destiny freefall.

The grass was shimmering with starbursts on the dewy fronds of each tip. As she walked along the dampened earth between the fields, pale green seeds clung to her jeans. She shielded her eyes against the glare and made for the combine harvester which was still making its sluggish way across a field of alfalfa, leaving a shorn patch in its wake. At the wooden fence line she paused then climbed up onto the fence to watch. The peaceful labor had a Zen-like quality that drew up through her body, connecting her thoughts with the warm sun on her face and the mellow honeyed scent of the sticky grass. As the harvester cut a new corner, the rays caught on the windshield glass and the driver noticed her sitting there. The engine cut out and a man with long bandy legs swung down. He strode along toward her, giving the grass a jaunty kick with his boot as he went. He was tall with a big hat. Sue-Anne was right; he must be Kip.

He tipped his weathered hat at her and Gloria grinned, delighted at the ritual.

"Sue-Anne sent me to tell you it's breakfast time."

Kip's dark blue eyes were steady in his tanned face. "Did she now?"

Gloria thought that on any other day, at any other time, she would have been happy to have Kip's eyes on her, but now she felt quite immune.

"Gloria." She extended a hand down to him but instead of shaking it, he helped her down from the fence so she was standing on the wrong side of it with him. His hand was firm and damp with perspiration.

"Kip Preston. I knew a Gloria, real pretty lady. Looked something like you."

"What happened to her?" Gloria climbed through the gap in the rails and surreptitiously wiped her hand on her jeans.

"Well," Kip said, placing a muscular hand on the top of the fence and vaulting over. "Poor gal, she died of a broken heart."

Gloria raised an eyebrow. "Congenital defect?"

"Nope, no. Official diagnosis was lovesick. Say, Gloria, where'd you get that cute accent?"

"Melbourne, Australia."

"You're a long way from home, little lady. What brings you out to these parts?"

"I'm here to help with the horses."

Kip looked sideways at her as they walked. "You going to help me with the branding?"

Gloria laughed. "Well, I hadn't considered it, but I guess I'll do as I'm told." She fixed her eyes on the red barn between the converging fence lines. "So this is a working ranch? How many horses are on the property?"

Kip kept his long legs deliberately in step with hers. "Oh, about forty, give or take. Every year we have a big auction which ties in with the county fair. People come from all over to get a look at these horses."

"Quarter horses?"

"Finest in the country. Have you seen our big boy, Freddy? Well, Fast And Loose, that's his stud name."

Gloria smiled. "Fast And Loose? Is that how they breed them out here?"

It was Kip's turn to grin, showing front teeth slightly overlapping in the middle and a chipped eyetooth, which only enhanced his roguish looks. "Silky manes and barrel chests, powerful hindquarters and neat legs. Turn on a dime. If you don't believe me, you can see for yourself."

Gloria lifted her chin and took a great breath of air. Every separate smell was sweet and wholesome, combining to create a fresh perfume. Kip was persistent but it felt harmless, his usual way with women, and she was sure many appreciated it as more than mild flattery. She listened as he told her about the rodeo circuit and his mother who had left them when he was eight to ride trick horses with the circus. At the entrance to the barn he hollered for Samuel, and a young-looking kid came scooting out to stop abruptly when he saw Gloria.

"This is Gloria," Kip said proudly. "She's here from Melbourne to show us a thing or two with the horses."

Samuel turned a bright red and bleated out a greeting.

"Take your hat off for a lady," Kip said, nudging Samuel in the ribs.

Samuel whipped his hat off and Gloria laughed. "Please, gentlemen, keep your hats on. I don't want anyone removing any clothing on my behalf."

Samuel almost tripped over and Kip clutched his heart. "Gloria, it's too early in the day to be making a man's heart start like that."

Kip sprang up the steps to the lean-to and opened the back door. "Ladies first."

The smell of buttery herbs was a powerful force and Gloria was looking forward to sitting down with Sue-Anne so Kip could stop his manic courtship dance. With another tip of his hat, he departed with Samuel to "clean up."

Sue-Anne was skilfully sliding sizzling eggs onto a platter with ducks painted around the edge. "Where's Dolores?" she demanded immediately, her heavy presence and tone a distinct shift from Kip's jaunty manner.

"I didn't have the heart to wake her."

Sue-Anne gave Gloria a withering look and wiped her hands on a tea towel and threw it down onto the counter. "It's not healthy for someone to sleep all day. A good meal and some fresh air will do her a world of good."

Gloria couldn't stop looking at the mountains of food on the table: golden wobbling eggs, fluffy pancakes, thick toast, jugs of maple syrup, pats of butter, ruby jam, steaming coffee, a jug of orange juice, crisp bacon. Despite Sue-Anne's assertion that she wouldn't be feeding everyone, it appeared as though she was attempting to.

Kip and Samuel appeared, somehow diminished without their towering hats, their hair newly combed and gleaming with water above the white strip of skin on the foreheads of their suntanned faces. While Sue-Anne was rousing Lo, Kip pinched a piece of bacon from the platter.

"She'll notice that," Samuel said, blushing at his own daring.

Sue-Anne came bustling back in. "Don't just stand around staring. Food's getting cold." Gloria looked past her but didn't see any sign of Lo. "Dolores will be out presently," Sue-Anne confirmed. "Gloria, sit here by me. Samuel, you can say grace please, we'll just wait for Dolores to appear. Dolores!" she yelled immediately, obviously unable to wait. "Ooh, I hate it when food gets cold." She swiped away a fly. "And now the flies are starting. Kip, can't you do something?"

Kip held up his hands in mock defense. "Ma'am, no matter how many times I tell those flies that we ain't friends, they just keep showing up."

Behind Samuel's rigid shoulder, Lo appeared in the doorway, still dressed in the same clothes from last night. With an expressionless face like a paper cutout of a woman, she looked across at them all and blinked at the table. Kip and Samuel stared at their empty plates in front and Sue-Anne huffed.

"Dolores, hurry up, the food is getting cold on your account."

Lo walked slowly and purposely, one foot in front of the other, as though each step required thought. "I do beg your pardon, everyone. Please begin." Kip pulled out a chair at the head of the table, closest to where she'd come from, and she sat down with a thump. Her eyes widened in surprise at the thump then she sat very still, hands in her lap, her body looking limp as though she might fold to the ground like empty clothing. Sue-Anne sat down and gave Samuel the nod. He said a halting grace, his face deepening to a dark pink which clashed with his blond hair. As soon as he looked up, Sue-Anne began forking pancakes onto Lo's plate.

"Juice," Sue-Anne said, as though to a child, filling Lo's cup.

Gloria realized she was staring and helped herself to a cup of coffee then to toast and eggs. She silently marveled at the piles of food on the men's plates and the quiet that descended, apart from the sounds of chewing and cutlery clattering. Sue-Anne kept looking around at them and nodding in a self-satisfied way, her chin disappearing into the folds of her neck.

"Dolores, eat up." She put another egg on Lo's plate even though she hadn't touched the other one.

Lo lifted her glass of juice to her lips with both hands and lowered it carefully, still managing to spill it on the white tablecloth. Taking her fork in her hand, she speared a piece of bacon. Gloria watched its trembling ascent toward her mouth. When it finally made it, Lo seemed to have lost the will to eat, and she chewed slowly, her eyes on the pool of orange juice being absorbed into the white cloth. Everyone kept their eyes cast down except for Sue-Anne, who ate rapidly and angrily, leaning closer and closer to Lo. Intermittently she flopped back against her chair with a huff of impatience, only to begin her gradual lean again. Gloria piled her plate too high and found she couldn't finish. The atmosphere was stifling. Kip put his fork down and looked at Sue-Anne.

"Well, thank you, ma'am, that was exceptional." He flicked his tongue across an eyetooth. "We'll get back to it. Ladies." He dipped his head slightly at Lo and Gloria and picked up his plate and took it to the sink.

"Leave it!" Sue-Anne began yelling before he'd even made his intentions clear.

Kip grinned at Gloria over Sue-Anne's shoulder then sauntered out after Samuel. Lo sat, hands wrapped around her juice, staring miserably into space for so long that Gloria and Sue-Anne began clearing up around her. Through the kitchen window over the sink, the combine harvester chugged back to life. Gloria almost envied Kip the predictable, practical task with its clearly defined lines and concrete outcome.

"Bit early for haying." Lo's voice was soft and creaky. She cleared her throat and repeated what she'd said, although Gloria had heard her the first time.

Sue-Anne laughed. "Best tell Kip that, he's halfway through middle field. Make sure it dries out then, that's all we can do. Here." She passed Gloria a tea towel. "Dolores, when will we be expecting Peter home?"

"Peter?" Lo stood and carried her plate across to the peninsula. "He's working."

Sue-Anne's mouth puckered up. Gloria could see the supreme effort held in her face as she tried not to say what was on her mind. They stood and began piling dishes beside the sink.

"How far is it to town?" Gloria asked, imagining she might go for a walk.

"Six and a half miles to the gas station then another two to the stores." Sue-Anne scrubbed egg yolk off a plate under hot soapy water then handed it to Gloria to dry. "Maybe Dolores could take you in and show you around?" she said, directing her words toward Lo.

"Oh, Peter has the car." Lo had already started receding toward the corridor.

"Take the truck."

But Lo had faded into the shadows of the hallway.

Gloria's tea towel was growing ineffectual. "Does Peter usually spend the week in town? It's just that he's the one who made arrangements with me and I'm not sure what to do. Is there a phone number I can reach him on?"

"You can try. Oh, gosh. Things used to be different around here. Lo was a working woman, at the office, out with clients or with the horses. Nothing slowed that girl down. Even when she was a tiny thing, she was a busy beaver. Probably hard for you to imagine looking at her now. 'Joie de vivre,' that's how people used to describe her. Even when she had little Terrence, it didn't slow her down for long. I said to her, don't be passing him to me, you're his mother, but she did of course. Don't get me wrong, she is a fantastic mother, so fun. And I say 'is' because you never know what God's plan is. I think Peter used to worry a bit at first, how she would take to motherhood with all her other commitments, but she embraced it and loved Terrence.

He was her little cub, same cheeky smile, and well, once they put him on a pony that was it. He was in love. His first word was, 'Up!' He would hold out those chubby hands and want to be put on a horse. It wasn't Dolores's fault, what happened, it really wasn't." Sue-Anne paused in her dish washing and looked out toward the mountains.

"What happened?" Gloria threw the question into the ring even though it made her cringe.

"Accident, of course. Oh, dear." Sue-Anne used her forearm to dry a tear that was rolling rapidly down her rounded cheek. She pulled the plug from the basin and wiped her hands on her apron. "The horses, he was out with Dolores. It was a beautiful day, the sun was shining—because you know how those thunderheads can roll in real quick and send the sky crashing down—nothing to indicate there was anything out of the ordinary. No one could have known! God just wanted him close, that's all I can think." She dabbed at her eyes with a finger. "Horses are a way of life out here, there's no avoiding them on the ranch." She handed Gloria a platter. "Put this away will you, Gloria, bottom drawer. Bending over does my back no good. Thank you. Yep, Dolores needs to find the strength to carry on. There's no use sacrificing her own life, it won't bring him back."

"No, it won't. That's terrible." Gloria hung the tea towel on the oven handle to dry. "I can't imagine what it must be like to lose a child."

"Don't try to. But listen, honey. Don't tiptoe around her. Friends have stopped calling, even her family, they've gone quiet. Death is funny like that, it makes people shy away. Just treat her normal, don't put up with her moods. Get her up in the morning, make her go for a walk outside, tell her about yourself. People get scared to talk, scared of what they might accidentally say, how she'll react, but you can't worry about that. She's still here with us and she needs to feel people around her, even if she wants to stay hollowed out in grief. Don't let her disappear."

"I'm not sure she wants to talk to me," Gloria said.

"It doesn't have to be about anything in particular, just light conversation, the weather, anything really. Just keep her here in the land of the living. I bet she's shrunk off to bed now. Eats like a bird. Lies in bed all day. It's like looking after a child again. I have to practically wrestle her to bathe!" Sue-Anne's temper was agitating again. She let out a huff. "I have to stay calm, I know I do. It's no good for my blood pressure and I've got work to do. You got any clothes to wash?"

Gloria shook her head. "I can do my own laundry."

"Go and get it. There's barely a load these days. Peter's not here, Dolores wears the same thing day after day and…well, I'm not as busy as I used to be. Dolores keeps sending me away but I try to stick around as much as possible, even just for another soul in this big old house. I'm glad you're here." She squeezed Gloria's hand. "Now go and get your laundry. Bring it around to the washhouse."

Gloria hesitated. "I don't know if I'm staying, that's why I need to talk to Peter. To be honest, Lo, Dolores, wasn't even aware I was coming until I turned up on the doorstep."

"Do you want to stay?"

Gloria thought about it. "It depends, I guess. I came here to work with the horses, so if I can still do that, then, yes." Leaving now would feel like one more failure to add to her list.

"Those horses have been turned out to grow fat and woolly. They're starting to look like cattle, not imported dressage horses. Whatever Peter is paying you, it doesn't compare to the bags of money that are now sitting out at pasture."

"When I mentioned it to Lo, she didn't want me to touch them."

"Go and get your washing, honey. Just think about it. Those horses will still be there tomorrow."

Gloria sat outside on the back porch that extended along behind the house and watched Sue-Anne taking towels down from the line. A breeze was snapping them and pulling at Sue-Anne's skirt, but despite her irritation, she wouldn't let Gloria help. Gloria clutched her knees to herself and watched the sky deepening across the hills.

"Didn't I tell you that the weather changes quick? That's a storm coming. All this double handling of washing makes a woman tired." Sue-Anne said, throwing the leftover pegs from her apron pocket into a tub and dropping it onto the folded towels. "I hope you brought a big coat. The wind comes whooshing over the mountain and it is icy."

Gloria knew the contents of her small suitcase without doing an inventory. There was no coat. She wondered if she had been in a state of shock when she packed or even if she still was. She remembered once when she was ten and had fallen off the slide at the park and hit her head. She'd walked all the way home and stood ringing the front door for ten minutes, eventually sitting on the front steps to wait for her mother to get home. When her mother had arrived, laden with grocery bags, she'd asked why she hadn't just pushed open the unlocked door or gone to ask the neighbor for the spare key. Neither of those things had occurred to Gloria. A trip to the doctor had revealed concussion and she'd spent the next few days watching the kids playing in the street through the living room window. Now she thought of her stuff at home and wondered what Mike had done with it. She wouldn't blame him if he'd thrown it all out on the street or called a charity to pick it up. Perhaps set it alight in a massive bonfire in the backyard. She hoped he had; the thought was a balm on her searing guilt. She and Lo had something more than horses in common after all. At least Sue-Anne had her faith to refer to, a solid presence that assured her there was a purpose. Gloria had only her hastily packed suitcase and her own thoughts. She reached out a hand to help Sue-Anne up the stairs. "Sue-Anne, do you know where the paddock is with the horses?"

Sue-Anne tipped her head toward one shoulder. "Sure I do." She paused on the porch and pointed out past the field where Kip was bent over by the harvester. "Right down the back there. It's a fair walk. Take one of the jackets in the lean-to. You know she wants to sell all the horses off at auction?"

"Really? Do you think she will?" They went back inside, and Sue-Anne pulled a faded blue parka from off a hook.

"In her heart of hearts I don't think she means it, but she's said it several times. Kip doesn't pay her any mind and Peter's never here to listen."

"Maybe she's just trying to gain some control over her life."

"I think you're right. Trying to remove any reminder of her boy too. I don't think that's healthy. Now go find Samuel in the barn and tell him to grab one of the quiet horses so you can ride down. I reckon that cloud is moving in quick."

The barn with its towering ceiling and dim light was like a cathedral. The warm musty-sweet air was so still after the restless wind outside which was whining over the roof. The sun fell through the high windows in milky pools and everything was hushed. She found Samuel heaving sacks of grain into a storeroom, his hat placed on top a stack to the side. His arms moved with a practiced grace and surprising strength. She stood for a moment watching before she cleared her throat.

"Hi, Samuel, Sue-Anne said you might help me find a horse to ride. I want to go out to see Lo's dressage horses. Do you know where they are?"

"Sure thing, miss. In fact, I'm gonna go out there and check on them soon as I'm done here. I can show you where to grab a horse from."

"That's okay, you look busy. Just describe it and tell me where to find the stuff."

Samuel stood up straight. "You know how to handle a horse?"

Gloria nodded. "Just tell me where they are and I can do the rest."

"You won't hurt yourself and get me into trouble?"

"Nope. Promise."

"Okay then, grab a rope and head over to the pasture beyond the corral there." He waved his hand toward the west wall. "I'll tell you who's kind. Well, most of them are fine, just don't grab Yo-Yo, he's the big chestnut gelding, no markings, you'll see him anyway because he'll probably give you the stink eye, or Polly, the palomino with the walleye, she's got a bruised hoof. Else take your pick."

One of the rooms in the barn was dedicated to saddlery. It was nothing like the neat tack room in the stables. This room had gear stacked everywhere. Gloria found a rope and walked out feeling calmer than she had in a while. She was glad Sue-Anne had insisted she wear the jacket because the wind was bringing an icy chill. The field was huge, stretching away down a hill that dipped and curved back up into a plateau. Horses were scattered around grazing. The few nearest Gloria looked up, hoping for a treat. A buckskin with a full bushy tail and a forelock half covering his eyes came to investigate. "You're not Yo-Yo or Polly, so you can come with me." She looped the rope around his neck but he walked quietly beside her anyway. At the barn, Gloria put him in a stall and went to find some brushes to give him a once-over. As she was combing the tangles from his mane, Samuel came over followed by Wilbur and leaned on the half door.

"That's Dodger. I'll get something that fits him."

Dodger tolerated Gloria's affections with calm blinking eyes and an occasional whisk of his tail. He opened his mouth obediently for the curb bit, which Gloria wasn't sold on. No wonder the horses stopped on a dime. "Oh, you're a good boy," she said, taking his muzzle in her hands and kissing his velvety nose. "You smell good too." Dodger flicked his ears appreciatively.

Samuel reappeared with Wilbur in tow again, leading a gleaming light chestnut horse by the reins. "Well, nothing's on backward," he said, his voice cracking slightly. "We should head over if we want to beat that cloud."

"Let's go!"

CHAPTER FOUR

The smell of rain was on the breeze and Dodger's loose gait was steady as Gloria fell into the gentle rhythm which was as familiar to her as her own step. They waved to Kip, who held up a hand and stopped what he was doing to watch them until they disappeared from view as they dipped down into the flat. Samuel rode along beside her on Firecat, his well-muscled quarter horse, opening gates but not saying much. Gloria didn't mind; she was happy to take in the towering pines and the flat river stretching out toward the mountains with their sugar-dusted peaks. Wilbur paced happily by their side, at times blundering off through the long grass on the scent of something, returning with grass seeds stuck to his wet nose and pink tongue lolling happily from the side of his mouth. Eventually he disappeared into a field of corn.

"It's so beautiful. Do you ever get used to it?"

Samuel grinned. "I guess it is. I was born and raised just down the road there. I'm not really one for closed spaces."

"I can see why. What are those pink flowers everywhere? They're so pretty."

"That ain't pretty, that's paintbrush. It's a weed. It gets into the crops if you let it."

"The yellow flowers too?"

"All the flowers!"

Gloria laughed, glad Samuel was relaxing around her. She gave Dodger a rub on the shoulder, feeling that right in this moment things couldn't be more perfect. An isolated snapshot in her life.

"Shall we?" Samuel nodded at the open land stretching out in front of them. "Hold on tight, they get going quick."

Gloria didn't need to be asked twice. She picked up her reins and gave Dodger a gentle squeeze. Samuel was right—there was power in those rounded hindquarters. The cold air rushed at her as they raced to meet the cloud that was drawing closer. Lightning flashed across the sky, followed closely by a boom of thunder so loud it felt just overhead. Samuel slowed Firecat and indicated toward the right. Gloria sat back down and Dodger obediently dropped back to a trot. In a field to the right were two horses, disturbed from their grazing. Their heavy build and long clean legs gave them away as Lo's dressage horses. The bigger of the two, a bay with a white blaze down his face, still had strings of grass hanging from his mouth. Gloria recognized him from the photo on the wall as Hamlet. Despite being out of condition, both horses had the rounded crests and sleek lines of good breeding. The smaller of the two was a dappled gray, still dark enough in color to indicate she was young. They walked forward to the fence eagerly.

"Why are they all the way out here? These are good horses."

Samuel shrugged. "Don't know about good but they're expensive. These things are ballerinas, not good for much apart from trotting around a ring."

Gloria was barely listening. Thunder boomed again and the gray gave a little leap and trotted a magnificent circle, hooves flicking out like music. If that was all she did, it was fine with Gloria.

Samuel swung down from Firecat and walked over to the fence.

Gloria looked on in alarm. "What if he gets a fright from the thunder, will he just stand there?"

Samuel looked at her like she was crazy. "He'd better."

"Will Dodger?"

"They all will. That's how we train 'em. Else if someone takes a fall, they'll be over the mountain before we can get up again."

Gloria dismounted and tentatively stepped away. "Wow."

Samuel laughed. "And you say you train horses!"

"Look out, here it comes!"

A shoal of rain gusted through, and the gray mare lifted her head and trotted another anxious circle. Gloria squinted against the rain and followed Samuel over the post-and-rail fence. Hamlet stood with his head high and his ears straining while Samuel ran his hands down his legs and checked his hooves and inside his mouth. Gloria held her hand out to the gray mare, who stretched out her neck to waffle at her with delicate nostrils then squealed and reared and trotted off again.

"The gelding is sound as a bell," Samuel called over the splattering rain. "Don't bother with the mare, she ain't worth the bruises. If she can move like that, she looks all right to me. Let's go, and I mean quick."

Dodger and Firecat were looking very miserable, their haunches turned toward the driving rain. Water was running in rivulets down their fetlocks. Gloria vaulted up onto the squelchy saddle and they spun around and set off at a mad gallop through the fields, only pausing to open and close gates. When they finally got back to the barn, they were saturated and their cheeks were glowing. Poor Dodger's sides were heaving. Gloria walked him around inside the barn until he had settled and she was able to wipe him down. When she took the saddle off, steam rose from his sweat-curled back. Wilbur appeared, his white coat gray with water, his tail tucked between his legs. He lay down in front of the stall, his head on his big paws.

"Old Dodger has had a workout," Samuel said, bringing a bucket of water and sponge so Gloria could clean him up.

"What's her name, Samuel?"

"Who?"

"The gray mare."

Samuel blushed again. "We call her Sonnet, but don't you say that name back at the house. Dolores don't want to hear it."

"What don't Dolores wanna hear?" Kip asked, swaggering in with a saddle over his shoulder.

"Anything to do with her horses, it seems," Gloria said. "We need to bring them down here. It's only a matter of time before there's an injury."

"Lo won't like it," Kip said, shifting the saddle down onto his forearm.

"When I told Lo I was bringing the mare in to do her hooves, she burst into tears," Samuel volunteered.

"Don't tell her then. She won't know. Look, I'm here to work with those horses, I can't very well do it if they're miles away." Gloria dropped the sponge back into the bucket and wiped her hands on her sodden jeans. She had begun to shiver and her fingers felt clumsy. Overhead, the rain began to pelt down on the barn roof.

Kip spoke loudly to compete with the rain. "If you say so. We tried putting them in the stables but the mare went loco until she kicked out a wall and bumped her head. She's not right anymore, after the accident. You can't box her, can't handle her. We twitch and hobble her to do her feet. She'll follow the big gelding all right, if you want to bring her down. She yells if you separate them."

"So if we bring Hamlet in, then Sonnet will follow?"

Kip nodded. "Yup. Samuel, you can put them in the corral. A few days without food or water and she'll have a change of heart."

"No! It's okay, I'll look after her. Is there a smaller paddock close to the barn?"

"Samuel," Kip said. "Take Dodger back and let Gloria pick where she wants the horses. I guess we can't spare the corral at present anyway. We'll be going out to do a check later today, we gotta move the babies in closer. I've seen bear prints again."

"Up by the creek?"

Kip nodded. "Samuel, take this pony out so Gloria can get into some dry clothes. I'm stressed about the hay now. I think Dolores was talking sense. I was rushing because we got less help around here these days, but I may have cut my nose off to spite my face." He rubbed at his chin and stared into space for a moment. "I've got my work cut out now, making sure what we've got is dry enough. Yessir."

In her room, Gloria gratefully peeled off her jeans and T-shirt and stood looking at the inadequate object that was her suitcase. It sat like an apology on the foot of her bed, offering no more than it could. She was angry with herself for being so hasty. She remembered how she had been racing her own self-doubt out the door.

She put on her baggy gray shorts, black T-shirt, and the one windbreaker she had brought and realized she didn't even have any other socks. Garfield had succumbed to Sue-Anne's firm hand and was hanging on the clothes rack in the washhouse. She sat on the bed and pulled the quilt around herself. The magnolia tree by her window was taking a pelting from the downpour, its leaves bouncing up and down with each fresh spattering. The sky was a deep gray, lit up from behind. She was sure she had heard that Wyoming was hurricane country. Kip's haying wouldn't be finished anytime soon. As if reading her mind, Lo's shadow ghosted past the doorway.

"Lo!" Gloria called out. She saw the edge of Lo's shadow pause on the floor, then Lo followed it back until she was framed in the doorway.

"It's too early for haying," Lo said, as though they were mid-conversation.

"It's not very good weather for anything other than watering the grass. Kip seems to be remedying the haying situation. Hey, I was wondering if there is a clothing store in town? I didn't pack much."

Lo's eyes started at Gloria's feet and made their way slowly up toward her face as though understanding was slow to digest. "There is Hargrave's and also the general store in town."

"Okay, do you think I can walk into town? How long does it take?"

"In this weather? Tell Kip to drive you." Her gluggy gaze shifted back to the water gushing against the pane. "It's too wet to ride."

"Okay, thank you." Gloria looked up at Lo from where she sat with the quilt wrapped around her shoulders.

Lo walked over to the window and pressed her starfished fingertips against the pane. She stood looking out, the drips of water reflected on her pale skin like tears. She took a shuddering breath. "They don't listen to me anymore." She turned to Gloria, her eyes large in her peaked face. "Am I here?"

"You're here," Gloria said, opening the quilt. "We're here."

Lo stepped toward her, her fingertips lingering on the cold glass, the heat-frosted dots evaporating to nothing as she came to sit next to Gloria. Gloria closed the quilt around her.

"You smell like rain," Lo said, staring straight ahead at the wall, allowing but unwilling.

"My hair's still wet, it's probably dripping on you. Is it making you cold?"

"No. I don't know. Any sensation that makes me feel alive."

Gloria wanted to grab her and say *you are alive!* but instead she left her gaze on the wall beside Lo's and sat with her in silence. After minutes that felt like hours, she turned to look at Lo's proud profile with its upward inflections and downward planes. Her tiny gold stud earring was so close to Gloria's mouth that Gloria could pull it from the neat lobe with her teeth.

"Why don't we go and have coffee on the back porch and watch the rain come down?"

Gloria could feel Lo's reluctance to agree to anything, to agree to agreeing, to move with purpose. Even her breaths were infrequent and reluctant. "I don't…" She shook her head as though finishing the sentence might make her cry.

Gloria sat a moment longer, her hands folded loosely in her lap, before standing and letting the quilt fall from her shoulders. "It doesn't matter. Let's go and make coffee and then see if the rain will put on a show. The sun might come out and ruin our plans."

Lo looked up at her and her voice was sharp. "Does anyone ever tell *you* how to feel?"

"I'm not telling you how to feel about anything. You can have your coffee and be angry."

The quilt slipped from Lo's shoulder too. "Don't patronize me."

Gloria felt like she could sigh in frustration, could laugh with the strangeness of it all, could pick Lo up like an angry child and tell her what to do, but instead she was a blank canvas on which Lo could paint her choices. She wasn't sure if she liked herself for it, if it was the gutless thing to do or the right thing to do. She stood and waited for Lo to figure out what she wanted. In the end it was to stand and let the quilt fall back on the bed. Gloria didn't even bend to pick up the wet clothes in their path for fear it would break the web that Lo was hanging from. Instead, she let Lo trail along behind.

On the back porch, the swinging seat sat like a fancy from another era, its faded apricot cushions and dusty white fringe coquettish against the masculine contours of the house. Lo sat as far away from Gloria as possible with her hands wrapped around her cup and her feet tucked under her. The garden was green and sulky under the weight of the rain which dripped down apathetically, and Gloria began to wonder if her idea was so bright after all. Was it so impossible to think that Lo was an organic creature sprung from the same molecules that had formed into feathery stalks of wheat or vaporous clouds that ballooned and dissipated? Ghosts of the sky that no more minded if they were there or they weren't. A product of their environment. Lo, Dolores, cloudy eyes, and cloudy heart. At once both the landscape and the changing weather. Gloria remembered what Sue-Anne had said and crudely interrupted the dreary rain-song.

"When I left Melbourne, it was raining. I brought it with me." Lo didn't comment and Gloria knew it was an inane thing to say, unworthy of comment and hardly tantalizing to a prospective mute. She rocked the swing gently with her heels on the planks of the deteriorating porch. "When I was a kid I dreamed of places like this. I was so convinced that it would materialize somehow. Rolling hills dotted with horses, miles of free country. I'm not sure where I thought it would materialize from, but I was quite confident." Gloria took a sip of coffee. It was stronger than she was accustomed to and she was enjoying it for the warmth more than the taste. Something for her hands to do. "I used to draw sketches of houses and stables, plan out where I'd put the arena and the lunging ring." She smiled to herself.

"And it did," Lo said.

"Did what?"

"Materialize. Look around. Here you are."

Gloria did look around. Everything meek under the weight of the weather, the fields lost to mist in the distance. She had pictured something like it, yes, but not this. In her drawings of carefully ruled gray lines and white voids representing spaces, there had never been a woman with her lantern light dimmed low, grown so still her golden skin was turning marble. Never this sadness that sat like the mist.

Lo's voice was soft but clear. "I had dreams too, of being a city girl. I never wanted to stay here. I spent my college years purging the country girl from me."

"And what happened, you met Peter?"

Lo shook her head. "Dad passed and left me this place. It's selfish, but I was angry with him for that. I was working for a firm I loved, the name will mean nothing to you, but a big firm, and despite what Peter or anyone else might tell you, I got that job on merit. It took years of cutting my teeth on public defense work. I finally felt I was headed somewhere when he passed. That phone call is fresh in my mind, Mom's voice oddly calm. The time following it was something I'd never experienced before, it became a syrupy matter, like wading through molasses.

I think reality dawned on me in terrible sucking waves, that my life had to change being the final tsunami. To Peter's credit, he settled here with me. I think he liked the idea of playing house, and at the time I liked the idea of having someone to lean on. Mom didn't want to live here with us, she lives in Cheyenne with a gentleman named Casey who she refuses to admit she's romantically involved with. Losing Daddy was hard, but it still didn't prepare me for losing my child. There's no preparation for that. Sometimes in the early morning when I finally fall asleep, I have these dreams that I'm in a huge apartment overlooking a harbor. Inside the apartment it is dark and quiet but outside the city is alive with twinkling lights. I can see people framed in office windows, the headlights of cars on the busy streets below, lit-up billboards, ships bobbing on the inky ocean, and I know I'm at home, that's where I live. I feel happy and protected, but then I hear a voice. I know it's Terrence's voice, but he's older, it's the voice of a man. He's saying, 'There's still time.' The building starts to quake and I know that I've caused it by forgetting him. The building is crumbling and I'll plummet down through the middle, crushed by debris. It's the same every time. Do you think he's trying to warn me about the building, or is he telling me there's time for something else?"

Gloria cleared her throat. "I'm not sure. What do you think?"

Lo's forehead was knitted and she was looking at Gloria with a self-absorbed intensity. Suddenly, she laughed. "Jesus, I don't know, but you're easy to talk to. How did I end up here, so darn serious?"

Gloria patted Lo's leg. "I'm bound by equine therapist-horse owner confidentiality. It's all in the agreement you haven't signed."

"I'll get my legal team to look it over. But seriously, I'm sorry, Gloria. Can you tell I don't get out much?"

Levity seemed to be woven into the sails of Lo's grief and Gloria was getting better at standing tall against the winds of her sorrow. "But hang on, what about the horses? Don't you at least enjoy this lifestyle for the horses?"

"I do now, but I wasn't a horse-mad little gal like you. They were just a part of life out here. It wasn't until I discovered dressage that the love of horses really kicked in. Still, I'm sure I would love cocktail parties and apartment living just as much."

Gloria was doubtful, but then again the fringes of suburban Melbourne were hardly the big city lights. "But then what would have been left?"

"A high-powered career in law."

"No, I mean the city…a never-ending concrete tunnel. This place, it's alive, constantly renewing, a cycle of fresh promise that carries on regardless. The seasons are so evident, a fresh crop of foals…"

"There's nothing special about that, it's the most natural thing in the world. Birth, death. It's uncaring."

Gloria extended her foot so that her toe caught a drop of rain. How could she explain to someone who took it for granted that it was like witnessing a miracle each morning? She looked up, and at that moment a rainbow seemed to hurl itself through the gray, or perhaps it was just the trajectory of her gaze. Visions in the storm.

"I'm ungrateful and look what's happened." Lo shifted restlessly and Gloria stopped the swing's gentle rocking with the flat of her foot, thinking Lo would get up and go, but Lo merely rearranged herself and began to pick at the fringe on a cushion. "I'm telling you all these things, but happiness seems to me like a place I left. Like a big city, I can still see it on the map but I know I'll never go back there."

In Gloria's mind her childish pencil drew the wobbly lines of happiness, a place where Lo could live, but she knew it wasn't for her to create. She didn't even have the blueprint for her own. All she could say was, "Happiness is a strange idea." What she meant was that the raindrop that made the daffodils bloom was the same raindrop that made her boots wet. "Perhaps the times I thought I was happy, I really wasn't. Or maybe that happiness turned sour. It's hard to hold on to, isn't it?"

"It's the depending on others for happiness that's the problem. That tricky word 'love' again."

"Can we be happy without it?"

Lo's nose twitched. "Love for everything but not love for only one thing. You know, being a mother, the love you have for your child…it's intense and slightly terrifying, having someone need you so much. Suddenly you're the person who has to have all the answers. It's beautiful too, being needed like that. I don't think I appreciated it for what it was. I found it constricting, and I feel guilty for this, but sometimes I used to imagine my life without him. What I would be like, what my life would be like, without a child, without someone whose every need was my duty. And now I know how it feels. It's scary and bleak, having no one to need you."

"People need you, your friends, family, Peter." Even as Gloria said the words, her own brow furrowed, wondering who needed her and if it bothered her, the not being needed.

"Not like that," Lo said.

It seemed their conversations constantly found the deepest part of the woods. She made an attempt to lift it out again. "Will you show me the foals later?"

"The boys will be going over that way. It's not far, just by the barn there. Where the shelters are." She made a floppy gesture that somewhat resembled a pointed finger. "We keep them close when they're tiny. The pregnant mares too."

"Are they all quarter horses?"

"Mostly, yes."

"Ever wanted to breed a warmblood?"

"Maybe once."

Gloria thought of the gray mare and wondered if she had been part of that unrealized plan. She kicked her feet at the rain again. She wasn't used to all this sitting, the days stretching out in front of her like a slack piece of string. She desperately wanted someone to pull on the other end and set something in motion. "If the rain stops, I'll go down and see them. Are they all by, ah, Fast And Loose?" She couldn't say the name without smiling.

Lo's mouth lifted at the corners. "Yes, Freddy, he's the big daddy. We need an injection of cash to keep this place going.

There's a big auction that happens. I want to get rid of most of the stock. Let someone else have a turn at ranching with Freddy's bunch. Everyone knows he throws good working horses. I don't think he's lost too many championships at shows. Ask Kip, he'll remember. I never had too much to do with Freddy, but anyone could handle him, even Terrence." She seemed to shrink a few inches but she kept talking. "I should say his name, shouldn't I?"

Gloria looked at Lo for a moment before responding. Every now and then she had a feeling of déjà vu. It struck her now, the smell of wet earth and the look of fragile determination on Lo's face. She wanted to offer her something but she had nothing to give. She could picture how it must feel to speak of intimate tragedy, like sticking a finger into an open wound. "I'm no expert on grief, but they say it's good to talk." It wasn't sufficient, but she hoped it didn't make it worse.

Lo shifted again as though it was the seat making her uncomfortable. "Ugh! I'm so sick of everything…sick of myself, my own thoughts. I don't know why anyone would want eternal life. More like damnation. I think I understand the true punishment a prisoner faces. I feel safe in my room but it's the confinement of the mind that tortures."

"Won't you come to see the foals then? The rain has just about stopped and my hair can't get any wetter." She turned to smile at Lo but Lo wasn't smiling.

Lo's face had closed over. She stared for a long time at the rain-smudged line where land met mountains. "Don't bother. Is Peter paying you to be nice to me? Hang out with Dolly and bring her back to life." She looked at Gloria with glistening eyes and tipped her head to the side in a gesture of pity. "Naw, don't worry, you're not the only one. Sue-Anne is on payroll too, making sure I look after my skin, change my clothes, eat my food. No one wants a bony wife to hold, do they?"

Gloria felt hurt, even though she knew she had no right to bring it into the realm of the personal. How could one's interactions be sweet when one's emotions were bitter? "I know Sue-Anne cares about you, and I do too."

"You don't know me at all."

"You're right, I don't really know you, but no one's paying me anything. I'm sitting here talking because that's what I want to do." The rain had stopped but the gutters were still gushing and the eaves dripping.

Lo silently shed her angry tears. "I didn't ask to have you here." She scrubbed at a cheek with the sleeve of her cardigan.

Gloria felt angry herself. She hadn't asked for any of this either and had problems of her own to sort out. She stood up. "Lo, I'm sorry about your little boy but I can't be a punching bag for you. I think it's best if I get a flight out tomorrow."

Lo didn't turn her head, nor did she say anything to stop her. Gloria went into the kitchen and washed her cup and put it on the draining board. As she walked back to her room, she saw Sue-Anne in the living room dusting along the sideboard. She felt bold with anger.

"Sue-Anne, can you please give me a number I can reach Peter on?"

Sue-Anne stopped what she was doing. "There's a book right here by the telephone with numbers in it. Just call the office number, I think it ends in four-seven. You'll see it there. He's hard to catch but you can leave a message with his secretary, Crystal, is that her name?"

Gloria went and sat on the sofa by the phone. She could feel Sue-Anne's curiosity like a presence in the room, could see her mouth puckering without having to look.

"Candice!" she called. "That's her name."

Gloria picked up the little blue address book with its well-worn pages and opened it up to P. Inside was a business card with Peter Ballantyne, attorney at law, and a phone number, fax, and a street address on it. The card was thick creamy cardboard, frayed at the edges. On the page beside it, a child's hand had drawn a face like a misshapen potato in red ink, and underneath it was written *hores*. Gloria wondered if the innocent misspelling of Terrence's favorite animal had made Lo laugh until it hadn't. She gritted her teeth and dialed the number on the beige plastic telephone—now was not the time to be sentimental. The phone began to ring. Absentmindedly, Gloria poked her finger through the curly cord.

"Hello, Peter Ballantyne's offices. This is Candice speaking."

"This is Gloria Grant. Can I please speak to Peter?"

Sue-Anne began plumping the cushions on the other end of the sofa.

"Peter is currently in a meeting. May I take a message for you?"

"Please ask him to call Gloria back as soon as possible. He has the number."

"Well, would you mind giving it to me just in case?"

Gloria looked down at the telephone with its number written in a careful round hand on a slip of paper underneath the plastic. She read it out and Candice dutifully recited each digit until she began to recognize it as a whole and her voice slowed. "Oh, okay. I will have him call you." There was an itch in her tone, but Gloria didn't scratch it. Instead, she hung up and closed the address book and lined it neatly by the phone as it had been. Sue-Anne was not so withholding.

"Is everything okay?"

Gloria stood up and crossed her arms, then uncrossed them for fear of seeming angry, which she was. "I need to speak to Peter so he can arrange a flight home for me."

"Oh, no." Sue-Anne let go of the pillow she had been meticulously arranging and it fell forward. "What's brought this on?"

"This isn't going to work unless Lo is interested. I came here to train horses, but things have become complicated and Peter is nowhere to be found. I feel a bit as though I was tricked into coming!" She quieted her tone and began again. "It's my own fault, I shouldn't have flown halfway across the planet. I'm too impulsive."

"For what it's worth, Gloria, I don't think Peter is intentionally deceiving you. He has been so busy, running the business without Dolores. They were already busy, but his workload doubled overnight. I think he uses it as an escape and there's no one here to look after Dolores." She picked up the cushion and placed it so its colorful woven side was on display.

"With all due respect"—Gloria hated that phrase, but she uttered it anyway—"I'm not a babysitter."

"Just please wait until Peter comes back. Talk it over before you decide. What's one more day? Dolores has barely spoken two words the last few weeks and now she's sitting chatting to you."

Gloria tipped her head back in frustration and sighed. "I already feel bad. It's an awful situation but it's not something I can help with. Doesn't Dolores have a friend that she might want to see?"

Sue-Anne made a harsh sound in her throat. "Friend! What friend? Those useless women from town who baked casseroles and dropped by a few times then stopped bothering? Insensitive is what they are." Gloria didn't comment, so she continued, "Think on it, that's all. Just speak to Peter. He is paying for your flight after all."

Gloria didn't appreciate her sly dig. She was well aware that she was relying on Peter's generosity to get her home and it was making her uncomfortable. "Thank you, Sue-Anne, you've been very welcoming to me. I just don't see any other way."

Sue-Anne softened her tone. "Gloria, I just have a feeling that you were brought here for a reason. Please just say you'll sleep on it."

Gloria didn't see the point. Outside, the slow patter of rain picked up again. "Sleep on what? I came here because I thought there was a job. There isn't. End of story." Gloria took a deep breath. "Sorry." She turned away from Sue-Anne and went to sit on her bed so she could be within earshot of the phone in case Peter called. She didn't know what else to do. After about ten minutes, Sue-Anne came and knocked even though the door was open.

"Here are some books from the bookshelf in the study. There's cold meats and fresh bread if you're hungry, other than that, I'll call you when I'm plating up the supper." She gently placed a stack of books on the end of the bed, and Gloria thanked her and waited until she'd left before shutting the door and taking a look at the books. There were a couple of mysteries and a romance and a biography of a woman who'd survived a month stuck in a cave by eating moss. Gloria wasn't much in the mood for solving any more mysteries or hearing about people madly in love. Sitting in the solitude of a cave seemed somewhat appealing right now, being commanded by only the most basic of needs. She pulled the blankets over her and resolutely opened the biography. Twice she let it fall back into her lap when the phone rang but the call wasn't for her. Her stomach growled but she ignored it, determined to stay away from everyone. Cold meat was certainly no incentive anyway. Eventually Sue-Anne's authoritative rap on the door roused her from the damp depths of the cave. The smell of caramelized garlic and onion wafted in from the hall. Gloria was so hungry she was almost ready to eat moss herself.

CHAPTER FIVE

Outside, evening was beginning to drape itself over the landscape. This time the kitchen was noisy. Sue-Anne bustled around slamming pots and pans. Kip and Samuel sat at the table talking animatedly. Dolores was nowhere to be seen. Kip waved Gloria over and she was suddenly conscious of her fluffy hair and disheveled appearance. She sat down beside him, opposite Samuel, and Sue-Anne placed a platter of roasted parsnips, carrots, pumpkin, and potatoes in the middle of the tablecloth beside a bowl of green beans. Kip extended an arm across the back of Gloria's chair but continued his conversation about a man who worked at the hardware store who kept forgetting to order a certain hinge for him. Sue-Anne hushed them all for a prayer, and as they went quiet and bowed their heads—even Gloria, who wasn't accustomed to the ritual—a man walked into the room. Sue-Anne carried on regardless and it wasn't until he'd loosened his tie and seated himself at the head of the table that Gloria was able to get a proper look at him. He wore a blue business suit with a white shirt. His dark hair was gelled into a little wave above his forehead and his eyes were a bright blue that Gloria was somehow unprepared for. After Lo's evasiveness, his gaze was so direct. He looked around at them all and nodded.

"Sue-Anne, I have missed your cooking." He looked over at Gloria. "Hello, you must be Miss Gloria Grant, horse wrangler extraordinaire." He wasn't an overly tall man, but he was broad shouldered and well proportioned.

"People tend to call me Gloria. You're Peter?"

Peter unbuttoned his collar then laid both palms on the table. "Yes! Hello. I'm sorry I wasn't around to welcome you, but I trust Sue-Anne has been hospitable."

The playfulness had drained away from Kip and he soberly speared a potato with his fork. Samuel had turned pink again and sat waiting for Sue-Anne to give him a cue.

"She has, thank you." Gloria had a lot to say, so she said nothing at all.

"Where's Dolly? Still in bed?"

Gloria sensed that Sue-Anne also had a lot to say and was waiting for a private moment to do so. Sue-Anne looked reproachful. "She's exhausted."

"Yes, I suppose so. Do you think we should wake her?"

Sue-Anne looked at Samuel. "What are you waiting for, your ma to come and feed you? Start eating."

"Aw, Sue-Anne." Samuel ducked his head in embarrassment.

"Here comes the air-o-plane," Kip said and laughed.

Gloria was watching Peter, who was looking at the empty plate in front of him, his cutlery held loosely in his hands. After a moment, he looked up and stared straight at Gloria with a faraway look. She could tell he wasn't even seeing her. He placed his cutlery carefully back onto the tablecloth and said to no one in particular, "I'm going to check on Doll."

It struck Gloria that Dolores of the changing moods was also Dolores of the changing names. Dolores, Dolly, Doll…Lo. Who she was, Gloria wasn't sure. She had introduced herself as Lo, perhaps a reflection of her state of being. Dolores complete and factual to Sue-Anne, and Dolly, Doll to have and to hold to Peter. A pretty girl on the shelf. She supposed once, not so long ago, she had been Mom, Mommy, a name that had been cut from the cloth of her shirt. Sue-Anne leaned forward and plopped pumpkin onto Samuel's plate. Peter stood and placed the napkin that had been folded over his lap onto his plate. Sue-Anne's brow furrowed but she kept heaping Samuel's plate. Kip took a grim sip of water then started earnestly cutting up his pork. Sue-Anne turned her attentions to Gloria's plate and Gloria let her take it and pile it with food she probably wouldn't finish. "No meat!" Gloria almost yelled as Sue-Anne reached the tongs toward the pork. It was possible this would be her last dinner at Heaven's End. Kip picked up the conversation, ribbing Samuel about a girl he was sweet on.

"How old are you, Samuel?" Gloria asked, waving away Sue-Anne's offer of gravy. He was tall and lanky. A man's shoulders with the boyish markers of youth about his face.

"Seventeen, ma'am."

"Old enough to ask a girl out, ain't it, Gloria?" Kip said, obviously concerned with pursuits of the heart, or at least of the flesh.

"Sure, if you like her. Why don't you ask her to see a movie or something?"

Samuel's eyes widened at his food and he shook his head slightly. "Why is everyone so interested all of a sudden?"

Sue-Anne kept glancing toward the doorway, but she gave Samuel a flick of the wrist. "No one cares. Just buy the girl some candy and treat her sweet."

Samuel looked like he was ready to cry. Gloria wondered how she'd ended up at this table of mismatched souls. Kip turned in an exaggerated way toward her. "So, Gloria, tell us, do you have a beau back in Melbourne?"

Gloria prematurely swallowed the potato she was chewing. "No, I...I thought we were discussing Samuel?"

Sue-Anne flung her hands up in despair. "I've never known a bunch of people to make a natural thing such as courtship into such a difficult thing. I was sixteen when I met Earl at a dance. He asked me to dance, I said yes, and that was that."

"Well, Sue-Anne," Kip said. "We can't all be as winsome as you."

"Ooh, Keaten Irvine Preston, you don't give me that lip. I knew you when you were still on your mother's breast."

"Oh, Jesus, Sue-Anne. We practice kinder gelding techniques on the colts." It was the first time Gloria had seen Kip embarrassed.

"Don't you take the Lord's name in vain!" Sue-Anne bellowed.

Kip shook his head. "Talking about a man's mother's breast, at the dinner table, no less. It just ain't cool. You're putting me right off my food." He pushed his fork and knife together.

"Where do you think you came from? Your mother brought you into this world and I'm sure if she could hear you now the embarrassment would be all hers. Stop making an obscenity out of the facts of life and eat the good milk pork that's been cooked for you. Poor Gloria's never heard such disrespect in her life."

Gloria privately thought that Sue-Anne wouldn't last two minutes at the pub back home. Samuel covered his eyes with one hand as if to remove himself from all the fuss. Kip shook his head again and picked up his fork. His hands were tanned brown and there were calluses on his fingers. He didn't have the regular handsomeness of Peter, but he had a rugged dignity. The meal carried on without chatter, which made the atmosphere denser than the sparring had. There was a naturalness to the way they poked at one another, a familiarity that was better suited to terse conversations than rigid silence. Peter's chair was still pushed back away from the table, his tie slung over the wooden back. Despite Sue-Anne's demand that others focus on their food, she was a fractious person, constantly anticipating others' needs or misinterpreting them. Her eyes frequently slid toward the door until, despite adding more pork to Samuel's plate, she abruptly decided the meal was over and began clearing the plates.

"There's a pie in the oven. Gloria, will you get the brown china jug from up there?"

Gloria helped clear the table and opened the cupboards to find a jug. When she turned around, Sue-Anne was shuffling out of the room, probably to check on Peter and Lo.

"I'm gonna make a dash for it. See you folks tomorrow," Samuel said, depositing his plate on the counter and making for the back door. He closed it quietly behind him and Gloria gave Kip a look that said *Don't you go too*.

"You know what, Gloria. I'd like to invite you into town tomorrow. How about it? The grand tour. You can't hang around here all day with Ole Bossy Boots while Lo sulks in her room."

Gloria didn't like his use of the word *sulk* but she supposed she didn't have the history at the ranch that Kip did. Who knew what he'd borne to keep the place running and what insecurities hung over his head? "Thank you, Keaten Irvine Preston. We'll see."

"I deserved that, but please keep it to yourself." Kip smiled wryly. "How's about this—I'll get the morning chores done quick, then I'll take you in at noon? We could have lunch at the coffee house, my treat."

Gloria was aware of Sue-Anne's dull footsteps across the floorboards. "It's just that I don't know how long I'll be here. I'm hoping to head home in the next day or two."

Kip was interrupted from whatever response he might give by Sue-Anne announcing that Dolores was in the shower and would join them shortly. It seemed Lo's grief was a family affair that they all must wean her from. It made Gloria ashamed for her, that her emotional state was considered the property of Sue-Anne, the remodeling of Dolores through Sue-Ann's doughy handling. As if the strength of Lo's spirit wasn't guiding her, giving her what she needed. Just as Gloria felt it wasn't Sue-Anne's place to lay Lo's grief bare for them all to prod at, it wasn't Gloria's to bundle it up and offer it back. She turned away and tended to the pie instead. The sugary golden pastry had been produced by Sue-Anne's firm hand so perfectly that no one could object to its taste or texture.

Peter came and pulled back his chair, setting the atmosphere with the smooth, definite movements of hand and wrist. Once seated, he sat with his head slightly bowed, in a clear act of exaggerated patience so that the rest should follow suit. He made no comment on Samuel's departure. Gloria and Kip exchanged sideways looks at one another. It wasn't Terrence who was the ghost of the house, it was Dolores.

Lo eventually appeared, her shampoo-scented hair darkened to auburn by the shower, her white face throwing her freckles into sharper relief. The cuffs of her gray windbreaker were pulled into her fists, stretching the fabric taut across her shoulders and giving her an awkward tense look. She sat at the opposite end of the table, facing Peter at the head like king and queen. Gloria sat to her right. She gave Lo a small smile, but Lo was staring at Peter with a serene, almost lofty, expression. Gloria wondered what had gone on in the bedroom to make Lo victorious in her surrender. Peter's careful movements gave as little away as Lo's measured gaze. The meal picked up where it had left off. If Peter minded eating dessert before dinner, he didn't mention it. Sue-Anne lifted the mood again by telling Kip about who she'd seen by the pond at the public gardens (Malory Foster and Gregory Williams, who was apparently going with Hildy McEwan so it was quite the scandal) and what Mr. Ghertick had told her at the store about the brand new stock from Wisconsin that had gone missing from the lumber yard. He wasn't saying it was the youngest Gleeson brother, but he had been fired from the yard the day before. Kip occasionally commented and Peter listened with a serious expression that gave Gloria a glimpse of how he treated his clients. Lo's apple pie grew cold as she sat like a polite guest at a table of people speaking in a foreign language. Sue-Anne paused in her pointed conversation with Peter about the need for tourism in the area to sustain economic growth. She looked at Lo's plate and bugged her eyes in a meaningful way before returning to her conversation. Lo looked down at her food as though surprised it was even there. Gloria reached across and scooped half of Lo's pie onto her own plate while Sue-Anne was distracted. Lo didn't flinch, and when Sue-Anne glanced over again, her finger already tapping on her own plate, she did a double take and a fleeting look of concern crossed her face but she was too deep into her monologue about the woman who ran the guest chalet to investigate. "I've said it before and I'll say it again, the ranch should be reopened as a guesthouse." Sue-Anne glanced at Lo then back at Peter. "I mean, the way things are, this place will fold if there's not more income coming in. Ain't that right, Kip?" She continued without waiting for an answer. "Dolores is in no state to be at the office among criminals, but she could help me with the guests." She lowered her voice to an audible whisper. "It'll give her a purpose."

Lo's chest lifting with a deep breath was the only indication she'd heard. Kip cleared his throat and thanked Sue-Anne for the meal. Gloria shot him a beseeching look, and he said, "Gloria, won't you come and see the thing outside that I told you about before?"

Gloria stood, grateful for his inarticulate rescue. She turned to Lo, passing her the line of rope. "Lo, would you like to join us for a walk?"

"I might need a chaperone," Kip added. "In case Gloria gets any ideas."

Sue-Anne and Peter paused in their conversation again and when Lo went to scrape her leftovers into the bin, Sue-Anne nodded at Peter in a self-satisfied way. Gloria felt they would probably be the next topic of conversation.

"Peter?" Lo asked in a small voice.

"Doll, I've got some reports to go over, but go ahead. Gloria, I'll bet you've never seen the night sky until you've seen it from the plains here. Up in the mountains it feels as though you can touch the stars."

Gloria opened her mouth to say that perhaps they could talk later, but instead she said, "I'll bet it's magical."

In the lean-to Gloria reached for the blue parka, which was still slightly damp, but Lo took it from her. Gloria thought perhaps she wasn't allowed to use it, but instead Lo handed her a longer camel-colored coat with fringing along the sleeves. "Take this, you'll be warmer," she said. She pulled on a large dark green puffy jacket. "We'll both wear Peter's or else they'll feel they don't have a purpose." It was less a joke, more a release of tension from the power dynamics in the kitchen.

Outside, Wilbur materialized from the dark and began to follow them, his rump wagging with his tail. The clouds had shifted and the air was still. The smell of wet earth mingled with the oily smell of crushed grain. Overhead, the stars arched in burning dots and powdery clusters around a three-quarter moon.

"Wow," Gloria breathed, feeling herself relax.

"Spectacular, ain't it?" Kip said. "See that house way down past the long field?"

Gloria had to admit that she couldn't.

"Well, that's where they lock me at night, don't you, Dolores?"

"Keeps finding his way back," Lo said weakly.

"You two gonna walk me home in case of bears?"

"Bears?" Gloria asked, peering into the shadows as they walked along the path toward the barn.

"Grizzlies, black bears," Kip confirmed. They walked a few more paces before he pointed into the darkness again. "Look over there, can you see the foals?"

Gloria stared again before laughing. "I can't see a thing!" Something flitted above them and Gloria ducked, grabbing Lo's arm.

Kip laughed and Lo said, "Just an owl."

"So, you live here, at the ranch?" Gloria asked, staying close to Lo, her eyes following Wilbur as he vanished into the dark.

"For going on five years now, hey, Lo?"

Lo nodded.

"I'm always around. As you know yourself, livestock care is around the clock. Speaking of, I'm gonna bring the brown mare in tonight, she's close-to, I reckon."

"Foaling?" Gloria asked excitedly.

"Yep. There's a couple of them yet to go."

"Can I..." Gloria was about to offer to help. She'd been present many times when Mike delivered foals, but then she remembered she wouldn't be staying. She jumped slightly as something cold touched her hand. It was Lo's fingers, squeezing her hand for the briefest moment before it slipped away again, distracting her from the memory of Mike that was pressing in.

"If you were going to offer to keep me safe from bears tonight, it's all right, they hear me snoring and run away." Kip stopped and took hold of a fence railing. "I'd better bring that mare in."

"Kip," Lo said reproachfully.

"Goodnight, Kip."

Kip tipped his hat at them and swung easily over the fence.

"I'm sorry," Lo said as they watched his denim jacket fade into the dark. "Just tell him off if you have to. It's his way of showing affection, but not everyone finds it funny."

Gloria didn't mind. She found it harmless but could see how it could make someone uncomfortable. She was enjoying his freewheeling nature after Mike's cautious solicitude, which had sometimes bordered on humorlessness. "He's all right. If he bothers me, I'll tell him to buzz off."

"Buzz off…" Lo repeated. "You say the strangest things."

"Like a fly, I guess, buzzing away." Gloria squinted into the blackness. "Will he be okay? It's so dark."

"He's got cowboy vision. Sue-Anne makes sure he eats his carrots." Lo's teeth flashed a beam into the night.

They walked gently on toward the barn. Disembodied sounds of horses' movements and the rustlings of wild animals came from the darkness. Gloria kept her hand outside of her pocket but Lo didn't reach for it again.

"Are there bears here?"

"No." Lo didn't elaborate, but after a few steps she said, "I'm sorry. I didn't mean to be awful this morning."

Gloria wanted to squeeze that cold timid hand again but she didn't. "You weren't awful."

"No, Gloria, I was, and you don't deserve it. After Terrence passed, I kept going. I'd never had an idle day in my life. I'd worked through heartbreak and through loss before, my job always kept me anchored, but I couldn't do it anymore. I couldn't stand in a courtroom while someone was tried, knowing I was the guiltiest person there and I'm free to walk."

"Punishing yourself helps no one."

Lo's laugh was mirthless. "If punishing myself makes me feel better, is it negating the punishment?"

Gloria's stomach twisted for Lo, but she could only think in clichés which didn't bear repeating.

"What I'm trying to say is that I shouldn't punish others too. It's my own cross to bear. You know, when I worked as a prosecutor, and I was young and hungry for the win, there was a man. I went after him with everything I had. I don't think I slept more than three hours a night, poring over evidence. We got him in the end, the judge made an example of him. He hung himself in custody."

Gloria was shocked. "Was he innocent in the end?"

Lo lifted her gaze from the path. "No, only the guilty hang themselves."

Gloria's throat tightened. "What are you saying, are you telling me you want to hang yourself?"

"No. No. Only that now I understand how he felt. I thought we were different but we're not. We all have it in us."

"Intention, Lo, you know that." When Lo didn't respond, Gloria stopped walking and grabbed her arm. She wanted to yell at her and tell her that this was worse than the conversation that morning. She was prepared to shake her until her teeth rattled, but when they faced each other, there was no reproach. Lo's eyes were dull with despair and instead Gloria cupped the strained face in her hands and looked her in the eye. "Lo." How could she tell her that she couldn't be the one to save her from herself? She was more likely to run away when things became demanding. "Lo," she said again. "You're enough. You deserve happiness." Lo's hazel irises were like pools of night sky. She ducked her head away first.

Lo took a shuddering breath. "It's easier to just have nothing, be nothing." Gloria went to take Lo's hand but Lo pulled away and wiped at her nose with the back of her sleeve. "It's okay, don't get upset. I'll regain control. It's just an episode...an episode." She shook her head as though clearing it. Reflective eyes blinked at them from the fields, the smack of a tail whisking against a rump. "Am I crazy?" She looked back at Gloria, wonder in her liquid eyes. "Maybe this is what it means to be mad."

Gloria blinked away moisture from her own eyes. "Maybe we should go back. Have a cup of coffee? Bourbon?" She tried to keep the fear from her voice but its crack in the middle gave her away.

"You can go back if you want, but I'm going to the barn."

"The barn?" A desire to weep with the hopelessness of it all gripped Gloria. Lo turned and started walking with purpose, her hands deep in the pockets of the green jacket. Gloria looked back toward the lights of the house. She wanted to run back, away from graveyard eyes and rustlings in the grass, back to the irritating safety of Sue-Anne's gossip and Peter's reassuring stolidness. Instead she turned and quickly stepped after Lo, her heart beating at her temples.

The barn's large doors were closed but Lo wrenched open the smaller door in the side and felt around for a light switch. The lights up in the rafters swung slightly, casting shifting shadows over everything. In the artificial light, the barn resembled a tomb more than a cathedral, but the sweet smell of hay and herbivore was the same. Gloria followed Lo closely as she crossed the floor and made for a ladder at the side. She took hold of the first rung and climbed deftly. As soon as Gloria heaved herself up into the hayloft behind her, Lo flicked a switch and the lights went out. Gloria reached out and grabbed hold of the back of Lo's jacket to guide herself, stumbling through a bed of thick hay, terrified at any moment she'd fall through the floor onto the ground below. At the far wall, Lo stopped and there was the sound of locks scraping. The double window shutters creaked back, letting in a cold rush of air, and Gloria was looking out over the ranch at a velvety night sky.

"I come here in the night sometimes. It puts things into perspective. None of it really matters does it?" Lo sat down on a wooden reel and moved over so Gloria could fit.

Gloria felt at once insignificant and almighty, up there, closer to the stars but still so very far away.

"Stardust, it's all we are." Lo stared intently into the dark at something perhaps only she could see. "Touch me, Gloria."

The stars were like cream dollops in the sky, but Gloria turned away from them and looked at Lo, unsure if she'd heard correctly.

"Am I here?" Lo's profile, thinly foiled in the moonlight, the swan neck. Gloria reached out a finger and ran it down from Lo's chin, stopping to rest in the hollow of her throat. Lo closed her eyes and took a slow breath. Gloria could feel Lo's pulse, deep and strong. She let her hand fall back into her lap. Lo opened her eyes slowly and sat staring into the sky. A Grecian statue, the prow of a ship, the bronzed bust in a glass box, distant as the stars across oceans. They sat, turning through the universe, until the cold started to glaze their skin and Gloria took Lo's hand and they wordlessly reversed their steps.

At the house, the kitchen was clean and the light was on in the study. Gloria had been thinking about what she should say to Lo, but when they reached the corridor, Lo quietly opened the door to the study and shut it again behind her. Gloria stood, listening to the muffled sound of voices, feeling suddenly an outsider again, standing by herself in a desolate field. She was angry at herself for letting other people interfere with her emotions. She knew how easy it would be to run to Mike to quell the panic that was swelling inside her, but the remedy would quickly become the disease again. She stared at the closed door for a long moment, knowing that Lo would take comfort where she could find it, whether it was from her or from Peter or Sue-Anne in her own maternal way, and that she, Gloria, mustn't take it personally. The light from under the door was nothing to do with her and she turned away to begin the private bedtime ritual.

As she lay in the dark, her mind drifting through half-formed dreams, she remembered the relief teacher she'd had at school when she was seven. Miss Kennedy. The way she smelled like strawberries and her voice was kind and steady and she once brought them in a plate of biscuits with enough for everyone in the class to have two. It had taken Gloria less than a week to become absolutely besotted, and then one day she was gone and Mrs. Barry was back with her paisley vest and clompy shoes. Gloria had walked to school every weekday morning for the rest of the year hoping it'd be Miss Kennedy at the classroom door, but it never was.

CHAPTER SIX

Gloria awoke early again, the still unfamiliar sounds of farm life rousing her from a rapidly dissipating dream. The events of the night before drew into focus. There was no point getting involved in the ecosystem of emotions that grew in the house. She had to separate herself from that, and the easiest way was to create a physical divide. The house was too full of sleeping giants. Her same clothes that had seemed inadequate yesterday were a modest, self-contained symbol of the reason she was here and how little the personal should matter to anyone else. She was there to work, and regardless of what Lo had said, her job was to work with the horses and the horses deserved the care that Lo was unable to give.

True to Kip's word, the dressage horses were in a yard behind the barn next to where the mares and foals were. She wondered if the brown mare had foaled last night and decided a visit with the foals would be her reward if she made progress with Sonnet. The grass in the yard had been eaten down to almost nothing and although there was a large tub for water, there wasn't much in the way of feed. Along the fence closest to the path, there was a muddied track that Sonnet had trodden, pacing back and forth. When Gloria approached, Sonnet was standing behind Hamlet, who had his long neck stretched under the fence to catch some of the grass in the field next door. Hamlet carried on twisting his head to the side to try and reach the longer grass. Sonnet lifted her head in alarm and snorted once through quivering nostrils. "Why are you so scared, Sonnet, what happened to you?" Gloria went to lean against the fence, forearms resting on the top rail, her chin on her knuckles. Hamlet eventually extracted himself from his search for food and came wandering over. Sonnet stayed where she was and watched them through wary eyes fringed with white lashes. Hamlet nudged at Gloria, and she rubbed his face and ran a hand along the proud line of his neck, feeling where the solid muscle gave way to the vulnerable softness of his gullet. All the while Gloria spoke to him, telling him how he was a lovely boy and she hoped they'd be friends. Sonnet stood, her strong legs four-square, her ears flicking to catch Gloria's words, eventually dropping her head slightly. "That's okay, Sonnet," Gloria continued in a steady, predictable tone. "You're scared now, but you'll learn to trust again. Happens to the best of us, believe me. People are exactly the same. Something scares us and we find it hard to let go of that and try again. It's a primitive form of intelligence, I guess. We don't want to go on eternally making the same mistakes, but the outcome won't always be the same." She slowly climbed up onto the fence so she was sitting on the top rail. Sonnet threw her head up but didn't run. Hamlet placed his chin on her lap. "Oh, you're a big teddy bear, aren't you?" She could see what a willing type he was. "See, Sonnet, I'm not so bad." She had an impression of what he would be like under saddle and she was tempted to bring his gear from the stables and take him for a spin. "You're a luxury vehicle aren't you? Lo chose well with you. Where did you come from, Germany? Holland? Denmark? Do you speak English?" Hamlet turned his head to check on Sonnet. "You were keeping me warm. How about we get you something to eat? There's nothing on the ground for you." Gloria gently pushed him away and climbed back down.

In the barn, Samuel was holding one foreleg up of a muddy bay horse while Kip rasped at her teeth. "Morning," was all they said as she walked past them to find some hay. Back at the yard, she sat on the fence and watched Hamlet tuck in. After a while, Sonnet came shuffling forward with her head low to the ground and nostrils flaring. The wooden fence was rough under Gloria's hands, the morning air cold on her face, but she sat very still and eventually Sonnet came close enough to snatch a few mouthfuls of hay. The whole time Gloria kept up her one-sided conversation, even when Samuel came past with a wheelbarrow and shook his head at her. She was still sitting there when Kip came to call her for breakfast. Gloria climbed down, happy to see Sonnet eye her warily but not leap away.

Gloria grinned. "See, she's a bit calmer. I think I can work with her."

"Maybe so. Have you seen under her chest there?" Kip didn't look so convinced.

"What do you mean?" Gloria glanced back at Sonnet.

"No one's explained a thing to you, have they?"

The sheen on the morning quickly fell away. "Not really. Actually, I would love you to explain some things to me."

"This loco thing"—Kip gestured to Sonnet—"saw a mountain lion near the woods and took off hurley-burley with the little boy up on top. She didn't stop until she was tangled in a fallen branch, torn under the chest there. Take a look for yourself."

Gloria leaned forward until she could see a dark patch of scarring on the mare's belly. She stared at it for a while, wanting to examine it more closely but aware that Sonnet wouldn't tolerate it yet. "That would have been a big wound."

"It was. Do you know how much time I spent on this stupid animal?" Kip made a sucking sound on the side of his teeth. "They paid a lot to bring her over from Germany, else I would have shot her."

Gloria straightened up and looked him square in the eye. "What happened to Terrence?"

"Oh, that kid, he was a good rider, strong, but he either fell or was knocked off by a branch. They were a ways out over there by the tree line. By the time Lo brought him back, he was still alive but not doing too good."

"She brought him back?" Gloria swallowed against the thickening in her throat.

"What else was she gonna do? She put him up on this thing with her and rode back." He gestured toward Hamlet. "I think they tried to revive him in the ambulance. Jesus." Kip pressed his fingertips to his eyeballs. "I do apologize. It's…it was, is, a hard time for all of us. I can still see her riding up past here, the look on her face, I'll never forget it."

Gloria swallowed again and looked at her shoes to avoid embarrassing Kip while he composed himself. "But it wasn't her fault."

"Peter didn't want him up on the horses all the time, they used to argue about it, but Terrence, he had, almost a gift, you could say. An affinity with horses. You couldn't keep him away. Perhaps he was too young to be up on a big green horse like this, but for a little kid, he could handle a horse."

Gloria thought of last night, Lo's private anguish. "Was he wearing a hard hat?"

"No one does out here."

Gloria nodded, realizing she was assigning blame already. She didn't want to be that person. "Why does Peter want to get the horses fit to ride again?"

Kip's eyes were dry. He sniffed. "He can't get his son back, but maybe he can get his wife back. That'd be my guess anyway." He took a deep breath. "Well, Gloria, what's say we head in and eat before Sue-Anne serves us up on a plate?"

Gloria was slow to move. The very air felt thick around her.

When they got to the kitchen, Peter was shrugging into his jacket with a piece of toast clenched between his teeth.

"Peter!" Gloria said in alarm.

Sue-Anne looked up from the coffee she was pouring and Peter transferred the toast into his hand. Kip ignored them all and took a seat at the table.

"Sorry, I was hoping to have a word before you went back into town." Gloria still felt close to tears, the details of the past still fresh in her mind.

Peter jerked his arm so his sleeve moved away from the watch on his wrist. "I have a meeting starting, ooh, very soon." He looked up at her with his bright eyes. "I know, Gloria, we haven't even had time to talk." He dropped his piece of toast onto a plate on the table and dusted his hands. "I'll tell you what, if you feel like riding into town, we can sort out some terms. I appreciate that you've come a long way."

"Have some breakfast first." Sue-Anne's voice was desperate.

"Thank you, Sue-Anne, but I have to run. I'll take this though." He picked the toast up again and held it up for her to see.

"Well, take Dolores with you then. Take her into town!"

Gloria didn't want to contribute to the look of exasperation on Peter's face. "That's okay, Peter, you have things to do. We can talk later if you're free?" The idea of immediately entering into a conversation with Peter was overwhelming. She saw him in a different light now.

Kip's hash brown paused on the way to his mouth. "How's about I take Gloria in this afternoon when I go and sort out that idiot at the hardware store? I'll even bring Dolores in for the ride, how does that sound?"

Peter gave his tie a final tighten. "Very fine, thank you, Kip, if you can manage to get Dolly off the ranch. Gloria, if it pleases you, I'll be fairly flexible after about eleven. Kip knows where the office is."

"Of course." Gloria felt a reprieve for the moment and was pleased she would at least be able to shower and change before her first wander through the town.

"Oh, here." Peter reached inside his jacket for his wallet. "I apologize, we haven't discussed payment since you've arrived." He pulled a folded one-hundred-dollar bill out and skirted the table to hand it to Gloria. "You may need a few things. If you need anything for the horses, let me know."

"No, I haven't done anything yet!"

"Gloria, I'm not mean with money and I understand working with the horses is a process that may take time. I want you to be comfortable while you're here. My priority is regaining some sort of normalcy for my wife and contrary to what she may have told you, she loved those horses and riding used to make her happy. She's got a real talent. I'd give everything I have to see Dolly smiling again, and back to being a wife and who knows... maybe a mother one day."

Gloria was shocked by his honesty. He obviously cared for Lo, but hoping to make her happy so their hopes of children weren't dashed made her feel sad. She could only manage a feeble thank-you as Peter hurried out. She held the money in her hand not knowing what to do with it. Taking anything from Peter now felt wrong.

"Don't sweat it, Gloria. When a man offers you money, you take it." Kip took a bite of his hash brown. "You can spot me a beer at the bar in town. Rock's is a bar unlike all others."

Sue-Anne fixed Kip with a steely look. "Gloria doesn't want to waste her time with that rabble in town. An unsavory lot, Gloria. Don't let Kip and Samuel drag you in there. Speaking of Samuel, where is that boy?"

Gloria took a seat at what was becoming her regular spot beside Kip. "Are you sure you don't mind taking me into town?"

"Mind? I'd be proud as punch."

Samuel came in, holding his hat in his hands, his face red with exertion. "That pinto gelding was in the corn again. I think he's getting under the fence. I can't see any other way he'd be getting out. I know he's too fat to get over."

Sue-Anne began piling food onto a plate before he'd even sat down. "It's getting cold. I'm going to fetch Dolores. Eat up, eat up. I cooked extra for Peter and I don't want it to go to waste."

"She wants to fatten you up so you can't get a leg over either," Kip said as Sue-Anne toddled off.

"I heard that, Kip!" Sue-Anne called over her shoulder.

Gloria felt glum. She picked at a hash brown until Kip's recount of his most recent conversation with the man who owned the hardware store got the better of her. Eventually, she smiled and sensed he was trying to cheer the both of them up after their heavy discussion. Outside, the sun had emerged from the cloudy residue of yesterday's storm and was penetrating the kitchen window. She speared a corn cake with her fork and examined it before taking a small bite. It burst sweet and full of flavor in her mouth, and she examined it again before taking a bigger bite. Beside her, Kip tucked wholeheartedly into his food. Gloria chewed thoughtfully, watching Samuel selecting the crispest piece of bacon. Somehow she was here in this moment, totally foreign to any moments she had experienced prior to the past few days, surrounded by warmhearted strangers that had embraced her as their own. It made Melbourne seem like a hazy fog that she had stepped out of. She wasn't sure which was the truer reality or if one should be truer than the other.

Sue-Anne returned to interrupt Gloria's musings. "I can't find her."

"Probably in the can," Samuel said.

"Samuel, mind your manners. But no, she's not anywhere."

"Aw, Sue-Anne, don't fuss so much. She's probably found a quiet spot. You know how she is, just like the stable cats finding a patch of sunlight." Kip poured himself a second cup of coffee and offered the pot to Gloria, who held out her cup.

Sue-Anne fell into her seat and picked up her fork then put it down again. "Perhaps upstairs? You know I have difficulty getting up that staircase. Why anyone would make a staircase so steep is beyond me. I did holler up there several times to no avail. Gloria, I hate to ask but…"

Gloria pushed her chair back from the table. "It's no problem."

"The staircase to the attic, do you know the one I mean? You have to go upstairs then up again."

"Yes, I know the one you mean."

Gloria was happy to escape Sue-Anne's concern and do something practical even if it meant disrupting the cat in her pool of sunlight. She walked through the living room and climbed the large staircase to the bedrooms, then up again to the attic. The door was shut. She knocked lightly and then more forcefully, but there was no response. She turned the handle and eased it open. The long room with its expanse of wooden floor and sloping ceilings had a few furnishings, and cardboard boxes were pushed up against the lower sides. An old-fashioned wooden rocking horse with painted dapples and real horsehair was by the picture window, his yellow teeth bared, his beady eyes rolling. Pushed up alongside the window was a faded pink velvet chaise lounge where Lo sat, her arms resting on the windowsill, her gaze beyond the pane of glass, out toward the mountains. She didn't turn to look at Gloria, nor did she object when Gloria went to stand beside her.

"Breakfast is ready, if you'd like to come down."

"Not really. Tell Sue-Anne I'm fine. Please."

Gloria sat down beside Lo's curled-up feet; the cat in her pool of light. Although Lo had none of the proud contentment of a cat. "Kip and I are going into town later if you'd like to come?"

"No, thank you."

"I'm meeting Peter when he has a moment to talk."

Something made Gloria do a visual check of the window. There was no wire screen or locks on it. She imagined Lo floating serenely down toward the lawn below, how easy it would be. She pushed the thought away. There was a good view over the fields. Gloria followed Lo's gaze toward the part of the yard that wasn't obscured by the barn. She could see Hamlet with his head under the fence, still trying to get at the longer grass. She wondered how long Lo had been up in the attic, sitting by the window.

"Peter's moments are carefully lined up like ducks in a row."

Gloria could only assume that Lo's were not. That Lo's moments were not many, but one deep ocean of moment. She wondered when she had gone from being the person who was wondered about by someone to the one doing the wondering. She wanted to wrap her arm around Lo and kiss her temple, but she did not. Perhaps the urge to heal was rooted like a weed inside the soil of her being. She wasn't foolish enough to believe anything she could say would be the antidote to the vine wrapped around Lo's heart. At least Lo didn't appear upset that the horses had been brought up by the barn.

"Would you come into town, just to give me the tour?" Gloria tried once more.

"I haven't...I can't. Peter brought you out here. He'll look after you, just tell him what you need." Lo closed her eyes as though the conversation was exhausting her.

"Okay," Gloria said even though she felt wrong, almost dirty, discussing Lo and her horses without her there. She stood up and went to report that Lo was fine but she wouldn't be coming down for breakfast.

For the rest of the morning she sat down at the yard with Lo's horses. She wondered if Lo was up in her tower, watching what she was doing. She didn't let it alter her behavior. There was something about Lo up in her tower, keeper of both lock and key. Gloria was tempted to look up toward the attic, but she was sure she would see nothing but the sky's reflection, so she did not. After a while she went inside to shower and rearrange the clothes she had into a new outfit. Shorts, her oversize sweatshirt and her Garfield socks and sneakers were the cleanest option. She wasn't sure how proud Kip would be to accompany her after all. In front of the bedroom mirror, she scraped her shoulder-length hair up into a ponytail, wisps of it escaping immediately. She pulled it out again, staring at her face which appeared unchanged apart from the pink spread of sun across her nose and cheeks. The same dark brown eyes that had looked out at her before still looked back at her now. She examined her eyes, her dark lashes and straight brows, the upturn of her lip, trying to find something deeper in her own gaze, but her reflection stared back blankly. She tried to imagine how she must look to others but couldn't. She took the moss book out into the kitchen to wait for Kip. The story had reached a point where the main character, Kate, had developed a water filtration system using the moss. As Gloria sat on a stool with her book in her hands resting on the counter, she heard footsteps and from the corner of her eye saw someone enter the kitchen then stop. She turned to look.

Lo was caught halfway across the floor. She clutched herself around the ribcage. Something came to Gloria about the solar plexus chakra being responsible for personal power and she wondered why Lo's instinct was to wrap her arms around it. "Sorry, I didn't realize there was anyone in here…" Lo trailed off, as though she was an intruder in her own home.

"I'm reading this moss book, have you read it?" Gloria held up the book with its soft orangey pages and creased cover.

"Moss book?" Lo's expression was quizzical.

"It's about a woman who was stuck in a cave and ate moss to survive. Sue-Anne gave it to me, from the bookshelf. I hope that's okay?"

"Yes, you're welcome to anything." Lo dropped her arms but stayed a few feet away as though she might retreat at any moment.

"Thank you." Gloria kept looking at Lo waiting for her to say something, but when she didn't she returned to her book.

Lo came farther into the kitchen area and opened the fridge. "Don't tell Sue-Anne I'm snacking between meals." She peered at the contents a moment longer. "How can there be nothing I want to eat?"

"You could always lick the back steps," Gloria suggested.

"For moss?"

Gloria looked up from the book and they both grinned. "Or you could come into town with Kip and me?"

Lo let the fridge door fall shut with a gentle pop sound. She turned to face Gloria, leaning against the fridge with both palms placed against the door. "Why am I so afraid?"

"What are you afraid of?" Gloria was struck by a vision of Lo racing home with her dying baby in her arms. She squeezed her eyes shut for a moment.

"People talking. Or of enjoying anything ever again."

Gloria shut the book and laid it on the counter. She smoothed the cover with the heel of her hand. "Well, the people talking part you can't do much about. People will talk whether they see you or not. The guilt part, though, that's something you have to work on or live with or something. Have you seen someone to talk about things?" What Lo had experienced would cut a person to the soul.

Lo tapped the fridge with the tips of her fingers. "Only about ten different people. Apparently I'm holding on to the guilt. I know, I know. Intellectually I can understand that it's serving no purpose but it's the feeling...like a dead end. I just can't get past it." She gave her head a sharp little shake. "Sorry, I can't..." She blinked at the tiles on the floor then took a deep breath. "It's okay."

Through the window, Gloria could see Kip making his way up the path between the paddocks with Wilbur skipping along in front. "Okay, so if people gossip anyway, and you'll feel guilty anyway, why don't you come into town and get some lunch with me? I need to get some clothes and I would really appreciate your advice." She wanted to keep Lo by her side and chase the lurking shadows away.

Lo chewed the inside of her lower lip. "You don't need my advice on clothes."

Gloria stood up and swept a hand along her torso. "Are you sure about that?"

Lo glanced down at her own baggy house clothes then back up at Gloria. "Pretty sure."

"It would be great if you could be there when I chat to Peter. Wouldn't you like to be part of the discussion? They're your horses. Unless you want me to go home and then there'll be nothing to discuss."

Lo crossed her arms and her eyes found the ceiling. "That's not fair."

"None of it is fair but that's the reality of it. I'm not threatening you, I'm just saying that if there's nothing for me to do here then I'm going home to find a job." She didn't add that she had a waiting list of clients, none of whom she wanted to work with because they were all too close to home. She wondered how far through the dressage community the gossip had spread. Perhaps she and Lo weren't so different after all. Who was she to persuade Lo to step into the flame?

They both looked toward the back door as Kip came in. He was dressed in clean jeans and a pale green shirt that brought out the heavy blue of his eyes. His hair was combed back from his forehead and he smelled like cologne. Lo stood up straight and looked at him, chewing her lip again.

"Hey, Kip. I'll just put this book back and I'm ready." Gloria picked up the moss book and pushed the stool in under the counter.

"Sure thing." Kip nodded at Lo and came to swing his leg over a wooden stool beside her.

Gloria went back to her room and put the book on the bedside table and gave herself another once-over in the mirror. She looked so serious, all big eyes and worried brows. She took a deep breath and relaxed her face. As she was about to walk out again, she remembered the one-hundred-dollar bill that Peter had given her. She looked around for it, frantically trying to remember what she'd done with it. All this talk of town and she was about to step out without her money. She opened her suitcase and went through the side zips even though she knew it wasn't there. Then she remembered she'd been wearing her jeans at the table that morning and she had shoved it in her pocket. She had dumped the jeans in the washhouse. She hurried off to find them, hoping Sue-Anne hadn't started a wash. She chastised herself for not sticking to her guns about washing her own clothes. This was surely her punishment—she would never be able to look Peter in the eye again. In the washhouse the machine was gurgling happily. Gloria spied her jeans under a pile of dark clothes and gratefully snatched them out, whispering thanks to the angels. She groped around inside the pocket and withdrew the money. She put it inside the pocket of her shorts and went to find Kip. He was no longer in the kitchen but she heard a car horn from out the front. She went out to see him sitting in a white pickup truck, its motor thrumming noisily.

He hopped out to open the door for her and she saw Lo sitting in the middle of the front seat. Lo had changed into clean pale blue jeans and a cable-knit sweater in natural tones that brought out her rust coloring. Her hair had been let loose from its bun and it hung in messy coppery ribbons about her face and over her shoulders. Gloria sat down, her bare legs slightly mottled from the cold beside Lo's very neat denim seams.

"Peter's going to be surprised to see you, Dolores. He might give me a pay raise," Kip said, putting the car into gear. "Don't she look pretty, hey, Gloria?"

The question made Gloria slightly uncomfortable, but she said, "Yes," and made sure to keep her thighs to herself. Lo also kept her long legs in check, her knees pointing toward the dash.

Kip put the car into gear. "All right, Gloria, lucky for you, you have two of the best tour guides in the whole of Diamond Rock River. Dolores here practically runs the town, don't you?"

But Lo was pulling the seat belt away from her chest, then from her waist, trying to loosen it. "I don't think I can."

Kip reached over and unclipped the belt without slowing down. "You'll be fine. We'll go to the office and you can sit there and wait with Gloria if you want to. Or you can accompany me to the hardware store and serve some papers on old Barrett. Save me punching him in the snorkel."

Gloria thought Lo was going to object or even climb across her and make a break for freedom, but she stared glassily ahead. She was glad Kip was there to lighten the mood. Outside of the window, the fields were slipping by, swells and dips of uninterrupted green and yellow. It all looked so different now that she was in the cab of the truck, familiar with the ranch, without the anxiety of landing in a new place. The windows were down and the fragrance of the bright yellow flowers was streaming in dewy and sweet. The wind felt clean in her hair and on her face. She had to close her mouth and lick her lips because she could feel her teeth getting dry from smiling.

"It's so beautiful. It looks like the sky is lying right on top of the land."

"Isn't that what sky always does?" Kip asked, relaxed behind the wheel, one arm up on the window ledge. "Is Australia real different?"

"Usually there are buildings in the way! Where I am it's all gum trees and paddocks. It's not nearly this green but it's pretty in its own way."

"I'll tell you what, Gloria, I'll take you on the highway so you can get a look at the gorge. Or is that too far? It will probably only be about fifteen minutes out of our way."

"I'd love to if Lo doesn't mind. Lo?"

Lo shook her head. "It's beautiful and I haven't seen it in a while."

They fell into silence as Kip turned onto the highway. There was beauty in every direction, from the velvety green running up to meet the snow-topped mountains, to the clumps of sagebrush and orange soil. The grass along the highway was dotted with purple, pink, white, and yellow. The asphalt itself was a deep red.

"Why is the road red?" Gloria asked.

"It's the rock, ain't it, Lo?"

"They use the local rock to make the road. It's lava rock—scoria—and it just turns out that way." Lo recounted the fact almost robotically.

"I love it, it makes everything look so new, like I'm in another world. Like Dorothy on the yellow brick road." She looked at Kip. "You'd be the Tin Man."

"And I'd be the Cowardly Lion." Lo sounded so dejected that after a second Kip burst out laughing. It didn't take long for them all to join in. "Oh, look where you're going, Kip!" Lo shrieked as he swerved across the line into the middle of the road.

"There's no one in sight!" Kip said, wiping his eyes with a brown forearm.

"Just part of my cowardly nature," Lo said firmly.

The rest of the ride was more relaxed. Lo's leg flopped casually to the side and Gloria stopped feeling like any slight touch might electrify her. Kip slowed right down so Gloria could get a look at the gorge in the distance. She was humbled by the placid width of the river which seemed to sit still between the towering rock.

"That ain't nothing. That's a little bitty part of the river. If you're lucky, Lo will take you out on the horses or down the river for a float. It's strong this time of year with all the snowmelt. I don't suppose you like hunting?"

Gloria looked up at him from under her lashes. "Kip, I'm a vegetarian."

"You don't have to eat it, just shoot it."

"No thanks, that's even worse. Can you just watch the road?"

Lo laughed a little. "I like her," she said to Kip. "She doesn't take your crap either. I was getting worried that a defenseless woman would be stuck in the car with you all the way to town and here she is telling you off."

Gloria felt flushed with happiness in a way she hadn't felt in a long time. Being in the car with Kip and Lo, the smell of spring in bloom, a feeling of absolute freedom. The anxieties of the past few days seemed to have fallen away on the highway behind them. She took a mental snapshot so she could revisit the moment later: Kip's hand loose on the wheel, tendrils of hair being swept away from his long forehead, Lo's peaceful expression, her eyes lit up by the bright sun, the color of turning magnolia leaves.

Kip chatted the rest of the way to town, pointing out landmarks and telling stories of the various antics he got up to, usually involving alcohol, women, and horses or vehicles. It seemed to provide Lo with a distraction and although she remained silent, she smiled now and then. Gloria wondered how much of a smile Peter would need to indicate her womb was ripe for filling. She immediately felt guilty for having such thoughts; it was not her place to judge Peter, who had lost a son and his hopes of future generations with him.

CHAPTER SEVEN

Diamond Rock River was a town settled at the foot of the mountains that proclaimed itself "Cowboy Country" on a wooden sign by the school. The streets were wide and flat, the gray asphalt full of soldered cracks. The brick shops were painted bright colors which gave it the look of an old-fashioned film set, their purple, green, yellow, blue, and red awnings rolled out after the sun had chased away the winter thaw. Jeeps and pickup trucks were parked at an angle along the streets and Kip muttered something about too many folk sucking up the fresh air. Before he had even pulled into a spot in front of a beauty salon, someone walking along the sidewalk was coming over to say hello. Gloria felt Lo shrink back against the seat. She was looking at her hands folded in her lap and her lips were silently moving. Gloria couldn't tell if she was praying.

"Hey there, Jerry, long time no see!" Kip called cheerfully, leaning across them to wave.

Jerry stepped up to the car and peered in the passenger window. "Howdy, Kip. I heard you're jumping the gun there with that alfalfa." He leaned against the windowsill with meaty forearms and looked appreciatively and Lo and Gloria. "Hello there, Dolores. Nice to see you again."

Lo looked like she was trying to say hello but nothing came out. Jerry didn't seem to notice.

"This is Gloria Grant, she's staying out at the ranch with us. Gloria, this here is Jerry Sewell from over at the tire barn. Say, Jerry, how'd it come to be that you're hearing about my clumsy crops? You can hurt a man's pride spreading rumors like that."

Jerry laughed. "When I heard that, I said, that can't be true. If there's one thing Kip knows it's how to get the best out of a piece of land. Well." He thumped the windowsill with a fist twice. "I'll let you kids get on with your day. We've been real busy now that all the farm folk are getting their machinery in order after winter. The tourists and their damn snow chains have slackened off now, thank goodness. How a person can be allowed to operate a vehicle with no sense at all astounds me." He banged the car one more time, making Lo jump. "Ladies, enjoy your day. Good to see you again, Dolores."

As he walked off, Kip said, "Gossip spreads quicker than rabbits in a field out here. I'm going to wring Samuel's neck when I see him."

Gloria was watching Jerry saunter off, the pistol he wore at his hip gleaming in the noon light. "Don't you find it scary, being around people with guns all the time?"

Kip tapped the glove box. "Not many places I'll go without mine, so you'll be safe."

Lo let out a shuddering breath. "It's not the guns I'm afraid of, it's the judgment. A bullet would be a quicker death."

"Come on, Dolores, they're too busy talking about my failure as a farmer to bother talking about you. Let's go and see Peter, then Gloria's going to buy us a beer. She needs to experience Rock's at least once."

"I'm not sure if Rock's is as exciting as you think it is, but I'll need a beer," Lo said, sliding out of the car after Kip.

As they walked along the street, in and out of the shade of the awnings, Gloria gazed at window displays that seemed from another era. A yarn shop with needlework on display, an ice cream parlor with a checkered floor and gold script on the window, a toy shop with a tin train chugging merrily along its track, up and over a bridge and through a tunnel cut into a gray wooden mountain. Gloria felt she could watch it all day, but she pictured the room back at the house with its lonely little train set and didn't linger. A few people stopped to say hello, and Gloria sensed a friendly overeagerness in some of the greetings Lo received but she supposed it was small-town curiosity, as some of it was directed her way.

"Do people live up there?" Gloria asked, shielding her eyes against the glare and looking up toward the windows cut into the brickwork above the shop fronts.

"Most are offices or storage, but some are apartments that people rent out during ski season. We're lucky there is sustainable tourism all year round, although it's the bigger towns that get the traffic," Lo said. "Here we go, that's the office over there."

"Friends, I will leave you two to it. I'm going over to the hardware store to either get those hinges or wring Barrett's neck. I'll meet you at the coffee house when you're ready. If I'm not there, please bring bail money."

The building sandwiched between all the others appeared unremarkable and Gloria probably wouldn't have noticed it apart from the lack of window display. Neat white letters on the door spelled out the street address and simply said *P.E. Ballantyne & D.S. Ballantyne Attorneys Criminal, DUI & DWI, Divorce and Family*. If Dolores felt anything about her name being on the door still, she didn't remark. Inside the office it was dim and cool. At the far end of the small room a woman looked up from the computer at her desk and smiled. An indoor plant with large heart-shaped leaves climbed from its pot and a watercooler sat in the corner beside a few chairs lined up along the wall. The sterile carpet-y smell reminded Gloria of a bank. On the walls hung framed certificates and paintings of the local geography. She stopped to admire a small painting of a white slope with snow-laden pine trees.

"Peter's mother painted that," Lo said.

"She's very talented."

Lo nodded briefly and went over to say hello to Candice. Gloria took one last look at the painting. What at first had struck her as nature in all its glory, upon second appraisal appeared stark and bleak. She turned away from it toward Candice with her smiling Dutch face and neat white shirt. Lo introduced them and Gloria saw a glimpse of Lo in professional mode, as though someone had flicked a switch, the smooth flow of words and easy smile. Lo leaned against the high top at the front of the desk with one elbow, her body turned toward the door into the rooms as Candice answered the ringing phone. Gloria felt inappropriately dressed in her shorts and Garfield socks but there was little she could do about it. After a minute, Peter opened the door, his smile displaying very even white teeth. He took Lo by the elbow and kissed her cheek, then led them past a closed door with Lo's name on it to an open door with his own name etched onto a brass plaque.

"I'm so happy to see you! How does it feel to be back at the office?" His blue eyes shone like a child on Christmas morning. He breathlessly greeted Gloria and pulled chairs out for them on the other side of his oak desk.

Lo's confidence dimmed again and her expression was strained. "This feels odd. I feel as though I'm your client. I'm not sure I like being on this side of the desk."

"Bring your chair around here, Doll," Peter said, as though that would solve the problem.

Lo shook her head and crossed one leg over the other.

Gloria felt if she didn't take charge of the conversation, more time would slide by with little resolved. "The town is gorgeous. I see why you love it here."

"We're very fortunate, aren't we, Dolly?"

Lo smiled woodenly. Peter's smile fell almost imperceptibly but he plowed on ahead in a way that reminded Gloria she was dealing with two lawyers. "So, Gloria, we need to make a more formal arrangement. I've taken the liberty of drafting up a contract for you, to offer you more security. I appreciate that you've traveled a long way at my—our—request." At that remark, Lo looked down at her hands clasped in her lap. "If you wouldn't mind taking a look at this. I've marked the spots for you to sign. There's nothing to worry about, it's more of a payment plan." He picked up a sheaf of papers held together with a binder clip and slid it across the desk toward Gloria.

"Is this really necessary?" Lo asked, pulling the papers toward herself. "Sorry, Gloria." She scanned the first page and flicked it over to read the next.

"See, Dolly, it's just a standard contract of employment. Like we give to the ranch staff."

Lo's index finger with its one ginger freckle drew invisible lines across the page as she took in the words. "A one-thousand-dollar bonus if she gets the horses competition-ready for me by summer and two if she gets me on a horse again?" She looked up and a flush bloomed in her cheeks. "Peter." Her voice broke and her face twitched in its struggle against tears.

Peter looked worried. "Doll, why are you getting upset? It's the same contract I give the guys, with a few modifications. I just wanted to make Gloria feel looked after because you know how much I want things to be all right."

The expression on Lo's face was barely concealed fury. "Sign it, Gloria," she said, still staring at Peter.

Gloria leaned back in her chair. "No, thank you."

Lo turned to Gloria in exasperation. "Sign it."

"No." Gloria stood up. "Thank you." She stumbled over her own feet as she tried to get around Lo's chair. She opened the door and almost ran past Candice, whose head jerked up in astonishment, but before she could say anything Gloria was out on the street, the door banging shut behind her. It only took two seconds for the door to swing open and Lo to come rushing out after her.

Gloria could feel her own pulse pumping heat from her cheeks to her temples. She could barely look at Lo for fear she might cry herself. She had been so stupid coming all this way, into this train wreck that was the Ballantyne family. A woman walking by with a small dog on a leash skirted around them and gave Gloria a sour look. She realized how they must look, standing outside the lawyer's office, both close to tears. Lo spoke first.

"I've sat across from a lot of lawyers, and I've never felt so manipulated."

To Gloria, Lo looked changed. There was color in her face; passion and life. "Lo, I can't do it. I'd prefer to go home than be a pawn in Peter's game."

Lo wiped angrily at her eyes with the balled-up sleeve of her sweater. "Thank you." She took a deep breath and unballed her fists. "Let's go and get a beer and think about something else." She looped her arm through Gloria's. "At least I'm too angry to care what people are saying right now. I'm turning into a slave to my own emotions. Talk some sense into me when I get overwhelmed, please, Glo."

It was the first time Lo had called Gloria *Glo*, her nickname from home, and she had done it on her own. The simple gesture made Gloria resolute that she was doing the right thing, even if it meant being sent home. They started walking quickly along the sidewalk. "I can do that, if you'll promise to do the same for me."

"I can." Lo tugged Gloria's arm and they crossed the road to the side the hardware store was on. "I've got to apologize too. I've been so wrapped up in myself that I haven't even asked how you're feeling, thrust into this atmosphere. I'm sorry Peter called you without discussing it with me but I'm not sorry you came." Lo absentmindedly returned the wave of a woman with a toddler in a stroller.

"I'm not going to lie, it has been difficult. I still think it's for the best that I go home."

"Oh," Lo said, the heels of her cowboy boots striking the ground slightly more slowly. "I understand." She let go of Gloria's arm and they walked on past the beauty salon where they'd parked the car, past the barber's and a clothing boutique with a wedding dress in the window, to the hardware store. "There he is. Look at that, he's laughing his head off with old Barrett."

And he was. Any animosity Kip felt toward Barrett had vanished with the appearance of the hinges he'd ordered. When Kip turned from the counter his eyes widened. "I didn't expect you so soon."

"We'll be at Rock's," Lo said firmly.

"You don't need to ask me twice!" Kip said. "So long, Barrett. See if you can manage to get that wire in before next spring."

Barrett waved him away and Lo swung around before he could talk to her. "No chitchat from me today," she muttered to Gloria. "They'll have to take their gossip to the village well or something."

"Lola-Lou, Dolly-Doo, how'd it come to be that you intended to chaperone Gloria and me but now I feel like the chaperone?" Kip caught up with them as they strode along the side of the road.

"Keaten, just thank your lucky stars you have two dates this afternoon." Lo took Kip by one arm and Gloria in the other, a touch of the joie de vivre that Sue-Anne had described about her.

A pair of tourists on yellow rented bicycles whizzed past and yelled hello. The three of them laughed, infected by Lo's sudden good mood.

"Oh, wow!" Gloria said as they approached the Diamond Rock River Saloon with its wooden front and burgundy awnings. "This is just like in the Westerns on television. Will I be allowed in in these clothes?"

Kip laughed. "No dress codes at Rock's. You'd keep quiet though because if I know the men around here, they're going to get one hint of that Aussie accent and try to take you home to give you a tour of the bedroom, if you know what I mean."

Lo squeezed her arm. "Don't mind him, Gloria, he's just stirring. Most folk around here are gracious and don't pester a girl. It's only noon, after all! Despite what visiting a lawyer's office might lead you to believe, Wyoming has a very low crime rate."

As they passed under the leafy aspen trees, Gloria tore off a green leaf and twirled it between thumb and finger. "Reporting or committing?"

Lo leaned her head onto Gloria's shoulder for a second. "Are you sure you're not a lawyer?"

Outside the saloon two men sat at a wooden table, beers lined up along the length. "Kip!" one called. "How many girlfriends can one guy have? Can't you spare one for us?"

Lo turned to Gloria and whispered, "Sorry."

Kip nodded curtly and opened the door for them to enter. The men's laughter followed them inside.

They sat in a booth with a view of the street out of the window. They ordered a basket of fries and Kip went to the bar and bought them beers, despite Gloria's assertion that she should pay for things. Lo had gone quiet again, enlarged pupils darkening her hazel eyes. It didn't take long for Kip to find a group he knew who absorbed him into a game of billiards. Gloria still couldn't get used to the guns carried openly by both men and women. She sipped on her beer and looked around while Lo picked at the label on hers and sat back out of sight. The fries arrived, hot and salty, the grease staining the red checkered paper in the basket. Lo took a long swig of her beer, then another.

"What a day," she said eventually. "I actually can't believe I'm sitting in Rock's on a Tuesday afternoon. It's like an out-of-body experience."

"I'll second that. If you'd asked me two weeks ago what I'd be doing, I'd say same old, just giving riding lessons and breaking horses. It's a funny phrase, isn't it, 'break a horse'?"

"Sometimes they almost do out here. Break their spirit. That's why Kip is my main wrangler. He likes to gentle the animals instead of break their will. Still, I guess all of it is harsh. You're dealing with an animal with a mind of its own."

All conversations seemed to lead to sensitive topics. Lo stopped abruptly but Gloria picked up the thread. "Warmbloods are a different animal altogether. That heavy blood makes them docile in comparison to the Thoroughbreds I've worked with. Thoroughbreds are a dime a dozen in Melbourne. The racing industry spits them out. They make great sport horses—eventers, show jumpers, or stadium jumping as you call it."

"It's great that people retrain them from the track. We try to breed good-natured horses. No matter how pretty a horse is, if he's got a dirty temperament, he's no use. An honest working horse is what we aim for, good looks are a bonus."

"The perfect man," Gloria said and raised her eyebrows.

"No such thing." Lo held up her beer. "Cheers!" They clinked bottles and Lo took another long sip then set hers down on the soggy Coors coaster with a thump. "Where's the waitress? Lord knows I am not going to the bar, I'm going to hide here in the booth with you instead."

"Will Peter be looking for you?"

Lo got the attention of a waitress dressed in cowgirl attire, blue sateen shirt with white fringing across the bust and dark blue jeans with cowboy boots. "Peter doesn't have time to look for me."

The waitress came over and Lo ordered two beers with a shot of bourbon on the side. Gloria felt mild alarm but Lo set aside her protests. Every now and then Kip glanced over at them and gave a little nod. Gloria scalded the roof of her mouth with hot fries and soothed it with beer. Lo nibbled on a fry and stared out of the window at the light falling through the leaves. Gloria picked up the aspen leaf from beside her beer and handed it to Lo.

Lo smiled. "Penny for my thoughts?"

"Sure."

The waitress arrived with their drinks and they waited until she'd gone again to resume their conversation.

Lo raised her eyebrows. "You might ask for your leaf back." She brushed over the leaf's smooth surface with her finger. "I was just thinking how this time of year is perfect for riding, and how Terrence and I would go out or I'd go out with friends. The trails are amazing in the springtime. There's so much wildlife and everything is just buzzing, the river is swollen, it's really something."

"That sounds wonderful. There's so much uninterrupted country around here, perfect horse country. I'm dying to get out there." Gloria bit her lip at her choice of words.

"Kip would love to take you, they're just so busy at the moment, even though you wouldn't think it right now the way Kip's chatting up that brunette, but it's mainly my fault. The ranch used to be a thriving place. We took on guests, had more staff, and were a real point of interest for the township. I just can't face it now, which I feel bad about because people relied on us for work. I don't know how I managed it all before, juggling work, motherhood, the ranch admin, training horses. It seems ridiculous now, like I must have been doing a poor job of everything. Well, clearly I was."

"From all accounts that I've heard you were doing a fantastic job. Kip and Sue-Anne both have nothing but praise for you and I can see for myself the kind of life you've created."

"What does that even mean though, the life I've created? It's all falling away and I'm still here."

"Exactly, you're still here. I think I set mine alight and walked away," Gloria said gloomily. "Perhaps it's like clearing land; setting it alight so it can regenerate. Or we could be like phoenixes rising from the ashes?"

"Barbequed chickens, coming out of the oven."

Gloria laughed. "Less poetic but probably more accurate."

Lo raised her shot glass. "Let's chase this beer."

Gloria chimed her glass against Lo's. "To taking one step at a time."

They both tipped the bourbon down their throats and made faces at each other.

"This could be the drink talking, but I didn't think I'd ever want to make a step. Even trying to move on feels like a betrayal. I don't feel deserving of happiness. Ugh! Sorry, I'm not very good company, I know that." She picked up another fry and began her slow nibble. "It's weird that I'm getting to know you at this point in my life and the person you're getting to know isn't me...or is it the true me? Distilled to my bitter essence."

Gloria wanted to say that Lo's essence was vanilla, burning and sweet. She felt it so strongly that she was sure she could taste it, or maybe it was the bourbon still evaporating in her throat. "Any action that comes from love can't be bad, love is only good. Any example that results in a negative can only be because it wasn't from love, it was from fear. Do you understand what I mean, or am I speaking drunk?" Speaking the words diminished the sentiment she was trying to convey.

"I think I understand. But where does that leave me? The 'outcome' for my baby certainly isn't positive." She looked down and let a whoosh of air out that indicated a rush of tears might follow.

"Sorry, I didn't mean it that way. Random acts just happen beyond anyone's control, but love is a force—"

"God, Gloria, I can't." Lo cut her off, looking at the table like she might throw up at any moment. "Imagine a well of sorrow so deep and dark and every time you wake you're standing on the edge of it and the sorrow is sucking you in. It's mesmerizing, looking down into the sorrow. That's the way I'm shocked into being every morning. A long silent scream is coming from me all the time. At first I was in disbelief, fighting the idea every day, total denial that something so senseless and cruel could happen to an innocent child, to all of us." She looked up. "And now it's a numbness, like being coated in a toxic substance that distances you from reality and every morning that well is still there waiting for me. So forgive me, Gloria, for not being in the headspace for love."

Love came from someplace separate from headspace, Gloria thought. It was space itself, but she didn't argue. She was sorry she had spoken so expansively and so thoughtlessly. One beer and she was saying almost anything that came to her mind. Now looking at Lo at the edge of her well, staring down into the sorrow, it was infectious. Gloria had sent her there again and she tried to call her back. "Lo." Her name was the purest thing she could say but even *Lo* was not right. "Dolores." Lo was looking at her with tearstained eyes and she had to say something. "Why the name Dolores?"

"My mother wanted to call me Lolita because the book had come to popularity, or at least some kind of notoriety, around the time I was born. She just loved the name, but I don't think she cared what connotations the name would carry. She thought it sounded, in her words, 'upbeat and festive.' My father did not. I believe Dolores was a compromise and although my mother didn't dare call me Lolita for short—thank God—she called me Lola. Dad stuck with Dolores. He wasn't much for frills anyway."

"Lola." Gloria tried it out. "But no one calls you Lola."

Lo sipped at her beer. "Not since I had pigtails in my hair."

"Lola." It felt round and nice in her mouth. "I'd put you in a song only I don't know how to sing."

Their eyes met again and Lo searched Gloria's gaze, flicking from eye to eye. Gloria found she couldn't look away. "I think someone already wrote that song." After a moment they both smiled then laughed, like looking into a mirror.

"Not the song I'm thinking of."

"I knew you'd make a good lawyer. Full of hot air!" Lo said.

"Are you putting down your own profession?"

"Not really. There are a lot of great people, but some of those men that have been hanging around forever with their fixed views…let's just say that sometimes there's more bureaucracy than justice that goes on. It was disheartening when I started to learn how it really works but I still found it a compelling profession."

"Would you go back to it?"

Lo began peeling the label of her next beer bottle. "I don't think so, but you know, I didn't think I'd ever come into town again, so who could say?"

Gloria could feel the effects of the alcohol. Her movements felt fat and her face hot. Kip was over by the bar ordering more drinks. "Will he be all right to drive back?"

"Whoops!" Lo knocked her beer bottle and grabbed it before it toppled over. "I hope so because I think I might be loaded and it's only lunchtime. Oh well, it'll give people something to gossip about. 'I saw Dolores in town, drunk as a jackrabbit in a cider cellar, must be drowning those sorrows.'"

Gloria couldn't help laughing. She had only glimpsed Lo's comical side briefly and she looked so funny doing an impersonation. Lo waved at Kip and tapped her wrist to indicate the time.

"We should be going. I hope I don't stumble out of here."

"I just hope Kip is able to drive!"

Lo snorted, and when they stood up, Gloria realized they were both drunk. To Gloria's relief, Kip looked sober. "Will you be able to drive after all those beers?" she asked as they swayed over to meet him at the door.

Kip laughed. "What beers? I know how to behave when I have to. You two look like you were thirsty though."

On the ride home they were quiet apart from the radio softly playing country and western songs, Kip occasionally joining in with his low twangy voice. Gloria felt sleepy, the past few days crashing down on her. Lo also looked sapped, slumped in the middle, wearing her seat belt this time. "We forgot the clothes," she muttered.

"Doesn't matter."

Kip turned them onto the rutted driveway toward the ranch. Lo closed her eyes and leaned her head back against the headrest. A single tear slid over the tender skin below her eye and sat on her cheek, wobbling from the car's vibrations. Gloria wanted to wipe it away but instead she let her gaze be carried along by the unfurling fields. As they approached the house, Wilbur stretched his back and ambled down from the front porch to greet them. Without a word, Lo exited the car and for the next few days, Gloria saw her only on three occasions, and each time by chance. Once, when Lo was coming out of the bathroom and they almost bumped into each other, Lo glanced up as though she might speak, then hurried by as though they were strangers. The next night, when Gloria got up to get a glass of water, she found Lo sitting at the kitchen table in the dark, a bowl of cereal in front of her, and another time when Gloria was sitting on her bed reading with the door open and she saw Lo ghost past. *Lola*, Gloria thought. Like a pairing of musical notes: *lo-la*.

Peter was just as elusive. The first night, after their meeting, he came home when Gloria was in bed. Lying in the dark, watching the leaf shadows shifting in the moonlight, she could hear the rise and fall of contained arguing. There was a gentle dance to it, the shadows and the sounds, urgent but quiet, and she started to drift off, awoken by a door shutting with a decisive click. She heard purposeful footsteps pass by the room and then the sound of a motor. In the morning Peter was gone.

The days were made honest with work. Kip and Samuel were outside from sunup to sundown, out in the fields, with the horses, mending things. Clarence had appeared, a gruff old man with a limp and a yellow-tinged mustache. He made it clear he didn't think much of Gloria, or women in general, it seemed. She avoided him when she could. Kip tried to explain away his behavior by saying he'd been left by his wife who had taken up with the doctor the next town over. Gloria thought his behavior better explained his wife leaving. He had a habit of chewing tobacco and spitting it near where she was standing. Gloria helped out where she could—bringing horses in, checking fences, and generally assisting with ranch duties. She got used to being dusty and sweaty and wearing a big hat to shield her neck and face from the sun, even if she couldn't quite get used to the brutality of tending to animals. Muzzles were twitched, legs were hobbled, wounds were gouged, invalids were shot, animals were trapped. In between the ranch work, she spent time with Sonnet and Hamlet, getting Sonnet used to her voice and occasional touch. At night she showered and fell into bed with aching limbs and sore feet but still her mind would not stop reeling. She tried to ask Kip about Lo, but they were so busy she couldn't get him alone to chat, and although Samuel was a sensitive soul, he wasn't too perceptive. Sue-Anne had stocked the freezer and was leaving Lo to her own devices for the most part because she was reserving her fussing for her daughter, who was expecting a baby any day. Gloria had never been fussed over by anyone growing up. Her parents had been attentive but allowed for independence. They had already raised a son, Ben, eight years older than Gloria, who had tested every boundary and emerged relatively unscathed, so by the time Gloria came along, they were focused on work and let her get on with things. Ben left home shortly after Gloria turned ten and now worked as a plumber in Perth, so she rarely saw him. Keeping busy kept the intrusive thoughts about abandoned friends and family at home. She knew she had to contact people in Melbourne. With each passing day, the lump of dread in her stomach grew until it felt as though it was calcifying around her organs, making it hard to breathe, yet still she didn't pick up the phone. Kip had invited her to come and have a beer with him a couple of times at his place on the ranch, but she had declined. She wasn't sure why, because she enjoyed his company. Perhaps she was worried that she would succumb to an inconvenient urge that would leave her unsatisfied and regretful come the morning.

CHAPTER EIGHT

Without markers to identify them, the days blended in, and Saturday slid into place without Gloria realizing it was on its way until she got up and found no one about except for Clarence, who was pulling apart a water pump in a trough. She had decided not to let his gruffness intimidate her and she asked him where everyone was.

"It's Saturday. Your boyfriend's probably still in bed," Clarence said, spitting onto the grass beside the trough. He had taken to referring to Kip as her boyfriend.

"Oh, right." Gloria shoved her hands into the pockets of her jeans which were becoming ripped and stained from repeated wearing. Being around Clarence made her feel hunched and apologetic and it annoyed her. She looked over toward Kip's place behind the barn even though she knew she wouldn't go over. "See ya." She left Clarence to his tinkering and went to say hello to Sonnet and Hamlet.

"You must be sick of this yard by now," she said, climbing up onto the fence.

Hamlet came over immediately to nuzzle at her pockets for treats. Sonnet reacted in her usual way by first throwing her head up to stare at Gloria then eventually returning to grazing without losing sight of what was going on, her ears straining for any sound. Gloria swiveled around to look up toward the attic window. It was in the shadows of the eaves. She looked over at the barn and wondered if Lo had been doing any more stargazing up in the loft at night. She absentmindedly stroked Hamlet's silky ears. "You know what, goofball, you and I should go for a ride. We can bring your mate here with us." Without giving herself time to think she swung down and went to get a headcollar and lead and brought Hamlet out to the barn. She left the yard gate open behind them and Sonnet followed them out. Gloria knew it was a risk, that the mare could run away and damage herself or something else, but she carried on with her heart thudding uncomfortably. Hamlet stood like a perfect gentleman while she brushed and saddled him. Sonnet stood behind his quarters, whisking her tail. "You and me, mister, we are going to do some work. Both of us are a bit rusty, but I think we will get along just fine. Don't worry about Little Miss behind you, she can watch and learn. I know she has a few tricks she could show me herself, but let's see how you go." Gloria lifted the beautiful Swedish-made saddle with its soft brown leather onto Hamlet's back. He opened his mouth obediently for the snaffle bit and walked eagerly out of the barn, Sonnet following less enthusiastically behind. By the doors a wide tree stump served as a mounting block. Gloria placed her foot into the stirrup and tried to spring up as lightly as she could. "It's a long way to the top, baby," she muttered as she let Hamlet walk on. She was so high up. He had a large swinging walk and a no-fuss attitude. Clarence looked up from the water trough and then bent back over the pump, shaking his head. Sonnet walked along behind, her nose almost on Hamlet's rump.

Overhead the sun was traveling up the sky, promising a warm day. A single cloud like a puff of shaving cream sat halfway up the horizon, only serving to accentuate how clear the blue was. Gloria began to relax, heading toward the open pastures where the fences were few and the going was smooth. Hamlet picked his feet up and reached gently for the bit, asking little of Gloria. "Wow," she said as she let him step into his expansive trot. "And you're not doing too badly yourself," she said to Sonnet, who had begun to trot just as nicely, if not nervously, along beside. To Hamlet's credit, he paid her little mind and kept his focus on what Gloria was asking. She could see that Lo had a good eye for a horse. She felt so free, no one's emotions weighing on her, no one waiting for her to do something or expecting anything. Hamlet began to sweat, and Gloria slowed him to a walk and let him stretch his neck out. She didn't want to strain his muscles that hadn't been used in a while, but she could tell he was enjoying being out of the yard, watching the changing landscape. They turned for home and Gloria gathered Hamlet up into a collected walk, then extended walk, then trot, then up into piaffe. Hamlet responded without hesitation and Gloria could feel she was sitting on a brilliantly trained horse. "I don't know how much I can teach you, you know what you're doing. You, on the other hand"—she swiveled around to face Sonnet— "are a bit rough around the edges. You'll get your turn."

Back at the stables she hosed Hamlet off and put them both back in the yard where she knew he'd roll in the dust, which he did. She left him looking dirty and unrepentant while she went to knock on Kip's door.

Kip's house was a wooden cabin with red geraniums in pots by the door. A mat out the front read "Probably Riding" and there was a horseshoe nailed to the door for luck. Gloria knocked and Kip opened the door wearing a towel slung around his waist which he was holding closed with one hand. His hair was wet and shaving cream still striped the razor's path on his face. Gloria wasn't sure who looked more surprised. Kip stepped back and invited her in.

"No, thank you. Sorry to interrupt, I was just wondering which paddock I can put Lo's horses in. I want Sonnet to get used to having other horses around and eventually separating from Hamlet."

"Okay." Kip scratched at one firm pectoral muscle and looked past her out the door. After a moment he looked at her again. "Come in and sit down and let me put some clothes on."

Gloria nodded and made her way into the cabin, which was really just a living area attached to a kitchen and a bathroom and bedroom. It was neat, with a crochet blanket slung over an armchair and a small round table in the corner with two chairs. Along the kitchen ledge above the sink there were little plants in pots. It looked more like a granny flat than a bachelor pad, but Gloria found it endearing, testament to Kip's soft nature. The scent of shampoo and warm misted air was pungent in the small space. She went to sit at the table and leaf through a copy of *Quarter Horse News* which displayed a lot of horses that looked like bodybuilders. She hadn't even finished reading an article on barrel racing championships when Kip appeared in crisp jeans and a white shirt, smelling of cologne, his damp hair curling over the back of his collar.

"You must think I'm awful lazy, getting showered at this hour."

"The thought never entered my mind. I know you're always up at dawn, so you must like to sleep in on weekends."

"Actually, I didn't sleep real good last night. You want a coffee?"

Gloria pushed the magazine aside. "That would be nice, thanks."

Kip set about making a coffee, each action delivered with a little flourish.

"Why aren't you married?" she asked, saying it as casually as she thought it.

Kip looked up from where he was arranging some biscuits on a plate. "You offering?"

Gloria laughed. "If only you knew! Not at all. I don't think I'm the marrying type."

Kip brought a tray to the table. "Baby, we're all the marrying kind, it just depends on finding the right match and that ain't easy, at least not for you ladies. I think us men are simpler minded."

Gloria smiled. "Maybe. Well, it's true in my experience, but I'm sure there are plenty of different relationship dynamics."

"I thought you wanted to talk horses but you're here to propose. Sorry, Gloria, no woman has managed to drag me down the aisle yet."

"You ain't been lassoed by no rodeo queen yet?"

Kip grinned. "No. Nope, not yet." He regarded her thoughtfully. "But I guess there's still time."

"So, aside from proposing marriage, I thought I would run an idea by you." She waited for his confirmation and he gave a brief nod. "I took Hamlet out for a ride and I let Sonnet come along, she just trotted along beside and it was actually okay, but…I want to be able to work with one without the other."

Kip rocked back in his chair a little. "We can't put her in with the others, she's possessive of Hamlet and kicks and bites when anyone comes near them. I agree it would be good to separate them though. How about this: we put Yo-Yo in with them for now. He's usually dominant and he won't get beaten up."

"I don't want him hurting the dressage horses though. That's the last thing anyone needs."

"He's mostly bluff. We could put them into the field out the back where there's enough room for them to stay clear of each other if they need. There's plenty of feed on the ground. In fact, Hamlet drops his belly and gets a big fat neck when the feed's too rich."

Gloria laughed. "I know, he looks like Santa Claus at the moment. I could barely fit my legs on either side."

"I'm heading into town now, but I can help you this afternoon. I have to go out there anyway. We could keep an eye on them for a while, make sure they're not killing each other."

"Sorry! Am I keeping you?" Gloria took a quick sip of her coffee, scalding the roof of her mouth.

"No, I'm glad of the company." He smiled that easy smile. "You know there's a movie house in town. A cin-e-ma."

Gloria laughed again. "Is there?"

"Yep."

"Okay, thanks for that information."

Kip let his chair fall gently back onto all fours. "No problem, partner."

They looked at each other for a few seconds, Gloria unsure of whether he was drawing back the boundary or trying to lure her over it, or if they were two friends just sharing a moment. His twinkling dark blue eyes gave little away other than a veneer of amusement covering any true feelings. The idea made her worried more than anything, worried that she herself might wander across a boundary into difficult territory. She had never been good at boundaries with male friends, unsure of how much of herself she should give. Her recent experience with Mike filled her with caution and although she didn't know what she wanted, she knew what she didn't want: to plant a flower in the heart of Kip that would soon wither from lack of tending.

"Well," she said. "I'm not sure about the cinema but I'm still waiting to go for that ride up toward the mountains."

"Sure. You going to take Hamlet up there? We can cross over the river onto Uncle Sam's land. The trails will blow you away. You can ride for days without a reminder civilization exists."

It was a soothing thought, and she wondered how antisocial she would become, given the opportunity, and whether it was a state she desired or whether, like Lo, self-imposed exile was a punishment for social wrongdoing. "Once Sonnet gets used to being on her own again, I'd love to take Hamlet. He enjoyed himself today."

"You're funny, worrying about whether he enjoyed himself. He's just a horse."

Gloria raised her eyebrows. "He's not a block of wood, he's an animal."

Kip pushed the plate of gingersnaps toward her. "Eat a cookie and be quiet. Or are you worried the cookie might cry if you bite it?"

Gloria sighed. "All right, I'll take that as my cue to leave. Let me know when you're back and we'll move the horses."

Kip picked up a cookie and bit into it. "Yup. So long."

Gloria shook her head at him, but she didn't really mind. There was no malice to his teasing. He walked her to the door, and they said goodbye and parted as friends.

Gloria wandered back up the laneway between the fields with a long sprig of grass between her fingers, feeling it shiny and smooth and strong, letting it thwack against fence posts and running its feathery tip along the ground. The sun was warm on her back and the wind cool on her face. She pushed the back gate open onto the overgrown garden that no one had time to tend with its fruit trees and daisy bushes grown wild. It wasn't until she was almost upon the steps that she noticed Lo sitting on the swinging seat, looking down onto the back garden with Wilbur at her feet. It startled Gloria more than it should to see her there. She had almost forgotten Lo's presence was something she might bear witness to again; she had almost given up hoping she would appear. She slowed her pace and, under Lo's expressionless gaze, felt self-conscious in her dusty ripped jeans in a way she hadn't been sitting in Kip's house. Even her yellow T-shirt had a tear down the side from ducking through a fence. She stopped at the top of the steps, one hand uncertainly on the carved pole supporting the tin roof.

"Hello." Wilbur thumped his tail appreciatively on the wooden planks.

"Morning, Glo." Lo smiled and she looked serene.

Lo-La. Gloria curled her fingers with their dirty nails into a fist. Lo's eyes were clear, her hair brushed back into a loose bun at the nape of her neck, and she was dressed in a yellow gingham shirt with the sleeves cut off and denim shorts. She seemed to have sprung from the garden, a fully formed mystery. There was a control about her that Gloria had only glimpsed at in the office and talking to Peter.

"Sorry," Lo said. "I've been chasing peace for days and once I exhausted myself and gave up, I found it. For the moment at least."

Gloria nodded but looked at the ground. She suddenly felt overwhelmed herself, a relinquishing of the Lo she had been worrying about and an introduction to this stranger she had only seen from afar. Would this stranger care about Gloria, standing in her worn clothes with unruly hair and dirty face? It was painful to consider. She wasn't sure who she would find when she looked back up. She breathed to the bottom of her lungs and found Lo's eyes again. It wasn't just her eyes, she was a magnolia herself, delicate and strong, beautiful and easily bruised. "I'm glad you've found the sunshine."

Lo smiled softly. "I want to go into town. Will you come with me?"

"Yes, I'd like that. Will you wait for me to shower and change?"

"Yes."

Gloria relaxed whatever she'd been drawing tight and opened the door.

"Gloria!"

Gloria turned.

"Wait." Lo stood up and let a hand trail across Wilbur's head. "I have clothes if you need them. Come and choose some things."

"Oh, okay."

Gloria let Lo lead her through the house and up to her bedroom. Gloria had never seen inside Lo's room. The window was open, riffling the pale green-and-white striped curtains which matched a large soft green rug on the floor. The room had a faint smell of perfume despite the baked wheat air outside. The bedside tables on either side of the large, high bed reminded her that it was also Peter's room. She could tell by the stack of books and rumpled covers on one side where Lo had been sleeping. If Gloria was an intruder in a sacred space, Lo was not the keeper of it. She opened a chest of drawers and turned to Gloria. "Take your pick. If it were left to me they'd be a crumpled mess, but Sue-Anne keeps things neat." She pulled out a navy blue shirt with short sleeves and a sharp collar. "Dark colors suit you, I think. Come and take your pick."

"Will I fit into your clothes?" Gloria felt shy, faced with the choice, but she did as Lo asked.

"Try this." Lo passed her the navy shirt. "Jeans or shorts?"

"Either."

Lo opened the second drawer. "Don't be a drip. What do you prefer?"

"Shorts."

Lo passed her a pair of mid-blue denim shorts with white embroidery around the waist. "I like wearing these with that shirt."

Gloria carried the clothes in her hands, foreign and stiff with ironing, back to her room and went to shower, unsure if she'd even find Lo again once she finished. Once changed, she regarded herself in the mirror and ran her fingers through her hair to loosen it into soft waves that curled up around her face. She was browner than when she arrived, and she felt stronger with the use of muscle. The shirt did suit her. It felt like a new day. Before going to find Lo, she took the money from where she had put it inside her purse.

Despite her worries, Lo was waiting in the living room, sitting, staring into space. Her attention snapped guiltily toward Gloria and she said, "They fit real good." Her movements were assured and she didn't look back at Gloria to check she was following. She paced the corridor quickly and headed straight to the pickup truck and opened the door. Gloria walked around to the passenger side and swung up. The cab seemed bigger without Kip. The keys were sitting in the ignition and Lo fired it up, the radio springing to life, midway through a pop song. As she adjusted the rearview mirror, Gloria could see her hand was shaking.

"You sure you're okay to drive?"

Lo pursed her lips and jerked her head in a nod. "Yup." Her hands were strong and capable as she shifted the car into gear and spun the steering wheel.

As they drove down the drive and out onto the main road, Lo was tensed, checking the mirrors, her hands tight on the wheel. It wasn't until they gathered speed and the road began to roll away beneath them that she let out the breath she'd been holding and her grip loosened. She flicked the radio station away from an irritatingly repetitive song and found an Elvis song instead. Gloria had never been an Elvis fan, but it was like touching velvet after Velcro. Gloria relaxed too, and she was able to admire the scenery which she would never tire of.

"You know my Uncle Bobby claims he was sucked up into a twister?" Lo glanced over at Gloria then pointed a finger to the right, over the flat plain stretching out. "Over there. He reckons he was bringing back a wayward steer when he was about eight or nine and the sky changed from blue to purple. Apparently, the wind just whipped him up and sucked him right up into the sky and he could look down on the house, hurtling through the air. He says he heard the voice of someone, maybe a Pawnee or Comanche, a man, telling him something. He couldn't understand the words but he knew they were telling him he'd be okay. And just as gentle as a breeze, he floated to the ground, still running, only when he got home he realized his boots were missing and the steer was nowhere in sight."

Gloria felt goose bumps run along her arms. "Do you think he was telling the truth?"

Lo shrugged and glanced back at Gloria. "I don't see why not. Strange things happen on this country. It's a varied terrain with sometimes violent weather patterns. We don't get an awful lot of rain, but when it comes sometimes it's harsh. You've seen a storm firsthand. Tornadoes do sweep through here."

"What about the Native American part of the story? The voice in the storm."

"Whether that was a trick of the mind to soothe him or a guiding spirit, who's to say, but the first people of this land are spiritual people and their connection to the area is deeper than we can fathom."

Gloria stared out of the window with a newfound respect. "Was there evidence of a tornado?"

"I'm not sure. I think there had been a damaging storm, but my grandfather gave poor Bobby a whipping for losing his boots and a steer."

"So they never found it?"

"Nope, not a trace." Lo kept her eyes on the arrow of road. "You believe in spirits?"

Gloria thought about it, there in the warm cab of the truck with her bare legs sticking to the vinyl and Lo all the way across the seat by the other window, a lean slip of person in a big car. The notion of spirits seemed like something reserved for televisions shows, but there was something mysterious and all-knowing about the landscape outside, captured when the light was right. "I don't know," she said. "I haven't seen anything that leads me to believe in ghosts, but I believe in possibility."

Lo nodded. "To believe in possibility...I believe. I want to believe. I've seen things out here. You know what, sometimes when I wake up and I can smell pipe smoke, and I know Uncle Bobby has been checking up on things. He was like that, he'd wander around with his pipe between his teeth, making sure his staff were working hard. He'd want to know that I'm looking after the ranch. I reckon he'd sit me down and have a good talk to me about the way things are going. You know Clarence used to work for Bobby?"

Gloria curled her lip. "I don't think Clarence likes me much."

Lo laughed. "Don't flatter yourself, he doesn't like anyone."

"He practically spits on me. It's disgusting."

Lo indicated to turn onto the road into town. "Tell him off. It's a filthy habit and you don't put up with it."

"He'll love that!" Gloria gave a mirthless huff of laughter.

"Too bad. He needs to show some respect, rude old man. Once he told me that it was vulgar for a woman to be doing a man's work, meaning ranch work, and that 'lawyering' should be left to men because they had the nous to 'run things.' I try not to let it get to me. He's good at fixing things and knows about farming, and he's got no place else, so I just ignore him. He's not allowed to spit near people though! Pig."

Gloria admired Lo's ability to turn the other cheek even though she wished they didn't have to. The town rolled into view, the school first, and the red brick church with its peaked roof and glowering gray windows. The pink cherry blossoms were in bloom on the front lawn, a bright pop of color against the blue sky.

"Are you hungry? I am starving."

Gloria was. She hadn't been eating as well while Sue-Anne wasn't there with an endless supply of hot food. "Yes. Hey, Kip said he was going to be in town too."

"Probably on a date. The population is smaller than his dating pool; where that man gets a steady supply of women from, I'll never know." As they passed the office, Lo looked up toward the rooms above, probably wondering what her husband was doing. They cruised on by and she said, mostly to herself, "To believe in possibility." Gloria looked at her but didn't say anything. Lo pointed out Kip's dusty red car. "Probably over at Rock's. I'll take you for a little drive, if you like." They kept driving by, through the strips of shops to the houses of Diamond Rock River, the four blocks of wide faded roads and stretches of lawn dappled by the shadows of mature elm trees. A group of kids cruised along the road on bikes, a boy in front standing back on his pedals and pulling up the front wheel of his bike as they passed. "That's Courtney's boy, I can tell." Lo looked in the rearview mirror. "Wow, the little one at the back must be Billy, he's grown."

"Do you know everyone around here?"

The street stared straight out to the mountains ahead. "Not hard to do, that's all there is of the town. Trust me, I've been privy to most of these people's private dramas, directly or indirectly, and not just this town but all the farms around here and the towns around. If you dropped a pin on a map and drew a circle, well, I could probably tell you something about almost everyone in it, whether I want to know it or not." Lo was easy now, navigating the streets with one hand lightly on the wheel, the other resting on the gearshift. She pulled out onto the main road they'd used on the way in. "There's a small place up by the canyon, simple food and a clear view over the canyon. How's that sound?"

"I'd love that, thank you." Gloria was longing to find out what had brought on Lo's change of emotional state, but she was cautious of altering the mood. She felt almost intoxicated with relief that she had landed on her feet and was free for now. She would write to June at home, her parents too. Maybe pick up a postcard on the way back through and tell them that she was fine and apologize for minimal communication. She knew June would love it out here too. So many times she had longed for June's dry Aussie wit and grounded advice. She always knew where she stood with June, unlike this fickle ruined girl-woman who now seemed like someone who'd ridden through a storm and come out victorious, still in her boots, her steer at her side.

"Back on the red highway?" she asked Lo.

"The red road, that's what Terrence used to call it. You and Terrence, the only people I've met who thought anything of the red road. You know he came to me?"

Gloria looked at Lo, her steely intelligent profile, not pretty so much as clever, cultured-looking. "Who did?"

"In a dream. My boy did." Her eyes were calm as she looked at Gloria. "The night after we went into town, after we'd been at Rock's. That night I couldn't sleep and I went up to the loft, to watch the stars. Truth be told, I took the bourbon up there too, thinking it might knock me out. I was up there for hours, just talking with the universe, God, asking for guidance. I needed to know what was right, living for myself, or dying for my boy." Gloria started to say something but Lo glanced back at her. "No, it's okay. I went to bed that night and I lay there thinking as I always do, reliving certain moments, trying to distract myself from particular thoughts and let my mind go blank. Sometimes I close my eyes and imagine planting a garden, flower by flower, like a dot painting, until there's a whole sea of color, a wild garden in my mind. He liked flowers, he used to bring them to me sometimes in a posy, all big eyes and shiny pudding hair. His casket was white, a little bitty thing. There were flowers everywhere." She cleared her throat. "Sorry. Well, three days and nights I sat and thought. I'm not sure if there's order or chaos to the universe. I used to believe things happen for a reason, life sends us lessons, not more than we can handle. I wasn't sure I could handle this, so I sat with myself and thought about what the point of it all is. What the outcome for me is—I'm a very solution-based person—and I decided it's life or death and you know what happened? When I woke up, there were three buttercups lying on my bedside table."

Gloria realized she was staring with a bewildered look on her face, and she tried to compose her expression into a more neutral one. "You think it was Terrence?"

"No," Lo said. "I know it was Terrence. He was telling me to live."

Gloria's eyes pricked with unshed tears. She didn't know how to respond. She was touched by Lo's affected state, the evangelical gleam in her eye, born anew into the world. A world so uncompromising that she had had to compromise her own sanity, relinquish her will and kneel before the altar of her own soul and beg judgment. Salvation had come in the form of the residue of spirit, real or contrived, it didn't matter, the outcome was the same. Gloria had to accept it as real because it was. "Maybe he wandered through the wild garden of your mind's creation and brought you back some flowers."

Lo bit her lip and nodded but kept her eyes on the red road which had taken aim at the mountain, shooting through the yellowing grass. Strange rock formations began to rise from the thinning grass. The road dipped sharply and out of nowhere a canyon opened up beside them. The landscape was mesmerizing, ever changing, the colors shifting from green to yellow to orange, the mountains purple and white in the distance. Low clouds swept shadows across the grass as they hurtled along the highway. Lo had given up talking and was humming softly to herself, the radio long silenced by a fizzing nothingness. Lo stopped her humming for a moment and looked at Gloria. "I'm awake now. It's like I had to sleep through a night to realize what it felt like to be awake."

Gloria had a horrible thought. What if Sue-Anne had left the flowers by Lo's bed? There would be no retrieving Lo once she had tumbled from the manic cliff she stood on. Before, Lo had needed extracting from her own reality; now, Gloria felt an urge to pull her back toward it. "Is that an eagle?" she asked, spotting a smudge sprinting across the grass and looking up to see the cut of a bird through the sky.

Lo peered up under the sun visor. "A bald eagle. Isn't it beautiful?"

Gloria nodded. The eagle dipped and swung up again, accelerating until it was lost against the blue.

The restaurant was down a long tree-lined drive, backed out so it was almost hanging over a cliff that fell away into the canyon with its gushing stream below. Willows hung their lacy leaves over the outdoor dining area in green curtains, latticing them in shade and permeating the area with a sharp peppery aroma. They sat at a wooden table and chairs at the edge of the dining area where a railing kept them from falling into the gully below. The sound of water plying over rocks was enough of a reminder to patrons to keep their chatter low.

"You look like me," Lo said, her eyes shining.

Gloria's expression was quizzical as she compared Lo's straight pale hair to her own unruly dark waves, Lo's fine, gently freckled face with its long nose and generous mouth to her darker skin and demanding features.

"My clothes." They both laughed, and Gloria thought that when they laughed they did look alike after all.

The waitress brought them a basket of bread and they ordered salads and mineral water, which was enough on this warm day.

"This place has been here for as long as I can remember. It's beautiful at night with strings of lights in the trees and the bar over there livens up from about five in the evening. There ain't a whole lot of choice around here!" Lo said, pulling apart a bread roll with her long fingers. "It's pretty though, a fairy kingdom." She spread butter on a piece of crusty roll and passed it to Gloria.

"I've never been anywhere like this, it's magical." Gloria took a bite of bread and looked at an older couple holding hands across the table. "Oh, aren't they sweet?"

Lo craned her neck around then turned back. She'd stopped chewing and her nostrils flared slightly. "That's Paula and Greg. My parents used to go to church with them. I haven't seen them since the funeral." She dropped the chunk of bread back onto her side plate. A waitress was bearing down on them with two glasses of mineral water fizzing with lemon and mint. As she placed them on the table, Lo said, "We are going to need two large glasses of white wine. Anything dry." A crease formed between the waitress's eyebrows, but she nodded and took off with urgency. "Sorry," Lo said to Gloria. "I hate it when Peter orders for me, but if you don't want your wine, I'll drink it." She glanced back around at Paula and Greg. "Paula once told me that when a woman works, the child suffers. Imagine what she thinks of me now. I don't care. I don't care!"

Gloria cocked her head to the side. "Good, you shouldn't care. She's no one in your life." But she could see Lo's face had taken on its peaked look, pale and translucent around the pearly eyelids, and her hand shook as she lifted the glass of mineral water to her mouth. Gloria had reached across the table to take Lo's clammy hand in hers before she'd even known she would. She held it softly, running her thumb over the knuckles, over the smooth curve of her wedding band. "This minute here is isolated from all other minutes. Just a droplet of time still separate from the ocean of time. Lo, look at me." Lo's eyes traveled miserably up from the table. "It's just you and me, sitting in the fairy kingdom."

Lo nodded slowly. Her eyes seemed to have lost the clarity of only a few minutes ago, as though Lo had retreated back into the recesses of herself. "Okay."

"Here's the wine." Gloria let go of Lo's hand and made room for the waitress to put the two glasses down. "Not that I condone drowning one's sorrows."

Lo inspected the giant balloon of glass, tipping the liquid gently from side to side. "At this point, it has my full endorsement." She took a sip. "Sorry, I know it's pathetic."

"Not pathetic at all. You're speaking to someone who coped so poorly when their boyfriend proposed that they moved to the other side of the planet. Most people throw parties, some cry with joy, but not good ole Gloria, she scribbled a note and fled the scene. You'll receive no judgment from me." She gave a wry smile and took a sip of wine.

Lo drew a squiggly line in the frost of her wineglass. "I'm hiding and you're running."

Gloria shrugged. "Fight or flight."

Lo raised her eyebrows and sipped her wine the way a drowning woman would gulp for air. She put the glass down decisively. "I need to use the restroom."

Gloria watched her pick her way through the tables, avoiding the side where Paula and Greg sat. It gave Gloria pleasure to watch the quiet grace with which she moved. She noticed two men looking at Lo then making an appreciative comment to one another. Gloria felt a white flash of anger strike her unexpectedly. Even in Lo's vulnerable state, men still wanted to run their eyes over her body in judgment. Gloria's own appreciation came from a well of emotion, where Lo's physical body was the sum of her complex parts, a manifestation of her essence. The burning vanilla was lodged in Gloria's throat now. It wasn't Lo they were seeing, it was the picture of her they painted over the top and she deserved better. Gloria looked away until she'd lost herself in the view through the green lace.

By the time Lo returned, apologizing for bumping into a friend, Karen, the salads had arrived and Gloria wasn't feeling the least bit hungry, just slightly tipsy. At least Lo's eyes were clear again. She immediately took a sip of wine.

"Believe it or not, I went to school with Karen, although I was the year above. I dated her brother, Jim, when I was a junior. It was very chaste. We kissed once before school at the bus shelter. I still remember he tasted like peanut butter and his friends were all hanging around by the school gate pretending not to notice. Probably a dare! After that he didn't talk to me for a week."

"Must have used up all his courage to kiss you."

"He ended up dumping me and going out with Jessica Blartley anyway. She had boobs." Lo looked down. "I still don't."

Gloria smiled. "Do you know him now?"

"Who, Jim? I've seen him around. Actually, he came and saw Peter once about something to do with a land dispute. I don't think there was much Peter could do. Some people expect an instant fix or they can't afford to pay for assistance. He does a lot of pro bono work, there's a lot of poverty around too."

"Is it difficult working together?" Gloria was trying to establish a picture of who Peter was. He seemed both generous and benign, sweet and weak.

"Not really. It helps having Candice there. She's extremely efficient and lightens the load considerably."

"Don't you ever…" Gloria trailed off, realizing the wine was getting to her.

"Worry that Peter is sleeping with her?" Lo finished for her. "Not really."

"Sorry, it's none of my business."

"It's okay, he's barely home. I know everyone thinks it, even if no one says it, except Sue-Anne, she's said it. To tell the truth, if he was, I wouldn't blame him." She shrugged slightly.

Over Lo's shoulder, Gloria observed Paula and Greg approaching and Lo must have seen the recognition in her face because she turned her head slightly to see them from the corner of her eye. She stopped what she was saying and the Doll-Lo appeared, stiff posture and wooden smile. Gloria felt resentful that every time they fell into a natural state, something would pull Lo out again.

"Dolores!" Paula said, coming to place a gnarled hand on Lo's shoulder. "I was telling Greg it was you. How are you feeling, honey?" Paula's face was pretty, her blond-white hair nicely blow-waved, but her back was hunched and her fingers arthritic. Greg was tall and strong-looking for an older man, with a thick head of gray hair.

"Well, thank you, Mrs. Weston."

"Oh, Paula! Just call me Paula, you know that. How's Peter?"

"Very well, thank you. Paula, Greg, this is my friend, Gloria Grant, from Melbourne."

Gloria said hello and shook hands politely.

"From Melbourne, Australia? We went there once, Australia, to the Great Barrier Reef. My, it was something. Our friend Bert lives in Sydney now."

Greg cut in. "Paula, it's a big place, she doesn't know Bert."

"Oh, Greg, I'm making conversation."

Greg hovered at the periphery, his hands in the pockets of his woolen slacks, looking at the wedges of sunlight piercing through the trees. He turned farther toward the door.

"I hear you're taking a break from guests. It's for the best, I suppose. Nice to have some you-time, especially after everything that's happened. Things will calm down. You're young enough to try again. Same age as our Sheryl." Paula blinked her blue eyes stupidly and Greg looked agitated and stepped slightly away.

Lo went still and her face took on a hard quality. Her mouth worked at nothing as though it couldn't get comfortable on her jaw. When her words finally formed, they came with a stutter. "Mrs. Weston, my reproductive system is not your concern. One thing about having your only child die is that you no longer have to listen to bullshit like this."

Paula's head jerked back as though she'd been slapped and Greg took her by the elbow. "Let's go, dear."

Paula wasn't done. "Dolores, I understand how hard it is—"

Lo cut her off. "No you don't. You haven't got a clue."

Paula tried to speak again but Greg pulled her away, apologizing quickly over his shoulder.

Lo sat, her nostrils flared, her jaw set. Gloria reached out to take her hand but Lo snatched her own hand away. People had turned to see what was going on. Gloria started to say, "Let's go," but Lo shook her head and picked up her wineglass, clanging it against her plate, her hand shaking now.

"See, it's because of this crap that I'm better off at home, and don't you dare say she means well." Lo's eyes burned with unshed tears.

"Here, have my wine." Gloria pushed her glass toward Lo.

"She's a busybody, always asking pointed questions. I never liked her, even when I was young. Her daughter is just as stupid. I shouldn't have brought you here, it was a mistake to come."

"I'm glad you did. I love it. Don't let her get to you. What if this keeps happening? You'll end up a recluse."

Lo sniffed. "So?"

"So you'll let the Paulas of the world dictate your future?" Gloria tried to keep the frustration from her voice. "It strikes me that you've never let anyone hold you back from whatever it is you want, so why now?"

"Everything's different now."

"And yet there's one constant." Gloria didn't say *you*, but she knew Lo understood.

"I'm like one of the river rocks below, unmoving for all eternity while the river rushes by and the world grows around me."

"Without the rocks there'd be no river."

"I don't want to be a rock."

"Then be the river, be the sunlight playing on the river."

"I used to be it all." Lo sighed. "Sorry." She took a sip of Gloria's wine then passed it back. "Why is there so much fennel in this salad?"

"Because it's an orange and fennel salad?"

Lo let out a huff of nervous laughter. "Right. I probably knew I'd have no appetite." Her fork paused in its prodding of fennel. "Is it that generation or is that a huge generalization? I can't imagine foisting myself into someone's personal life uninvited like that."

"Maybe times were simpler back then. Paula probably got married, had her children, and that was her ambition fulfilled." Gloria didn't have an appetite either, but she forked up some salad and ate it anyway. "It's zesty. Nice. Much better than anything I could come up with. I'm not much of a cook."

"I'm certainly no Paula. Cooking's not my forte either. I don't care enough about food. I just eat what's put in front of me or manage grilled cheese. Not lately, I guess."

"Except fennel?"

"I've nothing against fennel, I guess I'm not hungry."

"You wanna go home?"

Lo's eyes were softly beseeching. "Would you mind?"

"Not at all. Let's go."

They stood and Gloria led the way indoors, proud to be walking beside Lo, no matter what people thought or said.

She'd never felt more happy to part with money in her life as she handed the cashier the hundred-dollar bill. Lo stood so close that she could feel the heat from her shoulder against her own.

As they began to drive home, Gloria wondered if Lo would retreat again. It had been difficult the first time, but Gloria felt it less personally this time. It was part of some process Lo was working through. Lo was quiet now behind her large sunglasses, watching the road, the sun falling in a heavy drape across their laps so Gloria could feel the pink burn of it on her bare legs. Instead of turning back onto the highway, Lo steered them purposely west toward the canyon.

"The river, do you want to see it?"

Gloria recovered from her slumped position by the window. "Very much so."

"Then you shall," Lo said.

Gloria had no idea what Lo's eyes were doing behind those large sunglasses, but her hands were steady as she shifted gears. The thought of an extra hour with Lo made Gloria happier than it should. These days she was evading introspection in favor of exploring the physical world.

The entrance to the national park announced various rules for existing among nature, signs with neat symbols for ease of translation. The gravel car lot was almost full, owing to the mild Saturday afternoon. Towering lodgepole trees cast shade over the cars, scattering brown needles across the floor and perfuming the air with pine.

"It's about ten degrees cooler here," Gloria said, shutting the car door and taking in the scenery.

"Are you cold?"

Gloria felt each sensation with pleasure, even the pricking of the hairs on her arms. "Not at all."

A family with bland faces came walking back to their car and nodded a vague greeting, the father holding a floppy toddler to one shoulder. They passed by over a boardwalk and out onto the trail. Wooden signposts marked with distances pointed in various directions. Lo took her sunglasses off and they stood looking at the options. They found the most direct path to the lookout and began to walk, Gloria slightly ahead, Lo walking behind, face tipped upward to watch the light falling through the tree canopy overhead. Gloria felt she was stepping above reality, gliding through a silvery dream where everything was new and anything might happen. Earnest hikers with backpacks, walking poles, and ruddy cheeks passed them, smiling exuberantly. Gloria appreciated the way her own muscles set happily to the task of walking after all the farm work she had been doing. If Lo felt the opposite of her own underutilized body, she didn't complain. In fact, when Gloria turned to smile at her, Lo was keeping pace, outwardly unaffected.

"I want to show you the river at home too," she said. "It's part of this same river."

Gloria stopped to pick up a pretty pine cone, then a few paces later she spotted another just as lovely, firm, smooth and regular in its shape and pattern. She handed it to Lo. "A Wyoming souvenir."

Lo took it and held it to her nose for a moment. "I'll put it beside my bed to remind me of life."

Gloria clutched her own pine cone, feeling happiness traveling from her hand into it and back again. She never wanted the walk to end, and a wild fantasy gripped her, of being out on the trail forever with Lo. She knew it wasn't possible, but it was nice to entertain.

They reached the lookout point on a wooden platform over the canyon just as a couple was leaving it. The platform projected them out over the edge of the canyon so they were looking down into the surprisingly blue waters crashing purposely through the banks of rock below. The air was cool and filled with the mysterious dank smell of churned rain and sodden leaf matter. They stood, leaning on the faded railing, casting their vision in a wide net, trying to capture the sudden blue of the sky meeting with the sharp points of the black tree line, the sunset rock of the banks, the jagged green grass, and the glassy blue and opaque white of the water. It was almost too much to bear.

"Not a cloud in the sky," Lo said, tipping her head back to catch the sun on the definite tip of her nose. As she uttered those words, a white feather, fluffy and curled, came floating down from the sky in front of Gloria, and she reached out and grabbed at it. It danced out of reach, propelled by the force of her movement, but she leaned forward and her hand found it. She closed her fist, careful not to crush it, and opened her fingers.

"Angel's wings," she said, presenting it to Lo.

Lo looked down at the feather, then took it between thumb and forefinger, a delighted smile warming her face. She looked up at Gloria, the sun catching on the gold in her hair and the flecks in her tawny eyes, and Gloria felt with a shocking bell of clarity all the feeling she had been concealing from herself. She dropped the pine cone she had still been clutching in the other hand and it fell swiftly and surely to the river below. Gloria stared after it, wondering how she would ever bring her gaze back and marshal her limbs to move again.

"Oh, your pine cone," Lo said. "We can find another one. Can I keep the angel feather? Are you okay, honey?"

Gloria dragged her gaze to the well-shaped shells of Lo's knees and nodded. "Maybe we should head back."

If Lo's voice carried a trace of disappointment, it was well concealed. "Sure. We can just follow the trail as it loops back, we're halfway anyway."

Gloria let Lo lead her back onto the path worn between the trees. Lo carried her pine cone in one hand, the feather she had put in the pocket of her shorts. Oh, to be that feather. Gloria looked away from the dusty heels of Lo's boots, embarrassed at herself, her own hands bereft of something to hold.

CHAPTER NINE

During the ride home Gloria was tensed, hunched against the door, her shoulder pressed against the window to gain control over the convulsions which shook her like tiny chainsaws at her bones. Once, as Lo checked for oncoming traffic at a road sign, she let her eyes stray toward Gloria, otherwise she kept her focus on the road. Gloria remained locked in her private misery until she was able to provide Lo a clumsy gratitude and flee from the car, heading straight for the barn to avoid further exposure to the object of her overwrought affections. If Kip was back from town, he wasn't anywhere Gloria could see. Clumsy in the thin skin of unrequited love, she made her way around, falling over her own feet, bumping her elbows and shoulders on miscalculated edges, until she'd oriented herself enough to put a headcollar on Hamlet and take him through to a larger paddock, Sonnet following along behind. She had a newfound sympathy for Sonnet's insistent attachment, the desperation in which she fought to remain within Hamlet's orbit. They could worry about Yo-Yo later. Lo's horses—Lo's!—seemed to breathe a double sigh, immediately rolling in the long grass, their legs flailing in the air like beetles stuck on their shells, then shaking themselves and settling down to nibble (Sonnet) and rip (Hamlet) at the grass contentedly. Gloria gave the fences and trough a check then fled back to her room where she could sit in solitude and no one was in danger of reading the truth in her dazed eyes or the judders of her regressed limbs. As though from a distance, she sat on her bed and watched the curtains billow in and out like labored lungs while the day rolled by unaffected. Gloria's own lungs labored with the heavy thudding of her heart and the electric news traveling her nerve endings. There was only one thing she was sure of: she was in trouble.

Time passed unbeckoned and there was a tentative knock at the door. Gloria jerked from her clammy stupor and quavered a response.

"May I come in?" Lo's voice, like funeral bells, poignant and beautiful.

Gloria snatched up the moss book from her bedside table and stood up before saying, "Yes!" then realized the awkwardness of her position and dropped the book onto the bed where it tumbled from the edge and that was how Lo found her, retrieving the book from the floor, her eyes wild and cheeks fevered.

Lo's bare toe stopped before the threshold of Gloria's quarantine and she wrapped her arms around herself as was her characteristic display of unease, squeezing the tops of her own arms. "Sorry to interrupt you, I thought you might like to know that Sue-Anne is a grandmother. Her daughter had a little girl. Hospital visiting hours are eight thirty until eleven, in case you're interested."

"Kip was placing bets in chalk on the barn wall: colt or filly."

Lo let one arm drop so it dangled beside her. "What did you guess?"

"Filly."

"What do you win?"

"Five dollars or something. Are you going to see the baby in the morning?"

"Oh." Lo's hand returned to cover her chest. "No, I couldn't. That hospital is where Terrence went and I...I don't think I can."

"That's understandable, I'm sure no one expects you to." Gloria stuffed her hands into her pockets, not quite looking at Lo.

"That's true. No one expects much of me, which is a relief and a cause for anxiety." She gave a small smile.

Gloria felt shy and stupid like a seventh grader in a circle of older kids. She couldn't think of anything much to say but didn't want the silence to become uncomfortable, so she shrugged and said, "We did a lot today." Their eyes slid away from one another as though the magnets that had drawn them together earlier now repelled them.

"More in one day than in a month for me." Lo looked down at the moss book. "You know there are many more books, they've been packed away in the attic. Please feel free to help yourself. Reading is the best balm."

Gloria said, "Thank you," and Lo said, "You're welcome," and turned and walked away. Gloria stood, watching the space where Lo had been, feeling the hollowness of the interaction, the sting of acquaintance. What right did she have to ask more of Lo? Now that Lo had stepped bravely out into the world, like sentries at the gate they must swap positions, Gloria retreating back into her own manageable realm.

The next few days ground by. Gloria declined to go and visit the baby even as Kip bounced off with a wooden mobile of colorful barn animals and a fluffy brown bear wearing a denim waistcoat. "From us all," he said, winking at Gloria. She'd signed the card and experienced relief that she wouldn't have to be the unwelcome stranger descending upon the new mother in an awkward ritual of politeness. Instead, she rose early to avoid breakfast interaction and went out to work with the horses in the clean dawn light. Sonnet was slowly getting used to her and would accept a carrot from Gloria's hand. They had put Yo-Yo in the field with them which had gone well with Sonnet, but when Gloria tried to catch any of them Yo-Yo was inclined to snake his neck and carry on, giving Sonnet worse habits, so he had been banished back to the field and they had brought in Mandalay, who was old and calm and, as Samuel quite harshly put it, no one cared if he was kicked and had to be shot. Sonnet tolerated Mandalay unless he tried to get between the two of them. He only tried it once and then kept his distance. Gloria hadn't yet had success going for a ride on Hamlet without Sonnet because she became immediately distressed and almost crashed through the fence. She was getting better at letting Gloria ride around in the field where she could graze and keep an eye on Hamlet. Hamlet was coming along well, displaying his athleticism and trainability despite his out-of-work condition. Gloria was longing to get him back into form. Having something to work at kept her distracted from her more pressing longing.

The day after her trip with Lo, she called her parents in Melbourne. They weren't angry so much as worried she was having a nervous breakdown. Apparently, they had spent many nights counseling Mike as he wept on their couch, at their table and over the phone. They were unable to offer him consolation; they had no clue themselves. Gloria's father offered to pay her flight home and said Klaus had been trying to get ahold of her about a hidden gem of a horse he'd found that he thought could be her Grand Prix hopeful. "They all miss you, darling," her father had finished. "No one's mad." But Gloria didn't believe him. Once she returned the relief would wear off and the accusations would start and then what? Her separation from Mike only confirmed that the flavor had waned from their relationship like a piece of gum chewed too long.

And love, love was sideswiping her every time her thoughts ran thin. When she was cleaning Hamlet's bridle and she wondered if Lo was the last person to do it, or when she heard soft footsteps creak past her room late at night, or when she'd been tossing and turning in bed and seen the barn light go on briefly. Peter's car turned up one afternoon, bringing an older woman who had Lo's fine bone structure and aristocratic air. The mother from Cheyenne with the non-boyfriend called Casey. Gloria saw them sitting at the table while Sue-Anne dished out steaming plates of something that smelled garlicky and herby and scrumptious that Gloria now couldn't eat. Instead, she stayed outside with the horses, cold and grumpy with her stomach crying starvation. Eventually she climbed onto Hamlet's back and lay there while he grazed. An electric blanket of warmth from his solid equine body. He was a good listener, and she knew he understood how unique Lo was. Eventually she could stay out no longer with the night biting at her through her thin jeans, and she went around to the front so as not to have to go through the back area which led to the kitchen. By the time she got there, Peter's car was gone and she crept to the bathroom to shower unnoticed. Even Sue-Anne had washed up and left, bustling off to see her granddaughter, no doubt.

During the day she was content with Samuel's companionable silence and although Kip offered beer and conversation again, it was easy to decline. She had the pleasure of watching him sell a horse to a local boy and his father who wanted to do barrel racing. He really turned it on, and Gloria thought he made a great salesman, suddenly seeing the walleyed pinto in a new light herself, not that she could afford to buy him even if she wanted to. Still, Kip and Samuel were generous with the horses, giving her free rein to do as she pleased. Samuel had even offered her a ride on Firecat, although she knew he hoped she'd decline. She did decline, of course, but it made her think of Klaus's offer back home of a Grand Prix horse. She'd never had her own, and working with Hamlet had ignited that fire within her again. She wondered if Lo had it too, that passion that time could dampen but not extinguish. She longed to see Lo ride, those long firm legs astride a horse. She knew she would be intuitive with horses and imagined how the grace with which she moved would translate to the way she sat on a horse. Gloria wondered where these erotic thoughts had sprung from; had she been burying them out of her own range or had Lo born them in her, fully formed? She found herself drifting off for minutes at a time, thinking about the way Lo's hands never stopped moving or the one freckle on her index finger, the way she drawled her words in a honeyed twang like syrup pouring from a bottle, the way each strand of hair looked painted in metallic orange under the light but all together it was strawberry blond. And each night she willed herself not to knock on Lo's door and ask her for a drink. It was a battle that she was proud she was winning. Lo for her own part didn't bother Gloria, although Gloria felt terrible that Lo had found confidence just as Gloria started to avoid her. A couple of times she was sure she felt someone watching from the attic as she worked Hamlet in the field, but it was probably her fancy. On Wednesday night, lying in bed with the covers pulled up to her chin and the romance book Sue-Anne had left in her room in her hand—the woman had survived her moss diet and lived to document her ordeal—Gloria heard Peter and Lo arguing, then the sound of Lo's sobs followed by the soft crooning of reconciliation. Gloria read the same paragraph of her book over and over, not taking in a word, eventually slamming it down in frustration and pulling the pillow over her ears in case the reconciliation should reach the bedsprings.

Thursday morning, Peter's car was gone when Gloria stumbled out of bed after a night spent offering herself to sleep the way someone might offer cucumber to a cat. Sleep evaded her and the cat stayed distant. Kip was already herding the yearlings in to get them ready for halter breaking and handling with a view of branding them en masse in a week. Gloria had offered to help with the handling, but she wasn't sure she wanted to be the one holding the hot iron. Kip had told her how one year they'd had four heavily pregnant mares stolen from the front paddock, never to be seen again, to try to make her see a purpose to the practice. She waved to him now but kept walking, keen to put as much distance between the house and herself as possible. She had to get used to drawing a line in the sand between employee and friend, and really, Lo's emotional welfare was her own to sort and her husband should be the one to support her.

Hamlet seemed unperturbed by the early morning routine she had set him, and he ambled over to greet her. Not to be outdone, Mandalay barged forward to check Gloria's pockets for treats. She let them say hello, then waited for Sonnet to step timidly toward her, stretching her neck forward to sniff at

Gloria. Even though she stayed where she was, Gloria counted it as a small victory. Clarence walked by with the clanking wheelbarrow, which made Sonnet trot her nervous circle and Gloria grit her teeth. She went to fetch Hamlet's gear and tacked him up to take him for a spin around the field where his jealous lover could keep him in sight. At least now Sonnet stayed closer to Mandalay; the plan was working. Hamlet trotted smooth circles and performed simple changes at the canter, his large strides eating up the distance. Gloria couldn't resist asking for a few steps of piaffe, a canter pirouette, an extended trot along the long side. When she slowed Hamlet to a walk and let him stretch his neck out, rubbing his shoulder, she looked up to see Lo sitting on the wooden fence by the gate. She felt heat spring to her cheeks and wondered if she'd been making her unattractive concentration face or babbling idiotically to Hamlet. Lo watched her approach, strands of her low ponytail blowing against her lips. She sat easily atop the fence, a hand placed on each side to maintain balance, her legs swept to the side. Gloria rode over, or rather Hamlet strode over to greet his mistress, shoving his face inelegantly against her chest so she was forced to grab him to avoid toppling backward.

"Sorry," Gloria said, checking him.

Lo rubbed his face with the palm of her hand. "Hamlet! It's been a long time. I'd forgotten how huge he is."

"Looks like he's missed you." Gloria swung her leg over and slid down, her knees almost giving way. "Sorry...I know you said you didn't want me to—"

Lo cut her off. "I know I said it, but you're right, it's not fair to neglect the horses. He seems happy to be working again. He tries hard, but he's not the most imaginative creature."

Gloria squinted up at Lo, shadowed against the horizon. She liked the view from Hamlet's tall back better. "He's a well-trained horse. I could get him ready for sale if that's what you want to do. I mean, not that you couldn't do it yourself..."

"He looks different with you on top. He goes well for you."

Gloria swept the compliment aside. "I'm sure he'd go well for anyone. I've ridden a lot of horses and this guy is impeccable."

She pulled the impeccable horse's head away from the grass so he wouldn't ruin his impeccable show bridle. She supposed she shouldn't be using that either, but she didn't know if there was another.

"He's a lovely horse but he doesn't look like that with me on top. Any placings we won at competitions were due to his good training, not my skill. I came late to the game. It's not such a fair sport, is it, where money can buy a degree of talent. I wish I could have ridden like you do."

"He's your horse, why don't you hop on? I'm sure you ride well." Gloria meant it.

Lo waved her hand in front of herself. "I'm done with that, but it was selfish of me to say that Hamlet is done too. You go ahead and ride him, he looks like the horse he should with you on top."

"So you're not mad?"

Lo shrugged. "With Peter maybe, but you're just doing what you came here to do." She slid down from the fence and watched Sonnet approach Hamlet and place her chin on his rump, which was almost too high for her to reach. "Say, Gloria, is everything okay?"

Gloria was only half expecting that, she had been so worried that Lo would be cross that she was riding her horses after being warned not to. She switched the subject to the logistics of the immediate situation, trying to avoid her own feelings. "Sorry, Sonnet has to come to the barn too. Do you mind shutting the gate before Mandalay rushes through?" She opened the gate and Lo did as instructed, walking with them toward the barn before she tried conversation again, her steps beginning to lag.

"It's hard to look at Sonnet without being reminded of that day. Her scar is right there." She gave her head a quick shake and started reversing back the way she came. "You know what, this is giving me flashbacks…Sorry, I can't. I'm going back." Her voice rose and she turned and began to jog.

Gloria stopped the horses and watched Lo lope all the way back to the house.

As Gloria groomed Hamlet, she contemplated what had just happened. Although Lo had run off, it was fair to say that she was slowly opening up to the idea of life after death. She tried to run the body brush over Sonnet's shoulder, but the mare threw her head up and dodged out of the way. "Get over yourself," she said, feeling like flicking her away. Instead, she led them back to the field and let them loose. Gloria walked back to the house feeling she owed Lo more than a sulky silence. Facing up to herself was much harder than running away, but she was trying. In her mind, Lo was at the table eating breakfast but after she'd washed up and gone into the kitchen, Lo was nowhere to be found. Gloria was waylaid by Sue-Anne, who was glowing with maternal pride. Gloria hugged her, realizing that it was lovely to sink into a warm embrace, and listened to the birth story and how wonderful baby Hayley was. She sat and allowed Sue-Anne to ply her with fluffy pancakes and orange juice. Then Kip, Samuel, and Clarence came in, arguing about how many foals Freddy had sired. Sue-Anne was no greater fan of Clarence than Gloria was, and she began clanging pans into the sink. Gloria made her grateful escape.

It took Lo long seconds to answer Gloria's knock on her bedroom door. Gloria wasn't prepared for the tear-blurred face that greeted her. She was so wrapped up in her own concerns she hadn't given enough weight to Lo's flashbacks. She should have been more considerate around the horses; of course Lo's last memories of them would come pouring back.

"I'm okay," Lo said stoically, smearing at her face with the sleeve of her shirt. "My skull is brewing a headache though, I can feel it."

Gloria forced herself to look Lo in the eye even though it made her feel laid bare. "Sorry, I should have thought that through."

Lo shrugged and wrapped her arms around her waist. "I came down there."

"Can I get you anything for your head? I might have something in my purse."

"Trust me, if it's available via prescription, I have it in my bedside drawer, but thank you anyway." Lo dropped her gaze to the floor, relieving Gloria's burning eyeballs. "Did I say something to offend you the other day? I mean, I was going over it in my head, thinking maybe it was all too much, bumping into Paula and Greg. I was rude, I know."

Gloria almost laughed at the absurdity of it all. Poor innocent Lo running through all the reasons Gloria could possibly be giving her the cold shoulder and never once imagining it was the heating of Gloria's affections rather than the cooling that was holding her out of reach. She shifted her weight uneasily and stuffed her hands in the holey pockets of her jeans, which were becoming more air than fabric. "I just don't want to crowd your solitude," was all she could offer in reply.

This time Lo's mouth lifted in a smile. "Crowd my solitude?" she said mockingly.

"I came here to work. I won't intrude on your space any further." Gloria's tone seemed to frame the statement pointedly and Lo's eyes hardened even as the tears were evaporating from her cheeks. She seemed to physically collect herself, standing a little taller. Gloria admired her self-possessed gathering of pride. That was one thing she'd give Lo; even though she was frequently a mess of emotion, she never seemed to lose control of her faculties. Gloria already regretted the words she didn't mean, but she could see it was too late. Lo's eyes glittered green and gold.

"Right, yes. You know what, I think you made a valid point earlier. Hamlet should be prepared for sale. He's no use here, wasting his talent, and Peter will want some return on his investment. The horses are in capable hands, so I'll leave you to it."

Gloria felt the sting even though she had set the stage for it. "Thank you." She turned and walked back down to the kitchen, already questioning herself. Kip, listening to something Sue-Anne was saying about childbirth, watched Gloria as she walked stiffly to the kitchen and made herself a coffee. He didn't say anything, but she saw reserved understanding in his eyes.

Gloria didn't need to be told twice; she made sure her schedule wouldn't overlap with Lo's. They existed in different time zones, Gloria rising early and going to bed early, Lo hours later and roaming the dark night alone. When they did meet, they were polite, friendly even. Lo asked Gloria if she would like a drink one night, but Gloria sensed she didn't mean it and declined. She did, however, accept Lo's invitation of access to the books in the attic. That was easier as she was left alone to pore over the books, like a pioneer exploring the recesses of Lo's mind, the cobwebby corners and crisp open fields. The fascination with the supernatural butting up against the factual. The thirst for psychological case studies and true crime, thick science journals and the proclivity for historical romance. Poetry books with notes written by College-Lo in soft-tipped pencil and fiction underlined in pen. It was a new secret world for Gloria to explore, and those notes on Plath and Whitman, Brooks and Frost, an all-American cast, were crumbs thrown through time for Gloria to follow. Follow where? Along the fault line of her heart where it tremored and quaked. Those notes scribbled in margins were more beautiful to Gloria than the cinematic fan of Lo's lashes or the silky skin on the underside of her wrist, the shocking length of leg or the scholarly bent of her brow. Those notes made Gloria swoon. It was a way of being close to Lo while keeping her distance. She didn't miss Lo while she was lost in her mind.

Keeping to herself also meant time with the horses, which, as she had pointed out to Lo, was the reason she was there. She helped gentle the yearlings and get them used to being led and their downy hair brushed. She had already developed favorites, like the compact palomino who picked things up quickly and the shy steel-gray filly who gravitated to her softer style rather than the men with their loud voices and rough movements. Kip promised she could help name them if she didn't pick "sissy" names (which made Gloria resolve to pick the most feminine names that suited, although she floated Lamington for the gray filly and was quickly shut down). The dressage horses were also coming along. Sonnet was finally tolerating brief periods away from Hamlet, and Gloria could touch her shoulder now but not her head. Hamlet was slowly beginning to unstiffen from his months at grass, and Gloria began to ask more of him. The more she worked with him the more she fell in love with him, and she regretted that Lo wanted to sell him. If there was ever a horse to give a rider confidence, it was Hamlet.

When Gloria wasn't riding or helping with the other duties, she was reading or writing letters home to her parents and friends. The first two letters that had arrived from Mike were long and begging rather than accusatory. They were hard to read and made her pity him and feel worse than she did already. The next letters that came from him she shoved under the stack of books, unopened. To try to prevent more from arriving, she wrote and rewrote letters to Mike but none felt genuine. Markings on a page failed to convey what she wanted to say— sorry—without the relief of their separation seeping in. In the end she opted for two lines:

Dear Mike,

I won't ask you to forgive me, that wouldn't be fair, but I am sorry. I hope you are well and that you now know why it was necessary to put distance between us.

Gloria

Her name, stark and unadorned by kisses or measures of love seemed out of place, but any combination she tried seemed contrived. She hoped it was short enough to give him pause.

She wrote to Klaus and received a brief, efficient letter back written using his familiar letterhead, which she had written on so many times herself, asking her to return and offering her full livery for a horse if she wished and telling her about the exciting young mare he had acquired, potentially for her. Gloria was touched, but wary of his generosity. It usually came with a price. To her friends back home she sent glossy postcards with glaringly bright pictures of the landscape that said about as much of what she was doing as the words she wrote on the back. A chasm yawned between her old life and this temporary one, that she found she couldn't bridge.

Now that Lo was leaving her bedroom more, Gloria frequently saw her on the swinging seat outside, staring off toward the mountains with Wilbur at her feet, or rambling off toward the fields on foot with a big hat on her head. Peter appeared more frequently now too, as though he had been waiting for Dolores to step back into a wifely role of her own accord, and he paid Gloria, thanking her for all the work she was doing with "the boys" and suggesting she might like some new jeans from town. Gloria was aware of how she appeared to Peter: wild hair, dust-streaked face, tattered clothes, and coarse limbs. Every day, she intended to go into town and buy a whole new wardrobe and get a haircut, but there was always something to do. Sue-Anne was back on board, cooking with fervor but less inclined to stay and eat with them now that there was a little person to coo over back home. Her little blue hatchback flew up and down the highway tending to her two babies, Hayley and Dolores. Dolores, like Terrence's phantom limb, unreachable but a persistent affliction.

The dinner table was often the scene of serious discussions pertaining to the ranch finances, in which Kip held his own against Peter while Sue-Anne went about her kitchen duties making agreeing noises in her nose and throat. Kip kept pointing out that there was no revenue coming in and if there wasn't more rain the crops wouldn't yield what they usually did. Horses were eating their heads off doing nothing and guesthouses were sitting idle, home to spiders and dust. No one spelled it out, but it was glaringly obvious that if nothing drastic was done, they would be forced to sell all the stock, if not the whole place. Peter grew angry time and again, saying things like, "What more can one family take?" and "Why must we ruin a perfectly good meal by discussing negative subjects?" but Kip hung on doggedly and Gloria felt the gathering of a storm that had been brewing off the horizon for a while. Lo stayed mainly silent on the subject, most likely dreading either prospect.

CHAPTER TEN

The wheel of time was slowly throwing them toward summer. The days were warmer now, the nights still chill with mountain air. Gloria had ridden out a few times to see the overgrown stream rushing fatly along and was getting to know the wider reaches of the ranch where the fences ran out and the fields grew feral. After one such ride on Dodger, who remained her faithful friend after their first encounter, Gloria's jeans completely gave out as she dismounted. She hobbled back to the house, trying to maintain some dignity as she passed Clarence, who spat on the grass and watched her discomfort unashamedly. Inside the house, Gloria bundled up her jeans and threw them into the trash. She showered and stood with her towel wrapped around herself, staring into the chest of drawers that contained hole-riddled Garfield socks and Mike's grass-stained oversized T-shirt. She could only laugh at herself. "Not even fit for a scarecrow." She cursed herself for letting it get to this point, embarrassed at her own inaction. Securing the towel around her breasts, she took a deep breath and steeled herself.

Facing Lo would be her punishment for letting things get this bad in every way. Before she knocked on Lo's door, she looked over the railing down toward the lounge room sunk into the floor. Tucking the towel in between her legs, she called down to Lo's head directly beneath her, bent over a book. Lo looked up sharply, her finger automatically wedging a place in the pages, her legs coiled up, a cushion on her lap.

"Sorry, Lo, I don't have any clothes."

Lo blinked up at her. "I can see that." A cold droplet of water rolled from a strand of Gloria's hair and splashed Lo's forearm. "Are you going to use water torture until I help you out?"

Gloria felt another drop fall. "Yes."

Lo's mouth pulled at its moorings. "I'd guess I'd better help you out then." She folded the corner of the page in the book she was reading and put it out of sight on the side table. Gloria wondered what it was. Something old and tattered looking. She tucked her towel more securely around herself and waited for Lo to follow the echo of her footsteps up the stairs.

"I was wondering when you were going to break," Lo said, pushing her bedroom door open.

"My jeans broke before I did. It was a mutual split really." Goose bumps rose on Gloria's arms as she looked around Lo's room while Lo rifled through her clothes. Her eyes stopped at the bedside table where she saw the feather tucked under the pine cone. Her heart jolted gladly.

"You're welcome to anything, but how about these?" Lo held up a pair of denim overalls. "They'd look super cute on you. Here, with this T-shirt." She pulled a black-and-white striped T-shirt from the drawer and held them up against herself to demonstrate what they would look like.

"Thanks, are you sure?"

"Sure I'm sure. Would you like a lift into town?"

Gloria was surprised that Lo seemed eager. "Actually, I would love that. My sneakers are falling apart, I have nothing left at all. Even toiletries."

"We are holding you prisoner at the ranch. Soon you'll have nothing left to wear and will be stuck here forever. It's the only way I get company."

Lo passed her the clothes then turned back and fished out a pair of very white socks. Gloria felt like a child who had wet herself at preschool but she took the items, stiff with Sue-Anne's zealous laundering.

"You can keep the overalls, I never wear them, they're for someone younger. Let me get my purse."

"We're practically the same age, but okay, I'll get changed. Thank you!"

Gloria went to her own room and slipped into the clothes, using the last of her deodorant. She ran her fingers through her stubborn hair and took a wad of notes from her purse and shoved them into one of the many pockets the overalls had. She looked at herself in the mirror; the yin to Lo's yang. In her clothes but nothing like her, except the smile maybe.

Lo was waiting in the kitchen for her, examining an apple from the fruit bowl. "You know what a client told me once? That she feeds her guide dog apple before he gets in the cab so his breath won't smell."

Gloria grimaced. "What are you trying to tell me?"

Lo laughed and tossed the apple to her. "I'm playing it safe."

Gloria arched an eyebrow. It seemed they both were.

By the time they reached town, they had both crunched their apples down to the core and had sweet breath and apple skin in the back of their teeth. Lo threw her core out the window into the long grass and instructed Gloria to do the same. Lo parked the car and seemed to gather herself, then gave a sharp nod at Gloria as if to say, "Let's do this." If people wanted to gawk at Lo in her yellow floral sundress they'd have to do it quickly because she strode straight into the clothing store, Gloria scurrying to keep up.

The store was larger than it looked from the outside. There were distinct sections for men, women, children, and babies. It smelled of clean-cut fabric and plastic. Mannequins in the window modeled city fashion two seasons old, but Gloria loved the quaint feel of it, the locally sourced hats and scarves and the way the bridesmaids dresses brushed up against the school uniforms. An older woman with glasses on a chain around her neck and a kind face came to say hello to Lo.

Lo smiled with genuine warmth. "Hello, Cathy, how have you been? This is my good friend Gloria Grant, she's visiting from Australia."

Cathy smiled at Gloria. "I'd heard you had someone new at the ranch. Pleasure to meet you, I'm Cathy." Her attention on Gloria was fleeting and she opened her arms for Lo to step into. "Come here, Doll. I've missed seeing your beautiful face around town."

Lo hesitated then fell almost gratefully into Cathy's arms. Gloria envied the warmth and easy familiarity Cathy had with Lo, who let her cheek fall onto Cathy's shoulder. Cathy dropped her head against Lo's like a mother comforting a small child and she rubbed her back. When they broke apart, they both had tears in their eyes.

"Oh!" Lo laughed wetly, rubbing at her eyes. She turned to Gloria. "I've forgotten how much I've missed y'all."

"Us too, honey." She kept hold of Lo's hand with her fingers. "Now tell me, girls, what do you need?"

"Just about everything. It's fair to say I traveled light!" Gloria said. "Do you have shoes too?"

"Sure we do, right down the back. Would you like me to show you?"

"No, that's fine, why don't you chat to Lo while I take a look?"

"That would be marvelous, honey. Feel free to browse and put things on the counter if you want. Just holler if you need a hand."

Gloria was happy to leave Cathy and Lo chatting. It was nice to see Lo melding back into the world she inhabited before the accident. All the negative imaginings that Lo had been so sure would spring to life had yet to manifest. The warmth which Lo was greeted with confirmed to Gloria what she felt was true; Lo was a lovely person and had once been a social butterfly and was still well-known and respected. She glanced backward into the mirror as Lo conversed with Cathy, Lo's long fingers playing with the tassels on a scarf as she spoke, her inner light freed, if only momentarily, from its lantern. Gloria felt a surge of pride, even though it was close to vanity, that she was a good friend of Dolores Ballantyne. She carried on along the racks of clothing: T-shirts arranged by color; dresses in lilac and forget-me-not blue and apricot, no two of a kind; berets and beanies and sun hats; riding clothes and ski jackets. The more she looked, the more entranced she became. She found some denim shorts and a white T-shirt and she was standing oohing and ahhing over a pale blue dress which wasn't really her style, but seeing how lovely Lo looked in her yellow sundress she felt inspired. The dress had thin straps and a sweetheart neckline and a pattern of small wildflowers a shade darker with green leaves rambling all over it.

"Try it on!" Lo said, coming up behind her.

"I'm not sure. Is it too girly for me?"

"You won't know until you try it. Here, pass me those clothes. Let's see how it looks."

So Gloria went into the changing room with its swinging saloon doors and slipped into the dress, realizing how brown her arms were in comparison to her legs. Her hair had grown past her shoulders to brush her collarbones. She felt different in a dress.

"Come out and face the jury," Lo called.

Gloria pushed the doors open and stepped out to greet Lo, who was sitting on the stepladder used to reach the top shelves. She sat up straighter when she saw her. "You're buying it!"

"I'm not sure if I can pull it off," Gloria said.

Lo stood up and came to grab Gloria's shoulders and swung her around toward the mirror so Gloria could see herself reflected with Lo beside her, two cotton confections in their dresses. Lo smiled at her. "See, it suits you." She tucked a strand of Gloria's dark hair behind her ear and smoothed the back of Gloria's head. "If you wear that around town, no one will notice me to gossip."

Gloria's heart thudded *Lo-La Lo-La*, Lo's apple breath on the curve of her neck, the ribbons of fair hair beside her own ebony tussles. "That would never happen," she said, standing one bare foot on top of the other.

Lo looked at her in the mirror with clear eyes and their eyes flicked from their own reflection to each other's until Cathy said, "Oh you look beautiful, Gloria, honey. You know, I remember when you bought that dress, Doll. It still looks fantastic. You two look like a posy of flowers. Now, Gloria, we have a sale on winter apparel if there are any slacks you fancy?"

And just like that the spell was broken. Gloria returned to the changing room to take the dress off. She stood in front of the mirror and touched a hand to the warm spot on her neck where Lo's lips had been so close. Her cheeks were hectic, and she stared wide-eyed at herself. "Gloria Grant!" she mouthed. "Get ahold of yourself."

"How's this, honey?" Cathy called, slinging a green woolen sweater and a pair of gray slacks over the door. "I'll do you half price on these."

Gloria startled away from her own reflection. "Thank you!"

Gloria walked out of the store with two large gift bags of clothes. She had bought the dress even though she wasn't sure she would ever wear it. It seemed special now, for no other reason than Lo had admired her in it. "Lunch?" she asked. "My treat."

"Yes, I think that would be okay, don't you?"

Gloria shrugged. "Why not?"

"I dunno." Lo looked across the street, suddenly self-conscious again.

"Are you worried that people will judge you for eating?"

Lo smiled faintly, her gaze still across the road on a family walking along the sidewalk in front of the barber shop. "I guess when you put it that way…"

"Would you like me to put on the dress? I can get changed in the phone booth like Superman and save the town from having to notice you."

"That would be immensely helpful, thank you. Here, let's put the clothes in the car so you don't have to carry them. Do you feel like burgers?"

"Veggie burger?" Gloria was skeptical.

Lo laughed. "We can ask. Would you settle for fries and a shake?"

Gloria would have settled for a bowl of oaten chaff. "How American."

Lo looked at her in astonishment as she unlocked the car. "Honey, that burger patty probably comes from one of our cows."

"Even more reason not to eat it." Gloria put the bags on the floor of the passenger side. "Will anyone steal them?"

"Darlin', Cathy probably doesn't even lock up at night. Let's go."

They ran gaily across the road to beat a car that was trundling slowly along and pushed open the door of Big Hal's Diner, which was surprisingly busy. Lo led Gloria to a booth with red cushions and a sparkly gold Formica tabletop.

"You did say you were buying, didn't you?"

Gloria nodded.

"I'm going to have a double beef cheeseburger then." Lo picked up the menu as Gloria slid in opposite her. "Oh, look! A vegetable burger." Lo flipped the menu so Gloria could see.

"Perfect. See, Diamond Rock River is more progressive than you thought."

Lo raised her eyebrows. "Try it first, then get back to me."

Gloria scanned the glossy pink menu. "Is it more American to have a shake or a Vanilla Coke?" Then, seeing Lo's bemused expression, "Well, I'm here in the grand ole US of A, so I want to experience what I can."

"Get both."

"That's even more American."

Lo laughed, showing her neat teeth. "Even more reason."

"I'll never finish it. All right, I'll give it a go. I hope you're not in a rush." She slid the menu back toward Lo.

"I think you know what my schedule looks like." She slotted the menu back between the napkin dispenser and condiments. "Do you think you'll travel around and see more of the country while you're here?"

Gloria was playing with a sugar packet, crunching the granules inside the paper. "I hadn't thought about it. I rushed over here without much preamble, unsure what would be on the other end of the plane ride, only knowing that I couldn't stay where I was. More traveling wasn't on the agenda. I suppose the future is just an unwritten page. Maybe I will, it would make sense."

"Not a traveler?" Lo asked.

"Not really. Apart from travel with Klaus and the horses, I've stuck pretty close to home. Life has always been rich with equestrian activities and new experiences. How about you?" Gloria looked up from the sugar packet.

Lo's eyes slid away as soon as Gloria's found them. "I love it, but it was always difficult to find time with everything that was going on. I'm not very hands-on with the ranch these days, but it's a full-time job, as well as the office. We did take Terrence to Disneyland when he was four. He was probably a bit young to enjoy it." She smiled sadly at the Formica tabletop. "On our honeymoon we went to Europe—Paris, Rome, London, then Hawaii on the way home. It was a very choreographed trip, but I would love to go back and take my time. There's something so freeing about the idea of wandering the streets of a foreign city alone. I see why you felt suffocated at home once things got too much." She looked up and this time their eyes held, two sad smiles meeting one another.

Gloria wanted to take Lo's hand and say, *Let's go. Let's wander the streets of Paris in the springtime.* But it was pure fantasy and Lo's husband was toiling away not a hundred yards across the street. The ranch had its own problems, and it was certainly not something one could run from. A waitress arrived to take their order, and Lo also ordered two drinks in solidarity.

"It's lucky you're in a dress and I'm in overalls in case our stomachs expand beyond buttonability." Gloria returned her crumply sugar packet to the dish and examined the jukebox list at the table. "Have you got a dime?" she asked Lo.

"I think so. What will we play?"

Gloria scanned the list of songs. "We've already done Elvis in the car. Why are you all so obsessed with country and western music? Who's Willie Nelson?"

Lo's hand dropped from where it had been cupping her face and hit the table with a slap. "Are you kidding me?"

Gloria looked up with large eyes. "I don't know any of these, except maybe Dolly Parton."

"I know Australia is a desert full of snakes and kangaroos but surely y'all have radio down under?"

Gloria narrowed her eyes. "The kangaroo pouch I ride around in doesn't have FM."

Lo grinned and leaned back, satisfied that her joke had hit its mark. "Put on a pop song then, or rock. Whatever you like. I have one dime and it's all yours."

"No, I want to put a country song on now."

"All part of the American experience?" Lo leaned forward again and pushed Gloria's hand out of the way. "Let me have a look. Now, what ails thee? A broken heart? Do you need someone to croon to you about their breakup?"

"I'm not sure I do have a broken heart." *Not yet*, she wanted to add. "Pick something happy. I want to hear about someone winning in love. Red roses and midnight trysts."

"You're a romantic, I can tell."

It was true. Despite Gloria's recent unsuccessful attempts at love, she was a romantic at heart. Wandering, sugar-dusted, and lovestruck along the cobblestone streets and leafy boulevards of Paris, ducking into sidewalk cafés and museums, in love in the city of love. It was bold in her mind. Any situation she could think of, it was easy for her to paint romance into the picture. So far it had been a blank face beside her, but now there was Lo, her face vivid to the point of iridescence. Lo's slim figure with its arm through hers, her lithe step beside Gloria's. It was easy for Gloria's mind to slip away to these dreamy images. But Gloria was not in Paris but in Wyoming of all places, sitting opposite real-life Lo, an unimaginable lunch date not so many moons ago. The thought had not entered Gloria's head, just as the color blue must surely be an abstract concept in the mind of the blind person, Lo was not yet born in Gloria's mind. She had been born part-formed on the day Gloria had first laid eyes on her, glimmering below the surface, a fully formed Venus yet to emerge from the depths. Gloria wasn't sure why the surface had been breached, but once risen it was as steadfast as any ship that could sink or steam forth. She wanted to know more about Lo and her past but was cautious of opening wounds that were beginning to scar.

"I like it here because they usually employ young people. No one knows me," Lo said, watching the waitress approach, balancing a black tray with drinks. The waitress—Courtney, her name tag read—placed the drinks on the table with only a slight wobble of the tray and beamed in relief.

Gloria watched her depart to the kitchen again. "Is there a high rate of unemployment here?"

Lo pointed each of her index fingers at her two drinks. "Which one first? Try to make headway with the shake?" Gloria nodded and they both took a sip before Lo answered, "Mmm, that's thick. I guess employment is seasonal in some parts. There's agriculture and tourism that have peak seasons. There are a lot of family-owned businesses and the town supports itself, however not ten miles that way there is a block of new superstores that no one is real happy about. It's a concern for these small towns that are more or less self-sufficient, we don't want these discount outfits leaning on local business."

"I hadn't thought of that," Gloria said, her brow creasing. "So I did well to shop locally?"

Lo stirred at her shake slowly, watching the white-and-red striped straw part a path through the bubbles. "Exactly. We sort of carved out a niche here with the legal practice, not that it was my intention, it just worked out that way. Peter is probably more suited to the city life as well, he's not much for ranch life, but he tries to do the right thing. We both did, coming to take over the ranch rather than selling it. It's been in the family for a good long time. We thought Terrence would take it over, it was assumed he would anyhow. You know…" Her straw paused and she looked up. "That was one thing I thought worked out well. Even though ranch life isn't for everyone, Terrence seemed to thrive out here. The horses, the open spaces, he was a happy kid, or do you think all children would thrive out here?"

Gloria considered the question before answering. "No, I think some children don't like the outdoors, they prefer to read a book or watch the television, they don't like dirt on their hands or wind in their hair. But from what you've said, Terrence felt comfortable in the elements, had a natural affinity with horses, and a talent. Perhaps another child wouldn't have felt the same way."

"Hmm." Lo returned to her milkshake stirring. "I suppose you're right. I don't know why that helps but it does. I guess it frees us up to sell it if that's what is decided."

"Do you want more kids?" Gloria wasn't sure if it was an okay question to ask but curiosity got the better of her. She had spent too many nights wondering about Lo. Far too many, if she was honest.

"I'm not sure if I could give myself to another person that way again. It wouldn't be fair, not now at least. And if not now, then when? I'm thirty-eight."

"What about Peter?"

"What about Peter?" Lo tipped her head back against the seat, looking slightly down at Gloria. Gloria's eyes flicked to the vulnerable underside of Lo's neck, the white flesh that remained hidden from the sun, hidden from touch, the pampered child who didn't like the elements. Lo let her eyes stay on Gloria, reminding Gloria again that Lo was practiced in both comfortable and uncomfortable silences. If she could outstare an unwilling criminal, surely she could outlast Gloria, who only wanted to steal her heart.

It was Gloria who spoke first. "Thirty-eight suits you." A telltale slip of the heart. She couldn't win the war against every inflated thought balloon that tried to rise within her, nor could she explain the loveliness that were the laugh lines beside Lo's mouth and the fine webs beside her eyes. It reminded Gloria of the finite span of a person, of Lo, and it made her all the more precious in her eyes.

"Thirty-eight. Like a bad sweater. I wear it poorly." She grinned, her gaze sliding down over her lower lashes to meet Gloria, an energy coursing between them like humming powerlines. "Now quit stalling and pick a song."

Gloria had to willfully snap the line between them, from the topaz-infused live wire to the blandness of pink paper beneath plastic. To pick a song that would spell out what she couldn't was perhaps beyond any courage she possessed, but to choose one to throw Lo off the scent was just as fraught. A pop song that she recognized from a movie that she couldn't remember the name of was rolling through repeated choruses in the background, complicating her musical memory.

Lo laughed. "You look like you've been asked to choose someone to throw off a cliff."

Gloria smiled. Sure, who cared, just pick a song. She inserted her dime into the little slot and selected item K17.

"What did you choose?"

"You'll have to wait and listen."

"There might be a queue of selected songs, then I won't know which is yours."

Gloria kept her facial expression nonplussed. "Then you'll have to guess. Oh, good, our food is here."

Gloria was unprepared for the quantity of food that was put on the table in front of her. The burger with its thick orangey-looking patty was packed with a riot of salad colors and oozed yellow cheese. "I'm going to need a hinged mouth to eat this."

"You have to sort of stuff it into your face and accept that you'll look as messy as the plate while you're eating. Like this." Lo held the burger up and searched for the best angle, squashing the bun down with her fingers. Sauce began dripping onto her hands. Her face disappeared behind the burger, and when she reappeared there was sauce on her nose and chin and she was chewing a mouthful of food. "See," she mumbled, holding the burger so Gloria could see the missing bite. "Just attack it."

Gloria examined her own burger and pressed it flatter with the palm of her hand then followed Lo's example. Things inside the burger began to slide and she had to push them back in with her fingers, but she managed to take a bite. They both carried on grimly, trying to ignore the food on their faces until they stopped to restore some dignity with paper napkins.

"Lucky I'm not wearing makeup. Oh, you've got mustard in your hair! Here." Lo reached over and pinched a curl of Gloria's hair between thumb and forefinger. "Whose stupid idea was this? Oh, wait!" Lo sat bolt upright. "This! This is your song!"

Gloria cocked her head as the first strains of "Please Don't Go" thrummed through the room. "How did you know?"

Lo smiled. "Because it reminds me of you. Kinda quirky and upbeat. I dunno."

Gloria nodded. "It seems appropriate."

They listened to the song in silence, taking small sips and picking at their fries, bopping along to the lyrics that had been sung a million times before that were suddenly new again. Gloria felt exposed and returned to rattling a sugar packet, but when she looked up, Lo had her chin in her hands, looking right at her. Lo smiled and winked.

On the way home, that moment was like a warm spot in the sun that Gloria kept returning to as she gazed dreamily out the window, not sure what it meant but happy they had shared something, her lips dry from the tepid wind, her stomach heavy with food. When she looked at Lo, Lo's eyelids appeared heavy, her limbs languid.

"Are you okay to drive?"

"Whatcha gonna do about it?" Lo said, not unkindly, turning her head to glance at Gloria.

Gloria flopped her hand onto the middle seat beside them, palm up, seeking Lo's sun. Lo let her hand fall into it and Gloria held it, the long slim fingers, running her thumb along the heartline, until they slowed for the crossroad and the gearshift reclaimed it. *It's nothing. It's nothing.*

They tripped up the veranda steps as though drunk, carrying Gloria's bags.

"You don't understand the joy of socks without holes," Gloria said. "A T-shirt that isn't patterned with stains."

Lo shut the door behind them and Gloria stood contemplating the framed photos on the sideboard. Peter and Lo looking younger and smoother, the edges yet to push through the flesh, a sidewalk café in Rome, beaming across the sharply creased white linen tablecloth. Colorful towels on a beach, maybe Hawaii, the sun melting into the water behind them so their expressions were shadowed. And family: a dull-toned portrait of someone, surely Lo's mother, long necked and slim faced, pretty in an eager youthful way. A black-and-white wedding photo of a couple with dark hair and soulful eyes that had certainly produced a son that looked like Peter. Many photos, but none of a small boy. Gloria had checked before and it haunted her, the absence of his face. She pictured it, Lo and Peter melded into a small boy with rounded cheeks and button nose, but knew whatever she was imagining was not him.

Lo steadied herself on the sideboard. "I felt so certain out there that things would be…" She trailed off like someone who had woken up and found herself somewhere unexpected.

Even Gloria could feel the weight of the old house pressing in with its demands for habit and its walls scarred with memories. The smell of worn wood seemed to speak in hushed tones of secrets. She kept her voice steady, trying to prevent the magic from lifting its quiet spell. "Let's get a glass of wine and sit on the back deck."

Lo wrapped her arms around herself. "I shouldn't have left him."

"Left who?"

"No, I should have stayed here."

Gloria's eyes flicked between Lo's but Lo looked stubbornly at the ground behind Gloria. Gloria suppressed the sigh she felt. This fickle, sad creature had been through enough. Was this self an addition to the other selves before it, a coat of paint, or had it consumed them all like an angry beast? Gloria couldn't tell one from the other, she loved them all. She held out her hand. "Can we stay here and just sit? You don't have to say anything."

Lo's hand was warm and inert like a limp piece of felt, and she looked up with glistening eyes. "Why are you here?"

"In the house?"

"Yes, the house. Yes, here at all."

"There's no place else I could be." Gloria meant it, in every way, ridiculous; sincere in her overalls and beaten-up sneakers.

Lo, ridiculous; sad in a gay summer dress. "Me neither."

They stood gloomily swinging their hands between their hips. Gloria kept holding on as though she was keeping Lo tethered to a life force. "Shall we go in and pour a drink?"

Lo loosed her hand and it returned to her own waist. "I think I need to go for a walk. I'll see you later. Sorry."

"Sure," Gloria said weakly, left under the gaze of carefree, two-dimensional shampoo-commercial Lo on the streets of Rome with her new husband, while flesh-and-blood Wyoming Lo receded into the corridor to join the ghosts of Heaven's End. Gloria had the thought that all these miniature deaths of the relationship, the sudden departures and change in mood were repayment for leaving Mike. Karma shaking her, *you silly girl*. She went to fold her new clothes into the cedar-scented drawers in the room that was not hers. What had seemed like such a haul diminished to a few items in the drawers.

Once she had packed the clothes away, she went outside to sit on the swinging seat, her legs in the slanting sun. It was a glorious afternoon, mellow and warm. The high wind that often swept a cruel hand down from the mountain was slumbering. Gloria knew there were plenty of things she could and should be doing, but she felt zapped. Like the wind, the emotions stirred at her and even though it was calm now, she felt dull and useless, her stomach full and sluggish. A pair of white butterflies chased one another across the lawn in flittery circles. Each time the butterfly tried to land on a flower, its mate flapped it away. Gloria's thoughts turned to Peter, the star of his own shampoo commercial, or more likely a disposable razor commercial, where the strong jawline and dark hair would mark him as virile enough to be presented as the man men wanted to resemble. The lens zooms in, a quick cut from Businessman Peter finishing a day at the office, jacket slung casually over one shoulder, to Adventure Peter, slicing the side of a snowy alp on skis. How did this plastic razor model feel when he came home to his wife, Dolly? Did he look forward to the fall of her footsteps, even now they were tentative, or the sound of her voice, even now it was hushed? Did he feel disappointed, like he'd been sold a lemon? The promised model failing to perform as advertised. Did accusation give him heartburn as he tried to swallow it? Or were Peter and Lo, Dolly, following a natural course, a gentle growing apart that had been hastened by tragedy? Gloria zipped and unzipped the front pocket of the overalls thoughtfully, staring into the space where the butterflies had been. Peter was a good man, she had no doubt. A man of some substance, if not a lot. Enough substance to carry on when his wife collapsed but perhaps not enough to forgive her, not for the death of their son, but for the death of his wife. The many roles a person plays in life, stepping out of one and into another so fluidly they don't realize it's happening.

Gloria noticed, first, a patch of corn rustling in the distance, and she stood up, thinking perhaps the horse was in the corn again, but instead Lo appeared through the rows of dry leaves as though emerging from a rippling ocean. She was walking slowly but purposely, her face bent down. Gloria watched her duck under the fence and begin walking back along the path to the house. Lo looked up and Gloria wasn't sure if she imagined it or not, but Lo's stride seemed to slow for a beat, then she continued on, making for the back garden. Gloria watched her approach in silence, not sure if Lo would stop or keep moving past on her trajectory into the house. She pushed the gate open and continued in along the fruit trees and toward Gloria. Without pausing she came and sat down beside her, rattling the rusting poles of the swing. There was a dark red scratch on her arm and dried corn silk in her hair.

"Hello," Gloria said.

"Look what I found," Lo said, holding up a fluorescent buttercup, the earlier sorrowful mood apparently walked back to where it came from.

"A flower."

"It was there, growing right out of the mound of rocks." Lo's color was high, her eyes hidden behind sunglasses.

Gloria saw her own reflection looking back at her through the tempered glass and it made her uncomfortable. She reached up and settled Lo's glasses on top of her head. Lo's eyes were bright and quick. "It's sweet," Gloria said. "When you were a child, did you hold buttercups under your chin so your skin would glow yellow?"

"I did!" Lo smiled and contemplated the buttercup, then held it under Gloria's chin and looked into her eyes with a serious expression. "The buttercup always tells the truth. Are you fair of face and pure of heart?"

Gloria waited a tense second while Lo divined whatever magic the flower was offering, feeling if the flower knew its stuff, it would cast a dark shadow down to her heart.

"Hmm. You're glowing, Gloria." Lo raised an eyebrow. "Do you feel pure?"

Gloria shook her head gently. "Not entirely. Does anyone?"

Lo leaned forward and kissed Gloria on the lips and a slow heat crept across them. Burnt vanilla. "Not entirely, no."

They both looked at each other, startled. Like a mirror, both put their fingers to their lips then smiled then their eyes grew serious.

"Sorry!" Lo said. Her eyes were so round and she looked like a small child who'd spilled a cup of milk.

"Don't be." Gloria took Lo's hand away from her chin and held it between them on the seat. She waited for a moment, their eyes reading each other's for clues, then reached a hand up to brush along Lo's cheek, stopping to cup her firm jaw. They continued looking at each other and Lo's eyes eventually softened and a smile eased back against Gloria's hand. She turned her face to the side, kissed Gloria's palm, and stood up.

"For you." She handed her the buttercup and walked inside, leaving Gloria with the spilled milk.

Gloria didn't look back to watch Lo enter the house and Lo did not hurry. She sat with the stigmata of a kiss on her palm, burning a hole, but she was not holy herself. Her thoughts were tangled and impure and, even more shamefully, she didn't care. Her head and her heart were both telling her stories and she didn't know which to believe. Her heart, she hoped, but her heart was swayed by her head, the same head that told her no, told her yes. It was exhausting and exhilarating. A paradox of self. It did no use to question her affection for Lo; it was as definite as an exclamation mark beside her name, a call that she couldn't ignore. An etching on her own skin that had been drawn painfully and visibly with little hope of removal other than time. Gloria who rarely suffered from paralyzing crushes was in a vise right now and the strange thing was, she didn't mind.

CHAPTER ELEVEN

The thoughts were a lot but they were quick, running hot as a brief spurt of water. Gloria cut off the flow and went back inside, conscious of her movements which suddenly required her attention. Had breathing always required conscious thought? Breathe in, breathe out. Left leg, right leg. Hand opens door. Gloria entered the kitchen and saw Lo standing at the counter, looking down at a rectangle of frosted cake on a blue plate. Gloria paused, watching her for a moment, still feeling her lips hot on her palm. Love's prayer. She went to stand beside her, close but not touching. She could feel the heat from Lo's skin warming her own. Lo leaned briefly against her side and Gloria knew everything was all right. Her throat ached with happiness. She felt like dropping a kiss on Lo's bare shoulder, but she did not. It was enough to stand close and know that they were riding the same energy. Gloria gave her attention to the cake. She had always been partial to cake and even though she had never been good at baking herself, when she was growing up her father had liked making Sunday night desserts: chocolate brownies, meringues, fruit crumbles. This cake was yellow inside and white outside with green piping at the edges. It looked spongy and gluggy with refined sugar. Lo already had a spoon in her hand.

"I'm so full but this cake looks so delicious, I think I have to have some." Lo looked for the best place to start.

"Are we allowed?"

Lo turned to fix Gloria with a withering look. "Sue-Anne is on a constant campaign to get me to eat. She'll probably break out into 'Good Morning' if I have a piece of this."

"Good morning?"

"You know, Gene Kelly, Debbie Reynolds, *Singin' in the Rain*?" Lo broke out into a tap dance, windmilling her arms and working her heels and toes against the floor.

Gloria slapped a hand over her mouth to restrain her laughter.

Lo ceased dancing and grinned. "I knew my mother was wasting her money with dance lessons but trust me, you haven't eaten cake until you've tried Sue-Anne's lemon sponge cake. It's like heaven."

Gloria was still biting back laughter. "She'd be very impressed with today's efforts. You almost finished that burger."

Lo stabbed the spoon down into the heart of the piece of cake. "Oh, shit, maybe that was a stupid idea. Too late." She leveraged a towering clump onto the fork and held it toward Gloria's face. Gloria quickly opened her mouth lest she be smooshed in the face.

"What is it with making sure my face is covered in food?" she asked, her mouth full of delicately lemoned, velvety sands of cake. "Gimme that." Gloria wrested the spoon from Lo's hand and scraped frosting and cake into one crumbling heap. "Your turn. I'm not saying my aim is awful, but I once managed to spear a dart into my own shoe instead of the board."

Lo winced and hesitantly opened her mouth but frosting still caught her lips and the elegant tip of her nose. Lo shot Gloria a look of mock anger, then ran a finger across the side of the cake and dotted the tip of Gloria's nose. "Now we match." She licked the top of her finger and shrugged one shoulder.

Gloria knew she probably looked absurd while Lo managed to look as cute as a Who from Whoville with a frosting nose. Lo reached up and wiped the frosting off Gloria's nose and licked her finger again. "Your nose is sweet."

Their eyes locked on each other, glistening with playful mischief that clearly neither had felt for a long time.

"You have some frosting on your lip," Lo said, her eyes shifting to the full swell of Gloria's blushing lips.

There was a sharp sound from the corridor and Gloria jumped guiltily, the spoon clattering to the ground as Lo's hand gripped Gloria's wrist in fright. A man stood inside the doorway watching them with a perplexed look on his face.

"Lola," Gloria said softly. "He won't hurt you." Then she looked at her ex-boyfriend and said simply, "Hi, Mike. This is Dolores. Dolores, this is Mike. All the way from Australia to surprise us both."

Lo relaxed her grip on Gloria's wrist but her voice was firm. "You're lucky I didn't shoot you. I thought you were a murderer."

"In this town?" Gloria said, taking the breath she didn't know she'd been holding back.

"Baby, I've got a gun up in the cupboard there. I can shoot the eye of a hare at a hundred paces while it's running through the grass. I still haven't decided whether or not I want to have a crack at Mike here."

"I come in peace!" Mike lifted his hands halfway in surrender, his Australian accent stark and unexpected. He had on jeans and a dark blue T-shirt, with a black backpack slung over one shoulder. His pale brown hair was rumpled and his jaw was stubbled with a couple of days of growth. Gloria reflected that he had always looked best when he was disheveled. It somehow counteracted the boy-next-door friendliness. She hastily wiped the frosting from her face with the back of her hand. She wondered if Lo thought Mike handsome, and the first red pokers of jealousy stabbed at her irrationally.

"Sorry," Lo said, pulling away from the counter and swiping her face with her hand. "You gave me a fright. I wasn't expecting any tall handsome strangers in my kitchen. Not today, anyway."

Gloria's heart lurched and tumbled down to her shoes. Handsome Mike and Beautiful Lo. It made her sick to think about it.

"Dolores, is it?" Mike came forward to shake Lo's hand. "Mike Lawson."

"Dolores Ballantyne."

Mike nodded and shifted his backpack strap on his shoulder. "Sorry to burst in on you and interrupt your food fight, Dolores. It's just that I'm not sure if Glo has been getting my letters and I've been…Do you mind if I have a word to her?"

"Be my guest," Lo said. She half turned as though she might say something to Gloria, their eyes connecting in a deep plunge, then changed her mind and walked slowly then more rapidly away.

Gloria watched her walk out, feeling things were spinning out of control. A food fight seemed the opposite of what they'd been having, but it certainly hadn't been a moment she thought anyone else would witness.

Mike placed his backpack on a stool and came to hug Gloria. Gloria allowed herself to be limply folded up into his huge warm embrace. The earthy smell of him in two-day-old clothes, his familiar aftershave, the strong breadth of his body. It was so different to the petite lightness of Lo. Like comparing a bear to a bird. They pulled apart and Gloria swallowed hard at the feelings of shame, unable to meet his eyes.

Mike brushed frosting from the side of her cheek with a finger. "Is there somewhere we can talk?"

"We can sit at the table." Without waiting for an answer, she pulled out two chairs. Her attention had followed Lo out the door. She sat down opposite Mike, the table creating a formality that she preferred.

"You don't look that happy to see me," Mike said, folding his hands across his stomach.

"I'm surprised, that's all. Obviously!" She failed to keep the resentment from her voice.

"Okay. I didn't know what else to do. You haven't replied to my letters, you've left no phone number."

"I did reply."

"That?" Mike smiled an opposite smile where the side of his mouth drew downward. "One sentence? I don't think that's much after years in a relationship." He scrutinized Gloria's blank face, and when she didn't respond, he continued, "Did I do something to you? Did someone say something?"

"No, no! Nothing like that, I just…" Gloria searched for words that wouldn't hurt and came up short. "You're better off without me."

"Is there someone else?"

Gloria looked up briefly and met his eyes, but she couldn't take it and she found the fruit bowl on the table instead. The red-and-green-streaked apples had begun their slide into decay. "Of course not. I have never cheated on you." Mike didn't say anything for a long moment, and when she looked back at him, she realized he'd been waiting for her to make eye contact.

"So you don't have anything to say to me after all this time?"

Gloria's hands flew into the air. "I'm sorry! It's all my fault. You're a lovely person, you treated me well. I just don't…I love you, but not…I can't marry you." A tear pricked the corner of her eye and she blinked furiously.

Mike leaned forward and reached a long arm across the table. "Come here. Give me your hand." Gloria obediently flopped her hand onto the table and Mike took her hand in his. "Hey, I love you. I am trying to show you how committed I am to this relationship. The last thing I intended was to scare you away. And the bloody cat misses you."

Gloria's eyes betrayed her by allowing hot tears to begin their descent toward her cheekbones. She pulled her hand away and rubbed her clogged eyelashes.

"Don't cry, Glo Worm, I'm here to take you home. We don't have to get married, ever. We don't have to have kids if you don't want to. I've had a lot of time to think, and perhaps I pressured you. All this talk of the future, was it too much?"

Gloria nodded and sniffed noisily. She knew she was an unattractive crier. Her cheeks went blotchy and her eyes bleary. She was listening to Mike and it was stirring up feelings that she'd been trying to stay one step ahead of. They were catching up to her now. To collapse back into Mike's arms would be a relief from these stressful months of adventure. A carefully woven past that would provide a comfortable cushion. Here with Lo was like stepping backward into the shadows. She had no idea what was awaiting her, but the comfortable cushion wouldn't be there forever—now was the time to choose. "I don't know what to do. It wasn't working," she said.

"Give me another chance."

"I have to think about it. I'm busy here, I'm halfway through a job."

"A job?" Mike asked, not quite keeping the skepticism from his voice.

Gloria wiped at her nose with the back of her wrist. "A rehabilitation job."

Mike nodded slowly. "Is that what that was?" Then he gathered himself and took a breath. "Look, I can understand. This was a total surprise. I'm staying in town at the Diamond Rock River Inn or something. I haven't even been to check in yet. Can we get together tonight? Dinner?"

"I don't have a car."

"I hired a car. This little red thing. I thought driving on the opposite side would be hard but it's not really."

Gloria slouched down into her seat. "That would be completely backtracking though."

"I just flew here from Melbourne, I don't think a few extra miles in the car will kill me."

"That's true. I guess dinner would be nice."

Mike visibly brightened and he gave the table a few happy taps with his wide hands. "*Perfecto*. You won't regret this."

"Mike, it's just dinner." Her caution was to act as a barrier against Mike's affections, yet still they were threatening to break the walls.

"Babe, you don't know how much I've missed you. It's not just dinner." Mike stood up. "I'd better go and check in to this inn place. I'll swing by and pick you up at about seven, then."

"Okay." The aftertaste of the cake had soured in her throat and she felt lightheaded, like she was having an out-of-body experience.

Mike stood up and looked around as though aware of his surroundings for the first time. "Nice house. Do they raise cattle here?" He walked over to the window and looked out at the golden expanse of land, fringed with trees and the river a silver thread in the distance. "Wow, is this all hers? Ah, Dolores?"

"Yes, she and her husband own it, right up to the state park."

"Impressive. Nice barn, just like the movies."

Gloria folded her arms and nodded. She felt protective of the ranch and Mike's judgment irritated her. No one had invited him here to give praise. On the other hand, she had been in his shoes not so long ago, a stranger turning up unannounced and unwelcome. She just wanted to go to bed and pull the blankets over her head.

When Gloria didn't comment further, Mike tore his eyes away and seemed to grow more aware of her too. "Do I smell that bad?"

"No."

"Then hug me once like you mean it and I'll go."

"You do smell a bit," Gloria said, softening into his arms, her smile against his T-shirt. It wasn't him she minded, it was the proud swell of emotion he carried. The expectant gleam in his eye.

"That's more like it. Just those manly pheromones, I know you've missed them." He pulled away and kissed Gloria on her hairline. "All right, Glo Worm, I'll see you at seven."

Gloria let him out of the front door and stood in the doorway watching him drive off, the back of his hand waving out of the window. She knew the back of that hand like her own. Had seen it unwaveringly deliver injections into horses' necks and the scruffs of puppies' necks, she had held it in her own, it had grasped her in fits of passion. She had longed for that hand's touch once, had quivered and squirmed beneath it, but watching it diminish in size until it was gone made her feel nothing but relief. Even after the car had disappeared she stood, watching the empty road until the only right thing to do was to close the door and move away, where to, she wasn't sure. The horses required energy she didn't have, reading required concentration she couldn't muster, and she didn't feel like being around anyone, even Lo. She could feel the eyes of the photos by the front door on her. She turned away from them and went to the living room where she poured herself a bourbon and sat on the sofa staring into space. In the whole time she'd been there, no one had turned the television on. It sat like an alien spaceship in the corner, utilitarian in an otherwise richly textured room. Gloria had a desire to watch something predictable and homely. Watching two smiling chefs turn ingredients into a family meal, or a drab house transformed into a vibrant living space. She took her drink with her and went to investigate the functions of the object. It sat on a low wooden table, underneath which was a square wicker basket. Gloria pulled the basket from under the table and was rewarded with a remote control. The basket was also full of VHS tapes neatly labeled with black marker on white stickers. There was Dolores and Peter's Wedding 1987, Terrence's First Birthday, and then every subsequent birthday, ominously stopping at the sixth. There were videos of dressage competitions and horse shows and family days out to the fair and into the city. Gloria got the impression that Peter was an avid videographer. Peter, yes, not Lo. She had no desire to intrude on these private memories, but she noticed that squashed down the back of the tapes was a pile of photos. She wriggled the first one free. It was slightly grainy and brown with exposure, but it was of a group around a table where a cake decorated with sprinkles in the shape of a 2 took center stage, and sitting in the middle of the guests, with a little boy on her lap, was Lo. She looked younger, her cheeks fuller, her hair darker red, and her smile open as she looked downward at the cake, one arm protectively around the boy who reached a chubby baby hand to point at the cake just out of his reach. The little boy—Terrence, he was Terrence—was looking down at the cake too, but the length of his eyes and the roundness of his lips as he made a word, probably forgotten now, was his mother's. The fair curls, which could have been any shade of blond, light brown, or pale red in the half-light, were loose and full; a healthy mop on a little boy's head. Gloria recognized the kitchen, looking darker in the shadows of the photo. It was strange that this house had had a different life, a life that hadn't included Gloria—and of course why should it, she was no one. This had been a family home with the busy business of a child going about his small affairs. No wonder Lo could not forgive herself one small act or one small moment. How many steps could one retrace to prevent that instant? Seeing little Terrence with his sweet face and curious finger brought his death to vivid violence in her mind. This person swept off the earth so quickly and cruelly. It was not a thing to get over. Gloria replaced the photo and slid the basket back under, then stretched her legs out and sat on the carpet with her back against the sofa. Bourbon wasn't particularly her thing, but it was something to do. She felt more than heard the floorboards giving under the weight of footsteps, and Lo came in and saw her sitting on the floor.

"May I?" she asked, standing over Gloria.

Gloria nodded listlessly.

Lo sat down beside Gloria and crossed her legs in a yoga pose. Gloria wordlessly passed her the glass. Lo took a sip and handed it back.

"It's that bad, huh?"

Gloria shrugged. She didn't feel great, but it was all relative. Crying over a boy she'd never known struck her as melodramatic and sentimental, but she did feel like crying. There had been too many changes of emotional direction today. She was spent, and the prospect of dinner with Mike required emotional reserves she was short on.

"You know, honey, there's nothing to prove. Just take this moment and move forward. If Mike has come all this way then he must care about you. There's a life for you in Melbourne, family and friends. Don't feel obligated here, okay?"

Gloria searched Lo's face for clues, but Lo was looking down at the inner curves of her bare feet. Gloria tried to keep emotion from thinning her voice and failed. "I didn't invite him to come. I didn't even tell him where I am!"

"He's a man in love. The way he looks at you, you may not want to throw that away."

Gloria felt her mood dip lower. She was trying not to sulk. She wanted Lo to fight for her, say she cared for her, but instead Lo was encouraging her to go. "It's just dinner." She repeated the phrase she had used on Mike, hoping to make it so.

"Well, enjoy dinner, honey. If he's got a car, why not go to Rivers where we went the other day? It's beautiful at night, fairy lights and the stars overhead. If that doesn't rekindle the romance, nothing will."

Gloria picked angrily at a loose thread on the overalls. "Sure, we have a lot to catch up on anyway. Do you want this?" She passed the glass to Lo then stood up. "I've got a few things to do. See you later." She knew she was being immature and doing what she always did when her feelings were bruised: running away. She was a terrible sulker, and letting Lo see how hurt she felt wasn't something she was interested in. Whether learnt from her mother, or some type of genetic infusion, she found cold silences to be the easiest form of communicating displeasure. She had worked hard on it, and she knew running from Mike had been cowardly because she had taken her silence where he could not reach it, but he had found her anyway. She had hated it when her usually mild-mannered mother had inflicted one of her prolonged silences on her or her father. She felt as though half her teenage years had been spent under a cloud of angry quiet. As her mother had once said, the fading hormones of menopause and the surging hormones of puberty sparked a fire hot enough to burn the house down, but Gloria had hunkered down into her bedroom like a safety bunker, or escaped out into the fields with the horses, and later into the stables and later still, the arms of Klaus Hofmann. Things had calmed but Gloria had retained the urge to run from conflict, both internal and external, and had rendered herself nearly mute when it came to the ability to speak her mind if it meant hurting another person. She had practiced on Mike during their relationship, showing him the compartments and boundaries of her tolerance, and she thought she had grown and developed interpersonal skills but perhaps they were superficial. Now, she was a coin with both sides spinning through the air. Love's archer, spearing a painful blow, and the wounded fool, clutching at her heart. Red, the color of love and of blood. As Lo had once said, love and pain were a pigeon pair. She stood under the shower sucking on the salt of her resentment.

By the time Mike arrived to pick Gloria up for dinner, she had worked herself into such a state of lethargic refusal that her energy was spent. She waited at the table in her new black trousers and mustard shirt which she could only pull off now that she was tanned, growing irritated even though he wasn't yet late. To her surprise, Mike walked in with Peter, who looked pink-faced with surprise at having a young man arrive at his door.

"Gloria!" Peter said. "I believe your date is here."

Gloria attempted introductions which had already occurred outside.

"Can I offer you a drink?" Peter asked, going into the kitchen and opening the fridge.

Mike looked at Gloria and began his response slowly to allow her time to interject. "No, thanks, Peter. The restaurant's booked for seven." Gloria did not.

Peter took out a foil-covered pie dish, lifted the foil, and took a sniff. "Enjoy, kids." He put the dish down on the counter and looked around. "Is Sue-Anne here at all these days?"

Gloria's eyes slid to the spot where the cake had been but the counter was bare and devoid of crumbs. "She was here this morning. Perhaps she's gone to help with the baby."

"Never mind. This quiche smells okay."

"She did mention something about a salad." Gloria picked her purse up uncertainly.

"Not to worry, I'm sure I can throw some lettuce and tomato in a bowl. Go have fun. Where are you going?"

Gloria hadn't wanted to go to Rivers. The place was still alive in her mind, Lo crystal clear with the sun on her copper hair and her shoulders bare under the dappled light. She could almost smell the river and the damp wooden boards. To override that memory with one of Mike—no, that was hers and Lo's.

"The Inn recommended a restaurant called Bailey's. Do you know it?" Mike asked.

"Sure, yeah. They're known for their steak but the pasta primavera is Dolly's favorite."

Gloria looked at her new black leather flats, feeling her face prickle with a flush.

"You're welcome to join us, hey, Gloria?" Mike turned to Gloria for confirmation.

Gloria hastily nodded and Peter said, "Thanks for the offer. It's been a long day. I only just got out of court not long ago, but you know what, it might be nice to get out, and now that Doll's been out a few times, we might take you up on that another night. Actually, I think it's a really good idea. Get Dolly into a dress and out among the world." He secured the foil back over the dish and nodded in satisfaction. "Gloria, I think she'd feel confident with you there too. You two have become friends, it's nice to see." He grinned at her before turning to peer at the oven dials.

"Sounds fun," Gloria managed to say, guilt filming her like sweat. "See you later, then. Good luck wrangling the lettuce and tomato."

Peter nodded distractedly, still concerned with the oven. "Enjoy!"

The restaurant had low lighting, softened by golden candle beam. The tables were full of couples enjoying a night together or groups of adults talking and laughing, not a sticky-fingered child in sight. Gloria felt the weight of romantic intent as they stood waiting for their table. Mike looked refreshed, hair gelled back, an ironed pale blue shirt and navy slacks, a polished look she didn't often see on him. His movements were hesitant and his manner reserved and slightly brusque, like it had been when they'd first started negotiating the formalities of dating. Only, his warm hands continually found her arm and back, indicating a level of intimacy that they shared, or had shared. He almost collided with the waiter as they both attempted to pull Gloria's chair back for her to sit. Looking around, Gloria could see the wealthier side of Diamond Rock River coming out at night, the chalet owners and out-of-town skiers. The women with jewels at their ears, necks, and wrists, wearing their evening outfits in subtle colors. One petite woman caught her attention, the tinkling laugh that kept ringing out, louder than her frame would suggest, her head tipped back, clearly conscious of the effect she had on the men at her table who were all focused on her despite the other women. She had smooth very blond hair and a little heart-shaped face which glittered diamond-hard. Her dress was brighter, her diamonds bigger, and her nails longer. Gloria reflected that Lo would know who she was.

"Are you all right?" Mike asked, reaching for her hand.

Gloria looked away from the woman. Even she was devoting her attention to her. "Yes, sorry. It's a beautiful place, isn't it?" She meant it sincerely. The abstract art on the burgundy walls and the baroque-inspired chandeliers lent to the rich ambiance, but she felt disconnected from the atmosphere around her.

"You deserve a night out somewhere special. I plan on starting from scratch and doing things properly this time." He held her hand softly, caressing it with his broad thumb.

Gloria felt panic suction at her, whisking away her confidence. "Mike, we haven't discussed anything yet. I'm not sure we should get back together, this is just a chance for me to explain some things."

It was Mike's turn to compose himself in the face of disappointment, but he covered it well. "I understand. I certainly don't want to pressure you."

Gloria took a deep breath. "Coming here unannounced, assuming we are working toward a goal of being together...that is pressure!"

Mike's hand withdrew, and hers with it. "I suppose you're right. Forgive me, but this whole thing is confusing and I don't know which part you want me to play."

A waiter appeared, filling their water glasses and asking them if they'd had a chance to view the wine list. They chose a bottle of red and thankfully the waiter receded politely to his duties.

Gloria picked up the thread. "I don't want you to play any part, Mike. Can't you just be yourself and I'll be me?"

"Okay," Mike said, leaning back into his chair. "Who are you?"

Gloria looked at him and blinked back the tension surging through her jaw. She hadn't wanted any confrontation, had gone to great lengths to avoid it.

"No, honestly, I thought I knew but perhaps I don't." He absentmindedly murmured a thank-you to the waiter, who'd arrived to pour their wine into the rotund glasses. The waiter sensed the energy and moved on without asking questions.

Who was she? The answer to that question was a mystery even to herself. But who was anyone but many different selves or projections of self to different people? "If you don't know the answer to that, then why do you think we should be together?" Mike's eyes were large and his face slack. He looked as though he might cry. Gloria felt suddenly sorry and protective of him. She let go of the breath she'd been holding and reached out her hand again. Hands, they could convey so much, they extended from the desire of the heart one way or the other; to hold, to slap, to comfort, to mend, to take what the heart wanted. "I'm sorry, Mike. You've caught me by surprise in a time where I'm just learning who I am myself. I think I lost that, maybe we both did, or maybe I never knew. We've shaped each other so much, and it might sound harsh or hurtful, but I need this space to figure out what I want."

Mike looked down at her hand, consciously or unconsciously caressing her ring finger. "Gloria," he said, looking back up. "I appreciate your honesty. Perhaps you're already changing into who you want to be, and I certainly wouldn't fight that. If we were able to be more open with each other in this way from the beginning, perhaps you wouldn't have walked into a proposal you felt unready for because, to be honest, the impression I got from you was that you were ready for that part of our lives. That was my mistake too, perhaps I missed the signs."

Gloria felt a weight lift from her shoulders. "I've been too passive. This isn't easy though. I'm actually dying inside."

Mike smiled. "You horse trainers are weird. You can get up in front of a crowd and perform or give a lecture on something but as soon as you have to speak to someone familiar about something personal, you're scared."

Gloria shrugged. "One thing comes naturally, the other doesn't."

"So I've laid my cards on the table. I've jumped on a flight and come as soon as I could to have a discussion."

"Pretty expensive discussion." Gloria took a slug of wine.

"Well, someone wouldn't speak to me on the phone."

Gloria raised her eyebrows in amusement. "You've got me there."

Mike gritted his teeth. "Ouch."

In her present state of infatuation with Lo, Gloria could imagine how that would have felt to Mike, the belly-dropping disappointment he must have experienced. It helped to make light of the whole situation though. She remembered that that was one of the things she liked about Mike—he was calm and able to laugh at himself. "Sorry, Michael," she said. "You may have wasted your money. I'm not ready to come back."

Mike smiled. "That's okay. I took the money from our savings account."

Gloria stared at him from a second before she started to giggle. "Shit."

After that, she felt some of her animosity slip away and she was able to relax and enjoy herself around Mike in a way she hadn't in a long time. She realized how stifled she'd become around him, how withholding of herself. She'd forgotten how funny he could be and his ability to find the ridiculous in situations, which was something they shared. She noticed he didn't order any meat for himself either, going with Peter's recommendation of Lo's favorite pasta. Gloria munched through porcini mushroom ravioli and listened to Mike talk about things back home with the vet practice and Mike's business partner Dustin—Dusty— who still hadn't grown out of womanizing and turning up bleary-eyed for surgery after a night on the tiles to tend to the small animal side. It was evidence of Mike's impatience to see Gloria that he'd left Dusty unattended to run the practice. She knew Mike was loath to leave the racing stables who had him on call. To be trusted with expensive horses was something Mike had had to work hard for.

Gloria was still full from lunch, so pasta wasn't the best option, but she managed to have a crack at a dessert too, under Mike's insistence that he was paying with money from their savings account, which was becoming a running joke. Gloria ordered lychee mousse with tangerine foam, practically flavored air anyway. Whether it was the wine or the relief of talking with someone who knew her well, Gloria couldn't stop grinning. By the time they'd finished, the restaurant was nearly empty, the large table with the pretty blonde getting ready to leave too, the waitstaff standing around stifling yawns and trying not to slouch. Gloria excused herself to go to the bathroom and let Mike pay from whichever account he chose. She was drunker than she thought, the floor sliding away at an unnatural angle. In the bathroom mirror she saw her reflection looking back at her composed and sexy, her hair for once curling nicely over her shoulders instead of wildly in all directions, her cheeks merry with wine and her eyes sparkling because she was desired. When she came back out it took her a moment to realize that Mike was standing at their table, one hand on the back of his chair talking to the blonde. Gloria's eyes narrowed and she felt a territorial welling of jealousy. As she approached, the woman extended a little hand for Mike to shake. Gloria could see her give him a simpering smile before she caught up to her friends, who were slipping into jackets by the door.

"Who was that?" Gloria asked a little too sharply.

"Kelly Armstrong, her name is." Mike expression was nonplussed.

"What did she want?"

"Nothing really, it was silly."

"Then tell me." Gloria could feel herself playing the jealous girlfriend, but she couldn't help herself.

Mike smiled in exasperation. "It was nothing. She works in advertising and said they're casting for a commercial and would I be interested in going to the casting."

"What?" Gloria's voice exploded. She looked over to the door where Kelly no longer stood.

Mike shook his head. "Come on, Glo Worm, it was nothing."

"Okay. Well, I'd better get back anyway. Let's go."

Mike laughed halfheartedly. "Sure, let's go."

Gloria let him follow her out onto the street. The stars were large in the black night, the air damp with dew. It was later than Gloria thought. She could hear car doors slamming and the sound of engines humming to life. Bloody Kelly Armstrong, was she so desperate she had to trawl restaurant tables looking for talent?

"I'm parked here, Glo." Mike stopped at his rental car.

"I'll get a cab, there's no point you driving me all the way back."

Mike tipped his head to the side. "Stop being a drama queen and get in the car. There's probably only one cab in this whole place, I'm not letting you stay out here by yourself."

Gloria had at least six snide remarks waiting to trip from her lips regarding Kelly Armstrong, but she clenched them in her molars. "What do you think I do when you're not around? I can actually take care of myself!"

"Yes, yes, come on." Mike held the door open for her. "Hop in before I ask Kelly if she needs a ride home."

Gloria covered the ground in two large steps, grabbed him by the back of the neck and pressed her lips firmly against his.

"You will not." Gloria pushed him aside and got into the car. Mike closed the door gently and went around to the driver side. As soon as he sat down, Gloria said, "And that doesn't mean we're getting back together because we're not."

Mike put the keys in the ignition but didn't turn them. "Would you like to come back to my room and I can tell you about the many other women who have asked me a question in the past few weeks?"

Gloria crossed her arms. "No."

Mike gunned the engine. "Go to sleep, you're drunk."

Gloria didn't want to do as he said but she closed her eyes anyway, feeling as though she were in a boat rolling around in rough seas. The world seemed very far away, a land mass receding on the horizon. She opened her eyes again, her forehead resting on the window, her breath fogging a circle on the cool glass. Mike glanced at her but didn't say anything, for that, at least, she was thankful for. Speaking was beyond her. The ravioli swirled unhappily with the wine and mousse and Gloria wished she could go back in time and refuse a second glass of wine, and there would be no third. Nothing seemed more important than going to bed. When the car pulled up outside the ranch, Gloria barely thanked Mike and unsteadily let herself in and tried to quietly get herself ready for bed, dropping a shoe and turning the faucet on too hard. Thankfully she flopped into her welcoming pillow.

CHAPTER TWELVE

Less than three hours passed before Gloria woke with the seed of a hangover and a dry mouth. Somehow the bed covers were on the floor and she was wearing the clothes she'd gone to dinner in. She pulled on a sweater and went to get a glass of water from the kitchen. Still in the grip of sleep, she banged her small toe on the post of the bed and had to stop to squeeze the pain from it, which only worked for as long as she was holding it. It immediately started to throb, and she limped off down the stairs, clutching the wooden banister for support. Everything was dark and quiet except for the muffled snoring of Peter, a sound she seldom heard. A strip of moonlight fell in a silver river across the living room floor. With painful clarity, Gloria recalled the evening. The way she had spoken to Mike had been uncharacteristically rude and she knew she shouldn't have kissed him, but the thought of Kelly Armstrong still sent a jolt of jealousy through her, indicating feelings she thought she'd buried. An urge to prevent Mike from continuing to live a life unfamiliar to her was there: new clients she didn't know, friends she'd never meet, parties she'd never go to, and yes, girlfriends that weren't her. She should have kissed him longer, she wanted to feel his strong arms around her, the way he would listen to her talking in bed, looking at her as though she were the most important person in the world. She had let him go though, and the narrative should continue on without her.

At the kitchen sink she looked out past her own reflection to the buildings stark against the pure night sky. The gray shape of the barn was like a boulder in the earth. Gloria wondered if Lo had been going up to her cathedral at night, close to the gods and the stars and the little boys in heaven. Maybe Peter's slumbering presence in the bed kept her tethered to the rituals of day-to-day life that could consume a person with distraction and prevent the mind from climbing through open windows in pursuit of spiritual or, at least, personal truth. She stood, sipping a second glass of cool water, her toe throbbing insistent flashes of red in her brain. The possibility of having feelings for two people at once had never occurred to her. A greedy sort of love that went against her generally giving nature. Mike's arrival had stirred up feelings, adding to an already complex situation. Her reflection which had seemed sleek and attractive, lit up with alcohol, in the mirror at the restaurant, now stared back diluted of its powers. Not for the first time that week she wished she had a crystal ball to consult. It seemed an easier alternative to asking Lo how she really felt. They had been skirting the situation, if there was a situation to skirt. Playing games with Lo was not something she wanted to do, especially at the risk of their friendship, but Lo's emotions were playing them all. A jazz tune with surprising interjections, sad and bluesy, upbeat and strong, meandering and pensive, and Gloria wished she knew the words. By comparison, Mike was a dependable pop song with a recurring chorus and repetitive lyrics. He was fun and popular, kind and predictable. Gloria drained the last of the water from the glass and gave her reflection a hateful look in the window. Mike was easier for her personality type to manage. His upfront communication demanded the same of her. Lo's hidden lunar emotions swirled uncertainly with Gloria's, combining in dark nighttime waters where intent went to drown. Outside forces like winds over the pool made waters murky. As Gloria turned for bed, movement caught her eye. Had it been her own reflection, or the opening and closing of the barn door in the night?

Gloria was late getting out of bed in the morning. Usually she helped Kip before breakfast, but he seemed unfazed at the table, already engaged in animated discussion as he forked scrambled eggs into his mouth. Lo was seated at the head and Peter was wiping his hands energetically on a napkin and standing to leave. Gloria dipped her head and mumbled a greeting, hoping to get by without an interrogation, but Peter had other ideas.

"Gloria, how was dinner? Doll, I told them you recommend the pasta primavera."

Lo smiled. "Did you go to Bailey's?"

Gloria sat down under everyone's watchful gaze and poured herself some coffee. "Yes, it was really lovely."

"How'd your fella enjoy himself?" Peter asked good-naturedly. "I was telling Doll that the four of us should go out tonight." He looked at Gloria expectantly.

Gloria's hand faltered on its way to the orange juice. "He did, thank you. I guess we could go out…I'm just not sure. Kip, do you need a hand with the mares that were close to dropping?"

Kip grinned at her, a piece of toast delicately between his fingers. "No, ma'am. Samuel can stick around, can't you?"

Samuel took a second too long to answer. "Sure."

Gloria felt like kicking Kip under the table.

Peter nodded once in a definite way. "I shouldn't be home late tonight. I'll get Candice to call and set up a reservation somewhere. Won't that be nice, Dolly?" He placed a hand on the back of her neck, and Gloria met Lo's eyes for a brief intense moment before they both dropped their gaze to their plates. The way they held eyes was a gentle but powerful force, something Gloria hadn't experienced with another person, and it spoke of a strong undercurrent that flowed only between the two of them. Lo twisted her head ever so slightly and Peter withdrew his hand from her neck and patted her shoulder instead. When he spoke, his tone was softened with a reticent, almost fatherly tone. "Well, I for one would like to return to civilization for the night. I'll see you all this evening. Doll." He patted her shoulder again.

As he left, Lo sat with her head still twisted away from him, her eyes on the table. An uncomfortable silence was interrupted by Sue-Anne bustling in from the garden with a fistful of parsley.

"Kip, I told you to wait until we could sprinkle some herbs on those eggs."

Gloria smiled and sang out a greeting, happy to have Sue-Anne's maternal presence to break up the tension. Sue-Anne paused to hug Gloria to her before she went to rinse the leaves, ignoring Kip's protests that he had to return to work.

"How's the baby?" Gloria asked.

"Yes," Lo said. "When are you bringing her to visit?"

Sue-Anne gave the wet parsley a brisk flick over the sink. "I wasn't sure if the child would be welcomed, things as they are around here."

"Oh, Sue-Anne." Lo looked genuinely hurt. "You know Hayley would be welcome here. She's family, just like you. I want to hold her while she still has that new baby smell."

Sue-Anne chopped quickly, then came to tip the green pieces straight from the wooden board onto the pile of eggs before anyone could escape them. "I'll ask Bethany when she's free. I think mornings work best for her, but you're usually still idling in bed at that hour, Dolores."

Lo raised her eyebrows. "I'm up now, aren't I?"

In response, Sue-Anne spooned a large dollop of eggs onto Lo's plate. "Eat up. If you stood sideways, we wouldn't be able to see you."

Gloria had to look down at her plate to avoid getting the giggles. The warm sparring wasn't something she had grown up with and Sue-Anne's turns of phrase were unpredictable. Kip's facial expressions were comical in response and Samuel's blushing smirks were no help.

Lo looked at Gloria and said clearly, across the food-laden table, "Can I show you something?"

Using his teeth, Kip stripped some crisp bacon fat from the rasher he had pinched between his fingers and looked from Lo to Gloria. Sue-Anne looked like she might burst with curiosity waiting for Gloria to reply. Gloria swallowed a mouthful of hot coffee too quickly. "Sure. Can I check the horses first?"

Lo nodded and Kip interjected. "Gloria, I forgot to mention that I had a word with Peter and he wants you to push forward with Sonnet. He wants the both of them ready for sale in two weeks unless Doll plans to ride again."

"Two weeks!" Gloria said in surprise. "He hasn't said anything to me."

Lo stood up suddenly, her fork clattering to the ground. "That's not his call."

Kip let the last piece of bacon drop back onto his plate and wiped his hands on a paper napkin. "Don't shoot the messenger. Y'all talk among yourselves and get back to me. I'm just the hired help."

Lo turned toward the door as though she might chase after Peter, then turned back, realizing it was futile. "Kip!"

"Dolores, something has to be done about this place. Have a look at your outgoings. They're outstripping income and we've pared the staff right back. Sam and I are worked to the bone and Clarence is only here every other day."

"But the horses don't make much difference."

Kip stood up and carried his plate and cup to the sink. "Dolly, I'd think you'd better talk to your husband. Those horses are just the tip of the iceberg." He drained the rest of his coffee and rinsed his plate. "Way things are going, this place ain't gonna hold out." He took his hat from where it had been hanging on the corner of the chair back rest and put it on his head. "I'll catch y'all later." He walked out, letting the door close too hard behind him.

Lo stood stunned and Sue-Anne forked more eggs into her mouth then set her fork down, then picked it up again before saying, "Didn't I tell you, Dolores? Open up those guesthouses and get this place running again. You feel bad now, well imagine how you'll feel if there's nothing left of this place. It's been in your family for generations."

"Right now I hate it." Lo's eyes were blazing, and she rose, picked up her plate, and scraped the eggs into the trash.

Sue-Anne's face puckered but she held her dismay in. "Don't speak like that, things will work out. Just talk to Peter."

"I think everyone is forgetting whose place this is!" she said fiercely, letting her plate drop into the sink on top of Kip's. She looked to Gloria. "Don't do anything you don't feel is right. Peter doesn't know a thing about horses, least of all those ones."

"Can't we enjoy one meal together?" Sue-Anne said.

"Beg your pardon, ma'am. May I be excused?" Samuel half stood, holding his plate in two hands.

"Just go!" Lo said crossly at the same time as Sue-Anne said, "You're a grown man. Stop that."

Gloria picked at a pancake, her head beginning to throb along with her toe. She made no move as Lo stalked outside, followed at a brisk pace by Samuel. Sue-Anne continued to chew as though she was working at a particularly arduous task that required completion. The pancake felt like a dish sponge in Gloria's mouth. Her gaze traveled bleakly across the colorful palette of food still adorning the table, the blueberry preserves gleaming dark sticky; fruitful and fruitless.

"Well," Sue-Anne began, "I think it's time for Dolores to snap out of it and take control of this place. She's half-right, it was hers, but now they're wed as husband and wife, for richer or poorer, for better or worse, in sickness and in health." She sighed and looked through the wall to something stirring inside her mind. "This place is a lot of work. It needs the boundless energy that Dolores used to exhibit. She really was the life of this place. I've never seen anything like it. She would get up early and ride with the floodlights on before Terrence woke up, then she'd be getting him ready for school and make sure he was on the school bus. I still remember his first day, the size of his blue backpack. I cried my eyes out but not Dolores. She stood waving him off, a proud smile on her face. She trained that child to be an independent boy just like her, she couldn't have it any other way, between working and mothering and the ranch."

"Do you think it was too much though? Like she had to keep on the hamster wheel to prove something?"

Sue-Anne leaned forward to top up their coffee cups. "The hamster wheel? Hard to say. That's something only Dolores could decide. You've probably seen by now that there's little use telling her to do anything. She knows her own mind. I try to get underneath her because it doesn't suit her, all this moping, but she'll figure that out in her own time."

"Thank you." Gloria moved her cup closer but didn't take a sip. "Do you think she means it when she says she wants to sell up, the horses, the ranch, everything?"

Sue-Anne scratched at her arm thoughtfully. "No, honey, I don't think so. Her fear of horses is doing her no good. She's forgotten how this place can give if you'll let it. At the moment all she can see is the taking. This place is in her blood. She loves the lawyering, but I do believe you need a strong head for that and perhaps Dolores needs a little more time. The ranch though, it'll heal you up if you let it. She just has to let it."

"It's hard when it seems the source of the pain."

"She'll have to come to terms with her new circumstances. You about done, honey?"

Gloria finished the last piece of pancake and nodded, thinking over whether there was an alternative to coming to terms with one's changing circumstances. Death maybe. She swept the thought from her mind. "Let's wrap this up. Can you take something home to Bethany?"

"She sure would appreciate it. She's been eating everything in sight since she's been nursing Hayley. I've got too much to do here though."

"That's okay, let me do it." Gloria carried the platters to the sink.

"Thank you, Gloria, but there's the dishes and the laundry and this walkway is full of dust. How many times I've told those men to leave their boots at the door. They just don't listen."

"Sue-Anne, I'll take care of it." Gloria scraped the eggs on to the platter beside the bacon and wrapped the pancakes in a snug cling-wrap spaceship.

"That washing machine is temperamental."

"I've used it before." Gloria stacked the wrapped plates and handed them Sue-Anne. "Take it to Bethany. There's no sense wasting food."

"We-ell." Sue-Anne wavered. "All right then. You're a good girl. I'll be back to cook supper anyway."

"Can't Kip and Samuel get their own dinner? I believe the rest of us are going into town."

"That's okay, I'll come and fix them something to eat. Listen, Gloria, when you're all out tonight, if it feels like the right time, it wouldn't hurt to remind Peter and Dolores that opening the ranch again is a good place to start. Just between you and me, when the phone rings, I jot the caller's details down into a book. I know Dolores doesn't want me to, but I figure it can't hurt."

Gloria smiled. Sue-Anne would butt in where she pleased and try to control situations, no matter what anyone said or did to discourage her. "If it seems like the moment is right, I will craft it into the conversation."

When Sue-Anne finally left, Gloria began washing and drying the dishes so the kitchen would be a blank slate for Sue-Anne when she returned. Outside the day was blooming in blues and golds, casting long shadows across the ground. The magnolia trees were in full flower in the garden, dropping heavy petals on the shaggy lawn that no one had time to mow. Gloria thought of the autumn thinning to winter back home, the horses' coats thickening and the sky beginning to hunker down close to the earth. She'd almost forgotten Mike, so caught up in the breakfast drama, but she remembered the kiss all too clearly. She compared it to the kiss she'd shared with Lo. Both had been almost accidental, a loose stitch in the fabric of daily life, and both made her blush for different reasons. She stood, looking out of the window, the cloth and plate still in her hands, so deep into a pink mist of memory that she was lost, reliving every detail of her kiss with Lo. The vivid fluorescence of the buttercup, the calm wanting she saw in Lo's eyes, the way Lo's jaw felt in her palm. Try as she might, she couldn't decipher the emotional code. It had only been the briefest peck, a friendly kiss, and Lo had walked away. She startled guiltily as the back door opened and she glanced around to see Lo standing in the doorway, holding the door open, still in her boots.

"Are you coming out?"

Gloria carefully placed the plate onto the stack she had dried. "I told Sue-Anne that I would do some things for her."

Lo's hip dropped and her head tipped to the side. "What things?"

"Laundry and sweeping."

"Oh." There was a beat of silence. "Well, let me do the laundry while you finish up here and then can you help me with something?"

Gloria was surprised. "Okay, I won't be long."

The door shut behind Lo and Gloria saw the top half of Lo, in her blue checked shirt, tramp along the veranda by the window and out of sight toward the washhouse door. She heard the thump of the laundry door closing and the humming of pipes as she finished putting the dishes away.

She found Lo outside hanging laundry to dry. Something about a cowgirl in jeans and boots hanging underwear on the line amused Gloria and she stood observing Lo for a few seconds. The flick of the wrist, the tendons along her forearms, her deft fingers.

"Practically newsworthy, I know," Lo said, reaching for another peg. "I like the peg colors to be matching. I'm very particular."

"The pegs on those jeans are two different shades of blue," Gloria said.

"Just like me." Lo smiled at her joke, or perhaps at the idea of having the blues.

"The color suits you, but so do many others."

Lo looked up at Gloria. "Are you going to critique the process or lend a hand?"

"Just critique," Gloria said, but she came down the steps and reached for the stripy top she had borrowed from Lo and shook out the wrinkles. There was something satisfying about scented laundry drying in the sunshine. "What was it you wanted to show me?"

Lo played with the peg she was holding, pinching it open and closed. "I'm not sure if you heard Peter and I talking last night."

Gloria shook her head. "I went out to dinner, remember?"

Lo let the peg snap shut. "In bed, but maybe you were still out. We had a fight of sorts. Anyway, I'm glad you didn't hear it."

Gloria stopped what she was doing and turned to Lo, feeling a rush of guilt. "About?"

"The ranch. He thinks we should sell." She looked out over the farmland. "What do you think?"

Gloria shrugged. "It doesn't matter what I think, but why does he want to sell?"

"He says he doesn't like being here because it's full of reminders and while we are here I'm unable to move on. Plus, on a practical level, he feels the sale could unlock our finances and free us up to buy a manageable place and just…be, I guess. Sit in twin armchairs and watch television." Gloom washed over her face and Gloria had to laugh.

"Oh, stop it. No one's going to make you sit in a chair watching TV. You're not eighty-five."

"I feel it."

"No you don't."

"He thinks the horses are an utter waste of time and money if no one is enjoying them. Kip barely has time for Freddy these days, let alone bringing on youngsters. I'm no help. Peter's probably right. What's the point?"

Gloria picked up the last item of clothing from the basket, one of her Garfield socks, without its pair and a hole in the toe. "Can you please pass me a color-appropriate peg?" Lo passed her a red peg. "Thank you." She bent to pick up the basket and stood facing Lo. "Do you want to sell the ranch?"

"I don't know. It's losing money, and this is peak season but crops are going fallow, horses are scenery, and Peter doesn't have his heart in it anymore. If there's no one to enjoy the place, what are we all working our guts out for? Well, not me, I'm sitting around like a piece of outdated furniture. Sue-Anne will start dusting me soon."

"Okay, but do you want to sell the ranch. Yes or no?"

Lo looked at her, chewing her lip. "No, not really. No, I don't."

"Then don't."

Lo laughed incredulously.

"I mean it. Let's clean up the guesthouses. I'll help you. Let's get these horses back into shape. The sale's coming up so maybe we can get ourselves out of trouble for now."

"I'm pretty sure Peter's made up his mind." Lo turned to take the basket back to the washhouse with Gloria.

"Did you always let Peter make decisions for you?"

Lo laughed again. "Never! Things are different now. He cares and I don't."

Gloria took her by the elbow and stopped her on the stairs. "You should care."

Lo lifted her chin resolutely. "There's nothing left to care for."

A wave of different emotions hit Gloria at once. She felt sorrow for Lo and hurt that she didn't count. But who was she? No one, just the hired help, bleeding her heart out onto the wooden steps, stupidly, irrationally, and inconveniently. She wanted to run and remove herself from the source of her hurt, but she did not. Instead, she reached out toward it with her free arm. "You don't have to care, but I care for you."

Lo pulled away and opened the washhouse door. "Pass the basket here." She tossed the basket on top of the machine and let the door swing shut again. "Gloria." She clutched her arms against her stomach, pulling herself in. "Don't…It's easier if we don't." Her eyes were beseeching.

Heat flashed across Gloria's cheeks. "You don't have to say it."

Lo nodded once. "Thank you."

"What did you want to show me anyway?" Gloria had lost patience with her feelings as she had with this perfect blue sky on a perfectly horrible day.

Lo hesitated, looking out toward the barn. "It's nothing really. Just something I noticed. Are you going down to the horses?"

"Yes, I'm going to keep getting them ready for sale if that's the plan."

"All right, come on."

They walked down to the field in silence, Gloria aware of Lo keeping her distance at a professional level. As they approached the dressage horses, Hamlet looked up and ambled over and Sonnet came along behind.

"Do you think her hock is puffy?" Lo asked, pointing to Sonnet's back leg.

Gloria took another look. "It does look swollen. I wish I could get closer." She climbed through the fence and Sonnet backed away, her head low, watching Gloria intently.

"Don't be silly, little mule," Lo said.

Sonnet lifted her head and regarded Lo. Hamlet delightedly came to push his way past Gloria to hang his head over the fence for Lo to pat. Gloria tried to get near Sonnet, but she whisked out of the way.

"Oh, you're right, she's lame. Shit, this could be my fault." Gloria glanced over at Mandalay, who was ambling slowly toward them from the other end of the field. "How are we going to get a look at that now?" She made another attempt to slowly approach Sonnet, but she wasn't having any of it.

Lo patted Hamlet once then backed away. "Not again."

Kip came along the fence line, leading two pregnant mares in one hand. He stopped to watch Gloria make another attempt to reach out toward Sonnet. "That mare ain't never going to recover. Best thing for it would be a bullet."

Lo turned sharply. "It's none of your business. Don't you have some place to be?"

"Yes, Dolores, I do. These are the last two to drop, then we're done. You turned soppy in the head or what? If you ain't gonna ride that thing and she ain't fit to breed with, with that temperament, then might be time to face facts. Not so long ago you would have shot her yourself."

"Kip." Gloria tried to steady him.

"Well, she's the only one that can handle her and she won't." Kip sighed. "You're right, I got stuff to do. Just don't hurt yourselves tending to that thing." He tipped his hat and clicked his tongue for the mares to walk on. Hamlet reached out his neck inquisitively to sniff at the mares but Kip swung the end of the rope, catching him on the nose, and Hamlet pulled back and tossed his head.

"Is that true?" Gloria asked, turning to Lo.

"Is what true?" Lo blinked.

Gloria could read her face by now. "That Sonnet will let you handle her?"

Lo scratched her cheek. "She used to, of course, but I haven't touched her. Listen, I'm going to go inside. You know what you're doing. I'll…I'll see you later."

Gloria watched Lo walk back toward the house, her head bent and her feet striking a hard path. Gloria shook her head and went to rub the soft skin between Hamlet's nostrils. "Kip's a bully. Ugh, people are the worst, aren't they? Horses are much better people than people." She slung one arm over his great neck and he stood quietly, taking her weight as she leaned into him. She watched Sonnet, her hind leg pushed forward as she grazed, her woolly coat beginning to shed in patches to reveal sleek dapples beneath. Gloria longed to get at her with a curry comb and rub away all that fluff to let her summer coat shine through. "We're all a bit rough around the edges at the moment, aren't we, boy?" Hamlet's ears swiveled but he didn't budge. "I wish I could afford to buy you and bring you home with me. I'd have to sell my house for that. And you," she addressed Sonnet. "I'd probably get you for a song, pardon the pun, but I'd still have to lug you back to Australia. I'm not sure how you'd find that after living in these lush fields. No big cats, I suppose. You'd have to get used to the kangaroos instead, I'm not sure you'd like that. Klaus would whip you into shape though." Gloria patted Hamlet's silky chest thoughtfully. A thought bloomed rapidly in her mind. She wondered what time it would be in Victoria. "You wait there," she said to Sonnet. "And you, mate, we'd better do some work."

She brought Hamlet into the barn and saddled him, then took him out the back to the arena where Sonnet wouldn't be able to see them. She could hear her whinnying but she ignored it and began to warm Hamlet up, slightly distracted. Hamlet was sluggish, preferring to lean down into the bit and shuffle along. Gloria had to work hard to get him off the forehand and engaged behind, which wasn't usually a problem for him.

"Are you trying to tell me you don't want to go to Australia and do any real work? Trust me, if I could keep you, I would. Well, I think Lo should keep you. She's forgotten how much fun you are, not when you do that, though." She gave him a dig with her heels as she spoke to get his attention as he fiddled with the bit in his mouth and slothed along. "Klaus always did like a challenge, horses and women included. I think he'd even take Sonnet on, provided we can get her sound again. I'm sure he'd take your mistress on too." Gloria's mouth set into a grim line at the thought.

After almost an hour she had to be content with Hamlet's efforts, which weren't his best. She took him back and brushed him and prepared a feed for him for when he'd settled and left him in a loose box, which she usually didn't do because of Sonnet. She went out to check on the mare who had found a friend in Mandalay and was grazing crossly. She appeared unharmed apart from her injured hock. "Good!" Gloria said, happy that at least one thing was going well. She put Hamlet's feed into his tub, filled up his water, and slung a haynet over the door. "Remember this life? The life of a busy competition horse?" Hamlet ignored her, too busy with his grain. Gloria left him like a pig at a trough with sloppy feed sticking to his face, and went to find Lo.

Lo was on the phone in the living room, her back to the door, nervously wrapping and unwrapping the curly cord around one index finger. The living room seemed static after the constant motion outside, like stepping into a drawing. Gloria waited for a moment, hoping Lo would notice her, but she was hunched down into the receiver, the lines of her body burdened with tension.

"I don't see why you changed your mind so suddenly. I thought we were on the same page." There was a pause and Lo turned her head slightly to look out of the window. "You keep telling me what's good for me, but I'm not your surrogate child. The ranch means something to me in a way that it doesn't to you." Her voice was bitter and she sighed as she listened to someone on the other end talking. "I don't see how when there's an elephant in the room the shape of a child, our son! It wouldn't matter if we're living here or the moon, I'm not suddenly going to forget him and move on." Her voice broke as she started to cry. "I know I owe you something that can never be repaid…" Gloria silently left the room, scarcely trusting herself to breathe. *Oh, Lola, stop.* She went to the kitchen to make coffee, spilling it onto her hand and the counter. Outside the window, birds were chirping hysterically from their nest in the eaves. Gloria sat down at the table, warming her hands on the mug. It was pink with white cursive writing that read "Home is where the heart is" inside a curling heart. It seemed improbable that Lo had bought this mug, perhaps a Sue-Anne purchase or Lo's elusive mother with her pastel paisley scarf. Gloria wasn't looking forward to dinner, a mishmash of motives coming together to eat food and skim the surface of conversations. Thank goodness there would be alcohol involved.

After a couple of minutes, Lo came into the room and looked startled by the sight of Gloria. Her face was blotchy, her lashes darkened.

"Oh, sorry. I didn't expect to see you there."

"Coffee's hot if you want some. I actually came in to speak to you, but I couldn't find you." The lie slipped easily over Gloria's tongue.

Lo looked at her a beat too long before she spoke. "I was on the phone to Peter." She looked away and skirted the table to help herself to a cup.

"How do you feel about tonight?"

Lo looked up, one hand on the open cupboard door. "Tonight? Oh, right, dinner. It wasn't my choice, but it might be okay?"

Gloria took a gamble. "I wish it was just the two of us." She was not rewarded. Lo filled a plain white cup and let the comment hang without response. Feeling slightly angry, Gloria said, "I think you should help with the horses."

Lo leaned against the kitchen counter and held her coffee cup with both hands. The steam snaked up toward her chin. Gloria turned in her chair to see her better.

"I don't think it's a good idea," Lo said.

"So you're totally fine with the horses being sold?"

Lo shrugged. "Not really, but there's no other choice."

"Lo, you could try. Isn't that the age-old expression, 'Get straight back on the horse'?" Lo took a sip of coffee but didn't respond. "Who's your trainer? Aren't they interested in what's going on?"

"It was Caroline Bandiana. We're no longer on speaking terms after Peter threatened her with legal action for the accident. He blamed her poor training but there was no basis to it, he was just looking for someone to lash out at." Lo's voice was thickened from her earlier tears, her face expressionless. "So, evidently, he does hold someone accountable and that someone would have to be me." She looked down into her cup. "Sorry. Sometimes I feel bad for you walking into this mess. Peter is just running around trying to fix something that can't be fixed."

Gloria's facade of anger dissipated. "Maybe you have nothing more to lose. Get back on the horse. I think you're the only one who may be able to help with Sonnet."

"Gloria, I don't think I can."

Gloria's eyes flicked over Lo's, searching for something more. "Then Klaus may be interested in buying them. I could take them back with me."

"When?"

"Well, Mike is here, so it would make sense if I went back with him. He could help me with both of the horses. Start thinking about a price and we'll make Klaus an offer. At least the mare has good bloodlines as a breeding prospect, and Hamlet is an easy sell."

Lo's eyes filled with tears again and she started to weep softly, one hand shielding her face. Gloria stood up and took the cup from Lo's hand and placed it on the counter. "Come here." She took Lo in her arms, the fragile animal of her, strong and vulnerable, and held her against her chest. Lo wrapped her arms around her and cried into her shoulder, repressed sobs like little speed bumps along her spine. As close as they physically were, Gloria felt Lo's desperate aloneness, the way she constantly reached out to find there was no one who could catch her. Gloria wanted to hold her there forever, a transfusion of strength and knowledge that it would all be okay.

"Life is just a series of departures." Lo's voice was tearstained.

Gloria squeezed her and pulled back to look at her face, brushing a strand of dampened hair back from her forehead. "New beginnings." She sounded calmer than she felt.

Lo nodded and wiped her cheeks with the inside of her wrist. "Can I come with you?"

"Back home?" Gloria was surprised.

Lo smiled through her tears. "Outside."

"Oh." Gloria smiled too and took her hand, feeling the scar from the glass cut on her finger. "Of course you can. You can give your opinion on the mare's hock from a distance if you'd like. We'll ask Mike to come and look at it."

"Thank you," Lo said, giving Gloria's fingers a squeeze.

Gloria had Lo's answer to the question she hadn't posed. Gloria's practical side wanted to exit unfettered by emotions, but in her arrow-speared heart, the wound was split open. Lo hadn't begged her stay, hadn't said a thing. It was okay, the heart was there to pump oxygen-giving blood through locked chambers and malleable tunnels, to nourish the mind and body. *That* was all. That *was* all. That was *all*.

CHAPTER THIRTEEN

That evening, Gloria's hands shook as she applied lipstick from Lo's cosmetic drawer in the bathroom, a dark shade of browny-red, provocatively named, *Third Date*. It smelled of waxy perfume and Gloria pressed her lips together, pouting into the mirror, as close as her lips would get to Lo's now, a kiss by proxy, traveling via lipstick through time. She had on an evening dress of Lo's too, navy blue and a little tight on Gloria. It hugged her figure and she self-consciously tugged it down at the back even though it was too snug to travel either way. Lo's silver pumps fit perfectly. It had been a long time since she'd been dressed up, but she felt fatalistic about it and pleased in a doomed kind of way. She stepped away from the mirror and turned to catch herself from another angle. She looked nice, pretty, but unsure of why it mattered. There was a knock at the door and Gloria called for the person to come in. It was Lo, for who else would it be? Lo stepped into the bathroom, dressed in a silk olive-green dress with black shoes. Her hair was parted to one side and swept back into a knot. Gloria's eyes drank her in appreciatively. *Lola*, dropped from the heavens onto a Wyoming ranch, an unconscious angel learning the human condition.

"Aren't we pretty?" Lo said, lifting her chin in challenge.

The smile Gloria returned was crooked, one side cast upward to meet the challenge set by Lo's chin. "We are."

"Here." Lo held her palm out. "Earrings to match the shoes. Go on," she said before Gloria could object. She watched as Gloria fixed the diamond teardrop studs at her ears.

"They're beautiful, thank you. Thanks for all the clothes, it's been a long time since I was this dressed up. I hope I don't split the seams."

"You look stunning, ten out of ten for confirmation and balanced halt. Well, I'd better go and find Peter. This dress smells like mothballs."

Gloria watched her reflection leave. She didn't smell like mothballs, she smelled of French perfume and evaporated vanilla essence. Gloria could taste it in the back of her throat. She gave her hair a final arrangement but it bounced into the position it favored anyway, and she went out to find Peter and Lo in the hall, Lo fixing rustic gold earrings to her own lobes, Peter standing with his hands in his pockets, staring at the framed photos as Gloria had done earlier. He turned when she entered, and smiled.

"You look real pretty, Gloria. Are we ready, team?"

Gloria thanked him and waited for Lo to hastily shrug into a woolen houndstooth coat. They exited the house, Peter politely standing back for them to leave first, and they hopped into his car, Lo trying to make Gloria sit in the front beside Peter and Gloria refusing. It was like an awkward ballet of niceties.

Peter drove with quick, sharp movements, overtaking trucks and local vehicles meandering home, the scent of his aftershave mingling with Lo's perfume like the perfume section at a department store. The setting sun was radiating in electric pink waves, softening the edges of mountains and trees into solar burrs. No one spoke, Lo staring out of the window, Gloria watching the road through the gap in the car seats, and Peter concentrating on his game of king of the road. When they pulled up outside the motel where Mike was staying with its white and blue facade made to look like a chalet, he was already waiting out front in a brown suede jacket and the one pair of nice navy blue slacks he must have packed. With his white shirt underneath, open at the collar, he somehow looked very Australian without Gloria being able to pinpoint why. Gloria felt vulnerable to judgment in Lo's glamorous clothes, as though she had tried too hard for Mike. She was scared he would use it to bolster his feelings. Everyone turned their heads to greet Mike as he squeezed into the back seat, his long legs folded sideways. Gloria was reminded of the time her father had commented that Gloria and Mike would produce long-legged offspring. Even though it was intended as a compliment, Gloria had found it offensive, a commentary on their compatibility at a genetic level and in the physical sense. A broodmare or heifer waiting around to drop a foal or calf with the right breeding, an inquiry into their secret bedroom life. Thinking about it now, she frowned at the back of Peter's head while Mike's warm hand came to rest on her knee. Her eyes strayed to Peter's hand on the gearshift as he put the car into drive. His hand, different to Mike's, more manicured and pale, without the little nicks and scars from working with animals, the jagged white mark Mike still had from being bitten by a parrot. Peter, able to stand before a room of people and speak with clarity and confidence, fire articulate missiles forged as they flew from his mouth. They were different men, but as Peter's hand slid to Lo's thigh, Gloria reflected that they weren't so different after all. Perhaps none of them were, because Gloria longed to touch that olive-green silk too and feel the firmness of Lo's thigh under her fingertips. *Lo-La*.

They drove out to Rivers, shooting across the highway like an arrow from a bow, the reflective markers beside the road blurring into neon lines. Peter asked Mike questions about the vet practice and Australia as though he were asking a travel agent for information before he flew out. There wasn't much to see outside the window in the dark, the occasional yellow glowing squares of farmhouses along the way and the opaque green eyes of livestock caught in the headlights. This drive was nothing like the previous time when Gloria had driven out with Lo, a quiet wandering that gave space for the two of them. This was a quartet with a score to get through. It seemed an age before Gloria caught sight of the fairy lights from the road and they pulled up at Rivers, Lo opening the car door for Gloria before Peter and Mike could butt heads over the task. As they were shown to their table, Gloria noticed people casting surreptitious eyes their way, some openly staring. Lo didn't look left or right but let Peter lead her by the hand toward a table inside by the windows beneath a yellow paper lantern. She sat beside Peter, who faced Mike, so she and Gloria were facing one another.

"I would have preferred a table outside, but we can always move outside with a glass of something later." Peter looked across at Mike and Gloria.

"I'm okay, mate. Glo Worm?" Mike turned to her.

Gloria shrunk a little with embarrassment at his pet name for her being spoken as a proprietary display of intimacy.

"I'm fine with whatever everyone wants." She picked up the menu and began to study it.

Mike and Peter seemed not to notice and plunged into a conversation about surfing, which Mike was good at and Peter was desperate to try. Gloria glanced over the top of the menu at Lo, who was studying the menu while one hand pleated and unpleated a fold in the white linen tablecloth.

Peter interrupted himself to address Lo. "Doll, why don't we get the banquet and pair the wines, hey? I'm sure they can do a vegetarian thing for you, Gloria. I'll inquire." He raised his hand to get a waiter's attention.

The waiter came and Peter negotiated what he considered the best menu for the four of them. Peter was a good showman, turning interactions into a performance, and Mike seemed taken in. Lo shot Gloria a look that said she wasn't as impressed. Gloria gave Lo's foot a small kick under the table, and Lo smiled into her menu before handing it to the waiter. When Lo looked up, she mouthed, "I need a drink." Gloria glanced sideways at the men, but Mike was already offering to take Peter to his family's surf shack and show him the basics.

"Looks like you might be coming to Australia soon," Gloria said.

"It won't happen. He just gets overexcited about stuff like a little kid, but if it doesn't materialize in the next month he will have moved on to the next thing. The big barn is full of exercise equipment, gadgets, bikes, even a jet ski. He's been given some great things by clients too. I told him to sell them, but he never has time to use them let alone sell them. The quad bike we use, that's about it."

"What are we selling?" Peter asked, catching the last part of the conversation.

"The toys in the big shed. We should get rid of them."

"Oh, right. When we liquidate, we can auction it all. Come to think of it, we can throw it in with the farm equipment."

Gloria noticed Lo's face frost over, but Mike, who was largely innocent to the whole situation, was interested. "You're definitely selling up? That must be hard, it's a beautiful ranch."

A white wine arrived but Peter was not to be derailed. "It's the best thing for us, moving forward. It was always a big ask, managing the practice and a working ranch and now that it's just sitting idle, it's a financial drain. If we sell, we can afford a beautiful place in town, there are some lovely historical homes, or we could think about a total change and chase the bright lights. I know Lo always wanted to have a city view. A high-rise with a view over the Hudson or something. New York, New York?" He turned to look at Lo. When she didn't meet his eyes, he shrugged. "We could travel, invest, start fresh. I wouldn't be opposed to building something here either." He reached an arm expansively backward to drape it over Lo's chair.

"I don't think we need to discuss this now," Lo said to no one in particular.

"Sure, Doll." Peter stroked the back of her neck and fell quiet for a moment, then resumed his discourse. "Did I mention that Brewster is very interested in our piece of land? It makes sense, as he's our closest neighbor and he knows we keep things in good shape. He'd keep Kip on too. As much as I want a good price, we'd want it to fall into the right hands. Brewster's keen on the stock too."

Gloria swallowed her wine too hastily and felt it singe her nostrils. She could see how serious this discussion was about to become and even Mike had found a thread on his cuff that required attention.

Lo cocked her head to the side. Her voice was dry like autumn leaves. "And how would that conversation have come about?"

Peter didn't flinch. "He stopped by the other day to ask how we were doing, so I told him. It makes no sense to hold our cards close at this stage. Wouldn't you prefer the place to go as a parcel to Brewster than be divided or sold to an outsider?"

"It's not going to be sold." Lo leaned back to allow the waiter to place a small plate with artichoke hearts with herbed baby potatoes in front of her. The waiter seasoned the dishes with a large pepper grinder and Peter waited with pursed lips.

Valiantly, Mike cleared his throat and commented that he'd never had artichokes before, piercing one on the end of his fork and holding it up to examine it before he put it carefully into his mouth. Gloria chewed on a potato, experiencing the crisp outside and the cloudy white inside. It was delicious, but her appetite was waning. Lo was also chewing slowly. She swallowed with difficulty and looked up at Mike. "I apologize for the tension that discussion created. Can we start again?"

"No problem, Dolores. Gloria and I can go outside and look at the stars if you need some time to talk."

"Oh, please stay. So, tell us how the trip has been so far. Have you had a chance to take much in?"

The conversation was halting at first but, assisted by wine, it began to flow again. There was still a darker undercurrent pulling at Lo and Peter waiting to come to the surface once they had privacy. Gloria was glad that she didn't have to stand under the weight of the night sky with Mike. As more food arrived and they grew warm and plush with drink, Gloria's thoughts thickened like whipped cream and she had to call her eyes to heel when too often they strayed to find Lo's red-wine-stained lips or her quick intelligent eyes. Mike's hand sought her thigh beneath the table, but it was Lo's gaze on her lips as she spoke that made her aware of her own skin in the candlelight. Gloria could see how Peter and Lo were a handsome couple, like a matched pair of carriage horses, sleek, proud, drawing admiring glances, but their temperaments seemed in disharmony. As much as she looked at Lo, she mustn't interfere, had already slunk in between the shadows of their union in a way which was unholy. Lo pushed a strand of chestnut hair behind her ear in a gesture that was painfully Dolores, elegant and unassuming, and Gloria put her hand on Mike's thigh and smiled at the waiter as he leaned in and confidentially told a story about the marriage of rosemary and thyme. Gloria listened intently, her face arranged correctly but her mind was elsewhere.

Peter kept his drinking to a minimum, happy to fill their glasses and join in just as merrily as the conversation got sillier. By all accounts, it was a successful double date, even despite Mike's inquiry as to why there wasn't a team of tiny Ballantynes running around the ranch. Peter laughed it off and said he hoped one day there would be. Lo smiled for her life and looked into the candle flame until the conversation had moved along. Gloria kicked her ankle under the table and when she looked up, gave her a wink, which brought a genuine smile, albeit a sad one, to her face.

"Let's go outside for a bit, hey? I want to see these famous fairy lights. Boys?" Gloria turned to Mike and Peter.

"Huh?" Peter paused in his animated story about a court hearing where the judge kept falling asleep.

"Would you like to come outside and look at the lights?"

Peter looked across the table. "They're about to bring dessert!"

"We won't be long," Lo said. "I'm full anyway, you can eat mine."

Peter rolled his eyes. "Okay, kid." And returned to his conversation.

Gloria and Lo stood in unison, an unspoken need bringing them to their feet, and put on their jackets. As they walked to the door, their hands brushed, their fingers whispering together then falling away. Outside the air was cool and clean. Music, a woman crooning gently, ebbed above the chatter of people sitting and standing in clusters. And the lights, caught in the arms of the trees like twinkling webs, holding them all trapped under the night. They found a bench along the railing and sat against one another for warmth with the sound of the stream below restlessly coursing its way from the mountains. Gloria could feel Lo's shivering thigh pressed against hers, and she wanted to take her on her lap and hold her close, wrap her arms around her and breathe in the scent of her warm body as it met the cold air. It was the solidarity of Lo beside her, pressed against her, that let Gloria know there was a secret, the kind that gets forged in the trials of girlhood; it was them against the world. It was that unspoken secret that made it hard to do what she knew she had to. She looked around at the people sipping drinks, laughing, yelling, dancing, hugging, scowling, kissing… people whose lives lacked the magic of Lo. She regretted it for them and envied it slightly, the push and pull of heartbreak that she knew was soon to enter her life like a dancer standing in the wings, ready to take the spotlight. They were quiet, Gloria collecting each part of her view, setting it in stone because it was happening now and wouldn't again.

"Glo?" Lo turned her face toward Gloria.

"Hmm?" Gloria had been watching the leaves shifting to-and-fro across the moon but she glanced around.

Lo's cold hand found her cheek and she leaned in and kissed Gloria, their lips meeting smooth and velvety. This time when they pulled away neither flinched nor got up and ran. "I'm sorry for the way I've been," Lo said, her hand dropping to find Gloria's.

Gloria smiled. "There's nothing to be sorry about." She gently drew Lo to her and kissed her again, deeper this time, their lips parting. Gloria could taste the alcohol and another taste like rain. *Lo-La*. She drew back and they looked at each other for a long moment. Lo smiled softly and Gloria ran her thumb along the silky terrain of her wrist. "Are you okay?"

Lo nodded. Then, as if suddenly aware of her surroundings, she swung her head to look around and the music seeped back into Gloria's ears, the cold ran its hand along her arms. The revelry continued on around them, but Gloria knew they had taken a grave risk. "We should probably go in."

"One more minute. Give me one more minute with you." Lo's fingers intertwined with Gloria's and they sat side by side, Gloria's lips burning with the memory of Lo's. Lo's voice whispered like the stream below. "If I asked you to stay one more week, would you?"

Gloria watched Peter and Mike walk outside and look around, failing to notice them through the crowd. She wasn't ready to let go yet. "Don't, Lola, I can't. What's a week? You have your life to sort out and I can't keep running from mine."

Lo nodded slowly. "How long then?"

"I'll call tomorrow and book a flight."

Lo was squeezing her hand. "Tonight then, give me tonight?"

"How? We can't." Gloria wanted to say that nothing apart from forever would be enough. One more day, one more week, one more dance before heartbreak stepped from the wings. They had never discussed Peter or their marriage—it would be reality crudely piercing their pink-edged bubble.

Lo seemed about to say something but Peter's voice was loud. "There you are. Is it martini time or home time?"

Mike looked full of bounce but Lo said, "Time to go home," and her hand slipped from Gloria's. No one disagreed.

On the way home, Mike and Gloria sat in the back holding hands across the middle seat and Lo sat in front with Peter, her head turned away, staring into the black window. Gloria could feel herself bodily in the car, the warmth of Mike's palm, her pantyhose grating on the seat, but she felt light and unmoored, bobbing somewhere above herself, being swept along. She participated in the conversation Mike and Peter were having, and every now and then she caught sight of Lo's sullen profile. She wanted to run from it all. She could tell Mike wanted her to say that she'd stay with him but she didn't, and as he leaned in and kissed her on the cheek, he whispered drunkenly, "You look sexy." Gloria smiled with her mouth and felt relief that there was one less person to interact with when he left the car.

At home Peter and Lo sat down in the living room and Gloria went upstairs to change into something more comfortable. Her feet were unaccustomed to wearing high heels anymore, and it was with something close to bliss that Gloria kicked them off and slipped into Garfield, chastened and stiff as he was from Sue-Anne's firm hand. She heard the unfamiliar sound of the television go on and Peter's laugh ring out. In front of the mirror, she removed Lo's earrings and placed them carefully on the dresser. The dress she hung back on its hanger and lined the shoes up neatly beneath it, ready to return. Her reflection looked tired. Her lipstick was just a faint stain and there were violet shadows beneath her eyes. Only her limbs looked toned and strong. She would miss Kip and Samuel too, Sue-Anne of course, and her delicious meals. Downstairs, Peter's laugh chimed in with the canned laughter of a sitcom. Gloria went to peer over the railing at the living room. Everything felt so final, the final time she would look down onto the household's evening rituals, as disordered as they were, Peter's ebony head, Lo's long legs folded to the side, her heels flipped onto the floor. Lo rested her elbow on the arm of the sofa and let her head fall into the crook of her arm. From this new vantage point she looked up at Gloria. She didn't say anything but she looked sad. Gloria looked down at her, a tiny Alice in Wonderland below. She felt like a giant tear might escape her own eye and plop down onto the miniature scene below, drowning them both. Lo let her eyes return to the television, and for the hundredth time Gloria's mind played tug-of-war with her heart.

Bedtime brought no relief. Her blank eyes searched the dark space in front of them, finding only the darker clumps of shadows and the lighter outline of the window behind the curtains. She wasn't sure how long she had been lying there listening to the wind rattle branches against the wall, half an hour or possibly three hours, when the door opened and she saw Lo's gray silhouette framed by the gentle landing light. She had on an oversized T-shirt and tube socks falling down around her ankles. Her voice was quiet. "Gloria?"

Gloria made a croaky noise and Lo's ghostly figure entered the room and came to stand beside the bed. Gloria opened up the blanket and Lo slid in beside her. Gloria moved back and they lay facing one another, their faces only inches apart, the warm spot where Gloria's head had been resting between them. Gloria wasn't surprised; instead it felt like it was predestined to happen, Lo's socked feet meeting Gloria's, her right hand wedged between her face and the pillow, her left hand finding the dip between the side of Gloria's hip and her ribcage. Wonderingly, Gloria reached up and traced a finger across Lo's satiny lower lip.

"Are you all right?"

"I just want to be near you," Lo said.

"Can we stay here like this forever?"

"Mm-hmm. Forever in this one long minute." They looked at each other for a long time without speaking before Lo said, "Will you fly back with Mike?"

"Yes. It's a long flight, and being stuck together might force productive conversation." Gloria pushed a strand of hair back from Lo's forehead.

"So you want to get back together?"

Gloria considered that for a moment. "I honestly don't know, but if there's something you taught me it's that running from problems doesn't solve anything."

"I taught you?" Lo's brows shot up into her wisps of fringe.

Gloria smiled. "You may not realize it, but you're a strong person. It's put my problems into perspective."

Lo's fingers played along the hem of Gloria's gray T-shirt. "It doesn't seem that way to me. I used to feel energized by a challenge, now leaving the house is exhausting."

"That'll improve, it has already, so much!"

"I still haven't been on that horseback ride."

"Tomorrow? We can get up early and go."

Lo twisted the T-shirt hem into a knot. "You think so?"

"Yes."

"One last ride before you call Klaus and the horses are gone."

Gloria couldn't make out Lo's expression in the dark. "He said it's my decision. How are you feeling about it?"

"Doesn't matter, ranch or no ranch, they're wasted here. You can send me photos from competitions. Hamlet wears a tri-colored ribbon well. You'll make a good team. You know, part of me wants to keep Sonnet, I'm not sure why. Is it twisted, knowing that Terrence was riding her when he fell?"

Gloria frowned. "No. Do you want to keep her?"

Lo thought for a moment, her socked foot running restlessly along the bridge of Gloria's. "I think she should stay with Hamlet. She suffered a trauma too, so it wouldn't be fair. Plus, who knows, one day there might be a little Sonnet foal running around. I'd like to see that."

"Would you come and visit?"

Lo snorted then hushed her voice again. "I can barely make it down the drive, I don't think getting on a plane to Australia is an option. Sorry, my love."

"No, I suppose not." There was a question that Gloria had been mulling over for weeks. "Can I ask you why…How do you feel?" At the last moment she drew back from articulating what she meant.

"I feel like new growth emerging from a burned and blackened tree stump. That was largely your doing, and for that I'll be forever grateful."

"But I haven't done anything."

"You've allowed me to find myself without patronizing me or putting expectations on me, created space so I can breathe while being there. It's a warm feeling, knowing you're there. It'll be really tough when you're gone. Even though I've been hot and cold, I've never stopped wanting you around."

Gloria understood that warm feeling, like sunshine on her face. She hesitated again, not wanting to pressure Lo or say the wrong thing. "I'm going to miss you. It's been a long time since I've felt this way about anyone."

Lo's eyes gleamed as she looked slowly over Gloria's face. "I never thought I'd feel anything at all and now here we are."

"Now here we are." Gloria's finger drew along the swell of Lo's cheek and along the ridge of her nose to the acute tip. She loved the definite way it announced the peak of her face. She traced her finger down its middle and back over Lo's lips, committing it to memory. "The day I met you was the day I started my goodbyes to so many things, my sanity for one. You really shook me up, but the strange thing is it never felt odd that you're a woman. It feels familiar somehow."

"I know what you mean. It's strange but also just the same. I didn't tell you because I didn't want to encourage you, but before Peter I was in love with a woman, Kate. We broke each other's hearts more than once, and in the end I chose the conventional option, probably out of pressure from my family. I loved Peter, I did, but not with the passion I had for Kate, or for you. I'm sorry I didn't tell you sooner. It seems silly that we've never discussed our own feelings, but I didn't want to go through another heartbreak. It may have found me anyhow. That's something I've pondered since my first crush, the vulnerability we experience with romantic love. Why does it take such courage to reveal ourselves to someone? Are we so hardwired to fear rejection?"

"On a primal level perhaps it's a governing force. You don't owe me your past, it's only now that matters, what we have left of it." Gloria smiled. "But my feelings…How much time have you got?"

Lo pretended to look at a nonexistent watch. "About six hours actually." Her lips curled up, and although Gloria couldn't see the smile lines forming at the edge of her mouth, she knew they were there. "Did this take you by surprise?"

Gloria took her time to think it over. "In a word, yes. I mean I certainly didn't come here expecting to meet anyone, let alone a woman, and you were slightly terrifying in the beginning."

Lo laughed. "I really didn't want you around!"

"I could tell!" Gloria pressed a finger into Lo's chest. "But to be honest, I didn't know if there even was a 'this.'"

"Yeah, this is nothing. I hold hands with every girl I meet, particularly Australian girls."

Gloria flicked her shoulder with the back of her fingers. "How do I know how you feel? You're the married one, it's not up to me to say anything. I never in my life thought I'd have an affair."

"You're not, I am."

"Are you?"

Lo shrugged. "I'm trying not to. Really we haven't done anything. Well, that's what I keep telling myself. I can't take any more guilt, I'm at saturation point."

"Do you still love him?"

"Peter? Oh, he's pretty easy to love in a sweet puppyish way. It may not seem like it, but I feel loyal to him, like I owe him my presence at least. It was my fault that our family was destroyed. As you can see, he is trying to salvage it, start again. He always wanted a big family. If he can't accept our new reality, then I'll understand. I don't need him, not in that way anymore, but I can't hurt him either."

"That's why I need to go. I can rebuild my life and you can rebuild yours. I hope I've helped with the horses in some small way. You have a buyer now and I think we'll be able to get Sonnet onto the plane if we sedate her and put her next to Hamlet. They've flown before, which is good." Lo made a little honk of agreement and Gloria swept the fringe from her eyes again. "Are you tired? Maybe you should go back to bed?" Lo shook her head slightly but her eyes were closed. "Won't Peter wonder where you are?"

"No." Lo moved closer to Gloria and entwined her bare legs with hers.

Gloria wrapped her arms around her, feeling the warm weight of her, the faded scent of perfume and shampoo, and lay watching over her while her arm grew numb and her shoulder cold. Eventually sleep took her too, and she was walking through her old neighborhood and she knew Lo lived in one of the houses but she couldn't remember which. She jerked awake and there was daylight framing the window and Lo, pale and pillow-marked, was watching her. Gloria blinked and a slow smile spread across her face. "Was I snoring?"

"Only a little bit."
Gloria winced. "Sorry."
"Are we going out on that ride?"
"You want to?"
"Let's go."

CHAPTER FOURTEEN

A pink light bleached the fields and the wind shook the spiderwebs still threading the grass with silver. For once it was Sonnet who came to the fence first, sniffing at the apple Lo offered but just missing out as Hamlet barged through to get at the treats and pats. Lo fed him apple from her hand and he snuffled at her pockets greedily. Gloria rubbed at his mane while Lo held out her hand for Sonnet to sniff at. Eventually Sonnet got up the courage to take a piece of apple before backing up behind Hamlet to chew it. Hamlet shook himself, spraying apple foam across Gloria's jacket.

"Have some manners, you Ham," Lo said, pushing him away.

"Let's bring him in," Gloria said. "Let me find Mandalay and put him in here while you get Hamlet ready."

Lo's face had taken on a grim resolve, and to any observer she was a well-trained horsewoman, doing what she always did, but to Gloria, a small miracle was happening. Gloria trusted that Hamlet would give Lo no cause for concern, and she went to fetch Mandalay and bring in Dodger for herself; she wanted a last ride with him too.

Lo stood at the mounting block, her hands poised on the saddle while Hamlet stood four-square, rattling his bit. "Goofball. Okay, I've got this."

"You're the goofball, come on, unless you want Kip and Samuel joining us too."

"No thanks!" Lo placed her left foot in the stirrup and swung herself up. "Okay, you're tall, Hamlet. I can't believe I was ever okay with being up this high."

"Where to, Lola-berry?"

"This way, ma'am." Lo applied gentle aids to Hamlet and he stepped smoothly out, as though understanding the responsibility placed on his broad back. Lo turned to smile at Gloria. "Thank you."

Gloria smiled and said nothing as they headed off along the path toward the tree line, Dodger jogging to keep up with Hamlet's long stride. The breeze pulled at Lo's ginger ponytail and mussed Gloria's dark hair more than it already was. Despite Lo's nerves, she sat loose in the saddle, her heels firmly downward but her hands light. Her gaze pointed between Hamlet's curving ears, she sang a quiet song, the wind catching words and throwing them Gloria's way. It was their jukebox song from the diner. They left the fenced fields behind and Dodger's stride quickened. Against the swaying grass, blond and fluffy at the tips, and the bruised mountains in the distance, Lo with her hair the same color as her boots, Hamlet's gleaming conker coat and his carousel carriage, they looked like a commercial for an all-American saddlery range. Gloria smiled to herself and locked another memory in the vault.

"All this open space calls for some coal in the boiler," Lo said.

"I'm willing and able, but I'll let you steer the train."

Lo grinned and urged Hamlet into his expansive trot and Dodger broke into his tight little canter to keep up. They coasted along, the swish of the grass and the thud of hoofbeats vibrating up through the ground, the smell of crushed seeds all around. Lo rode with as much grace as she did everything else, the little indefinable finesse all her movements carried evident in the way her body flowed and her hands directed. It would be futile to tell her how perfect she looked to Gloria, Lo wouldn't comprehend it, and she was lost in her own moment, the freedom and beauty gifted from horse to rider. She was in her own world again, the subtle push and pull from heel to knee to waist, to chest to elbow, to neck to head. Almost undetectable but she was communicating with Hamlet and he was communicating back. They trotted all the way to the tree line and entered into the sheltered trail through the pines, the smell of crushed needles and sap pungent. Lo slowed and turned to look at Gloria, one hand on the back of the brown leather saddle.

"Glo, I want to show you my favorite part of the river. I remember Dad and Uncle Bobby taking me fishing here when I was a kid. There's something almost sacred about this spot. I come here sometimes on foot. At first I used to just stand right there, almost paralyzed by memories." She pointed to the beginning of the trail. "But it was like I could hear Terrence telling me it's okay." She shot Gloria a steely glance. "Sorry, am I freaking you out?"

Gloria shook her head. "Not at all."

"Okay, because it's beautiful in here."

As they rode along the trail, dwarfed by the all-seeing trees, Gloria said a personal goodbye to her surroundings. She would have loved to stay and spend more time in the rugged nature, watch summer flare and fade to autumn, autumn succumb to the frosty grasp of winter. Lo chattered on, exhilarated by her own accomplishment, pointing out species of tree and birds that Gloria often missed because she wasn't quick enough to look. She felt it was the right time to leave. Peter was spending more time at home, Lo was gaining some independence again.

Through the trees Gloria heard the sound of water and they emerged along the banks of the river in full motion, rushing against rocks and lacing the bank's edges in white foam.

"See where the trail meets the water?" Lo asked, indicating with a finger toward a worn area of the bank. "That's an animal crossing. If you have a look in the mud, you'll probably see all kind of tracks."

It was true that the area was worn, the grass trampled, but from where she was, Gloria couldn't distinguish individual tracks.

"Plenty of fish in these rivers, not that you'll be impressed. Trout, perch, salmon…tastes different if you catch it yourself. You wanna sit for a moment?"

"Sure." Gloria slid down from Dodger's back and copied Lo, who threw Hamlet's reins over a branch, admiring how relaxed she was about her valuable horse. Klaus would have skinned her alive for being so careless. Once at a dressage gala, she'd left a horse tied up to the trailer still in its bridle and Klaus had thrown a wooden-backed brush at her and dragged her inside the trailer, where no one else could see, to berate her about endangering his horses. The only endangering she had done was to his bridle as the horse rubbed its face on the wall, but she'd never made that mistake again until now.

Gloria and Lo sat side by side on a log, Lo twirling a long stem of grass between her fingers, those restless fingers that always needed something to do. Among the green of the grasses and trees and the blue below and above, Gloria felt very small. It was a humbling experience to be far from anything she knew, surrounded by nature which would carry on regardless of her presence.

"It's a tiny feeling, isn't it?" she asked Lo.

Lo looked around. "It's a relief not only from others but from yourself, don't you think?"

"True. It's hard not to have deep thoughts when faced with the evidence of your own insignificance. Like contemplating the night sky."

Lo nodded and trailed the tip of her grass stem through her fingers. "That's all I wanted to do when I took Terrence out here, just let him be a part of it all."

Gloria watched her for a moment as Lo's eyes fell to the rushing water. "That's what any good parent would want."

Lo nodded and let out a slow sigh. "I've retraced my steps in my mind, over and over. I've imagined telling Terrence we would go into town instead, or walk on foot. I can't help it, it's like a movie looping through my mind. He was buried in the family lot, back that way." She didn't look up but indicated with the tip of her grass stalk over her shoulder.

"Do you go there to visit his grave?"

"Not once. You can judge me for that if you like, but I just can't face it. I have my spot, a ring of wildflowers in a clearing. It was a special place we used to visit and make castles out of sticks and rocks. He loved it there."

Gloria reached an arm around Lo's shoulders and let her head flop against Lo's. "Do you want to go and see it?"

"Oh, he's safe with his grandpop and all the rest."

"We don't have to."

Lo watched a dragonfly zip above the water grass. "I remember Terrence chasing after dragonflies, determined to catch one to see if it looked like the dragon in his book."

"That's sweet."

"He was a little boy with a big personality, let me tell you. Nothing scared that kid." She threw down her grass stem and stood up. "Come on then, he must have got that from someone, and it sure wasn't Peter."

Gloria smiled at Lo's back as she retrieved Hamlet's reins and performed near acrobatics trying to get her foot up into the stirrup, ignoring Gloria's offer of assistance. They set back out on the trail, Lo stiff-backed but determined.

The graveyard was in a cleared little field contained by a faded wooden fence leaning slightly to one side. Lo patted Hamlet's neck as they approached, soothing herself along with him. Dodger snorted and his head rose as he skittered to the side. Gloria wasn't sure if he could somehow sense that death was around. Hamlet walked forward calmly until he was asked to stop. Lo turned to look at Gloria, her lips pale and her eyes round.

"Here." Gloria rode alongside and took Hamlet's reins while Lo dismounted, looking small and fragile beside Hamlet's bulk. She stood for a moment, one hand on Hamlet's neck, watching the quiet landscape. Despite herself, Gloria shivered and tightened her grip on Hamlet's reins even though he stood patiently. Lo walked slowly over to the gate and tried to open it but the latch was weathered, so she climbed through the rails and stood looking at the stone markers. When she started walking again something in her gait made it all too easy for Gloria to picture a plucky little boy with Lo's stubbornness playing in these fields, the vastness around them no doubt bringing them closer. From her vantage point on Dodger's back, Gloria could see the newer little tombstone, too clean and shiny beside its seasoned companions. There was a stone statue of a pony lying down with a little boy kneeling beside it. Lo went to crouch in front, reaching out a hand to place on the pony's gray stone back. Gloria wished she was able to leave and give Lo some privacy, but instead she turned her face away to look toward the clouds skittering across the sky above the mountains. Lo wasn't long. She returned to take Hamlet's reins and hoist herself back up before turning and silently heading them toward home. It seemed natural when they reached the fields surrounding the ranch that Lo let Hamlet canter on, his huge stride eating up the ground and carrying her quickly toward home. She slowed to a walk as they approached, letting the horses cool down and enter the path at a sedate pace. She didn't hang around, avoiding eye contact and leaving Gloria to tend to the horses, which Gloria was happy to do. By the time Gloria was finished and went inside the house to clean up, Lo was nowhere to be seen, so she went to the living room and called Mike to check how he had fared with travel arrangements. He told her he was able to get them on a flight in the morning. Gloria hung up and rang Klaus. She could picture the phone ringing in the room beside the stables where people could eat their lunch or relax between classes. She used that phone rather than his personal one at the house, knowing he would probably be asleep or possibly busy doing something she didn't want to hear about. The eerie sound of her own recorded voice asking her to leave a message was surreal, but she stated that she would be home within the week, deciding it would be better to give herself a few days to sort herself out at home before Klaus began demanding her time. Home. She had made this moment feel larger than life in her mind, these small acts of organization had seemed insurmountable, but they were easy, really.

She didn't see Lo all afternoon, which was just as well. Goodbyes were painful at best and Gloria, with her ability to duck out before they could happen, was certainly no expert. She was concerned that she had done the wrong thing by encouraging Lo to visit the gravesite, especially on a day where she was already taking on a lot, but she knew Lo would do what she wanted regardless of what she said. Sue-Anne knocked on Gloria's door to tell her it was dinnertime and she'd made a vegetable pie in honor of her last night. Peter was already sitting at the table, a glass of half-drunk wine beside his expectant plate, and Kip and Samuel were clattering around by the back door. Gloria sat down in her usual spot and waited for the men to get settled, one eye on the door for Lo.

"I'll go and get her, don't you worry," Sue-Anne said, passing behind Gloria and giving her shoulder a squeeze.

"So, Gloria, you finally got Dolores back on the horse. How'd you do that?" Kip asked.

"Tie a carrot to a string?" Samuel quipped.

"What?" Peter's head swung toward Kip.

"I saw 'em coming back along the back field there. Dolores was burning the ground up on the big horse."

"Dolly was up on the horse?" Peter asked in amazement, his youthful eyes shining.

Gloria shrugged, feeling uncomfortable. "It was just a quiet ride. She felt ready, I guess." Over Peter's shoulder she saw Lo enter the room, changed out of her riding clothes and into gray sweatpants and a black hoodie.

"Well, I guess I owe you fifteen hundred dollars, was it or two grand? You've done a good job getting her to ride again, I was starting to doubt I'd see it."

Gloria's face fell as she saw Lo's step hesitate at his words, but she pulled out her chair and sat.

"I don't want any money!" Gloria said.

"Don't be modest, you really are worth every dime." Peter turned toward Lo, who had turned her miserable gaze to Gloria. "Doll, I knew you could do it. That's my girl. You'll see, from now on things will start improving. You'll be back to your old self in no time."

Sue-Anne placed a plate of mashed potatoes dripping in butter on the table. Gloria tried to catch Lo's eyes, but she had retreated into herself. The meal was delicious, Sue-Anne had turned it on for Gloria's last night although, much to Kip's vexation, she kept bursting into tears every time it was mentioned. She mopped her eyes with the hem of her apron and insisted they all eat two helpings of lemon pudding with cream to cheer themselves up. Gloria couldn't fault the food, and she was grateful for Sue-Anne's efforts, but she couldn't stop trying to catch Lo's eye. She wanted to nudge her with her foot under the table and make her look, but her feet were tucked away. Lo joined in the conversation but Gloria knew her well enough to know she wasn't really present. After dinner Lo excused herself and Gloria stayed to help Sue-Anne clear up and say her goodbyes. Sue-Anne hugged her and made her promise to come back. By the time Gloria could get away, Lo was nowhere to be seen and Peter was watching television in the living room with his socked feet up on the coffee table. He called Gloria over and patted the sofa beside him, moving a bowl of pretzels out of the way so Gloria could sit down.

"Gloria, honey, how's it all been? I must say, you really pulled a rabbit out of the hat at the last second there."

Gloria sat beside him, glad of the bowl between them. "Peter, I can't thank you enough for having me stay, but I can't accept any money from you. I really"—she looked away from his eyes—"care for Lo, and we went out on a ride, that's all." She looked back, measuring his gaze for any sign of mistrust. He was hard to read. Behind the boyish good looks lurked a sharp attorney, even though she could see no trace of it now. "I'm glad that she's starting to feel social again."

"Don't be silly, Gloria, I'm a businessman. Take the money. I employed you to do a job and you've done it. You've even found a buyer for those darn horses."

"Well, I've told Klaus that it would be a lease for three months with first option to buy for the price that's been decided. If it doesn't work out, he'll fly them back at his expense and you'll have two highly trained competition horses you can sell at a vastly inflated price, or he will sell them for you, or, if Lo decides to ride, she can keep them."

"I'll get that in writing," Peter said, and Gloria knew he wasn't joking.

"Draw up a contract then. I'll have him sign it and send it on."

"I'm serious about selling the ranch, you know. We won't be taking the horses back."

Gloria shrugged. "That's up to you. I'm going to bed, but listen, you will tell Lo that I didn't take the money, won't you? I would hate to think she thought our friendship was about money." On the television the audience clapped, and Gloria stood up.

Peter glanced back at Gloria, a grin on his face for the person who just won a lawn mower. "Sure, Gloria." He leaped up to hug her, the remote control still in one hand. "She's probably gone to bed or out for a walk. Why don't you knock on the bedroom door and say bye? Chances are she won't be sleeping."

"Will do. Thanks again, Peter. Klaus or I will be in touch about transport, pending the horses' passports being up-to-date. Kip knows what to do."

"I'll leave it to the experts. Can I give you a lift to town in the morning?"

"That's okay, Kip has offered to take me."

"Good stuff. If I don't see you, take care."

"You too."

Gloria went upstairs, her eyes on Lo's bedroom door. She stood outside and listened for a moment before knocking, but no one answered. She went to her own room and finished packing what little she had. Her new pale blue dress that reminded her of Lo she left hanging in the closet. At least at home she could forget Lo existed and go back to a normal routine.

Sleep came quickly but then seemed to take her in and out of consciousness like waves on the ocean. Every small sound, the house creaking, branches in the wind, made her startle awake thinking Lo was at the door, but when the sun rose, she was still alone. She rose with dread heavy in her stomach.

Kip was sweet and insisted on taking Gloria and Mike for coffee at the diner. Mike hit it off with Kip too and wasn't deterred by Kip telling him at least three times that he had tried to seduce Gloria and that she must be in love with Mike because she refused. Gloria rolled her eyes, but no one noticed. They waited in his pickup truck for the bus to arrive to take them to the airport, and when Mike got out with the bags, Kip pulled her in for a hug and said, "Our Dolly girl, she's going to be lost without you."

"I doubt it, she didn't even say goodbye." Gloria tried and failed to keep the quaver from her voice.

"She's been through a lot. She probably didn't say it, but seeing someone she loves disappear from her life again, that's gotta hurt real bad."

Gloria felt close to tears. She should have tried harder to see her one last time. "Say goodbye for me, please, Kip. Tell her… tell her I'll write."

Kip nodded. "They're waiting on you."

"Bye, Kip. Thanks for being a friend and teaching me how to neck rein and make a horse stay like a dog." She smiled.

"Thanks for all your help, honey. You were right, you do know your way around a horse."

"I'll be in touch with the flight details for the horses." Gloria swung down and jogged to the bus where Mike was waving for her to hurry up.

CHAPTER FIFTEEN

Melbourne

Gloria's thighs ached from cantering circles in the indoor arena without stirrups.

"And change, change, change," Klaus called in time with Hamlet's stride. "Those one-time changes need to be brighter. Up from behind. Go again, long side, tempi changes, from here to here." He indicated with his whip. "And halt at K."

Gloria gritted her teeth and tried to ignore the burning in her stomach muscles. She pushed Hamlet on down the long side, collected him, and asked again. He whisked his tail in an uncharacteristic gesture of impatience but did as she asked, coming to a slightly too-abrupt halt at K. Gloria loosened her reins and patted his sweaty neck, then took him into the center of the arena where Klaus was standing dressed in his quilted blue waistcoat and beige breeches. He slapped the top of his black leather boot with the end of his whip and looked Hamlet over thoughtfully.

"I think this horse has been very poorly trained."

Gloria's face was red beneath the peak of her hard hat. "He's a very giving horse. You have to admit he's trainable and his movement is amazing."

"Hmm. He has made progress in a little over two months, and I'm not displeased with him, but prior to that he's been idling in a paddock. I wouldn't say he's in peak condition yet." Klaus's accent in no way detracted from the firm tone he took with Gloria most of the time. He had built his reputation on tough love with both his horses and his pupils, and his affair with Gloria meant he had been even stricter with her in the arena. Even though it was years since their affair, he liked to show her he was still in charge. Hamlet began to rattle at his bit. "Are you going to let him do that?"

Gloria gathered her reins and sent Hamlet back into a walk to cool off before she could return to the stables. Her legs felt like jelly and her back was bruised from being bucked off Sonnet earlier in the week. Klaus's tough love was working wonders with Sonnet, who was already back under saddle and furiously looking out for any chance she could to dismount Gloria.

As Gloria stood under the shower in her room above the stables that night, she let the hot water pummel her back and her thoughts slipped from her aches and pains to Lo. She had written her a letter apologizing for not saying goodbye, letting her know that the horses were well and outlining Hamlet's competition schedule and Sonnet's more placid moments, but she hadn't heard back. She hoped that Lo didn't think she'd been a false friend because Peter was paying her. She knew it was ridiculous; they'd shared intimate, fragile moments, just the two of them, but her rational mind kept returning to the fact that she hadn't heard from her. She had the horses as a constant reminder, even though she was learning to keep the thoughts at bay. Since coming back home, she'd been living in her old room above Klaus's immaculate stables. The tension on the plane ride home had felt like a thundercloud brewing, with Mike's frustrations becoming evident once Gloria's reluctance had also come to light. His expectations of picking up where they left off were vastly different from Gloria's expectations that they would begin again, taking things at a walk. All she had wanted to do was hide in a room and weep, but she was stuck with Mike's need and a plane full of strangers. It hadn't taken her long to realize moving back into her home with Mike wasn't an option. The house was on the market, and for the past few weeks she'd been looking after Klaus's stables in exchange for rent and pocket money. Still in its envelope, stuck to the bar fridge in her bedsit, was Peter's check that she refused to cash.

"Bloody Klaus," she said as she gingerly dried herself with a towel, careful not to flex her hands too much in case her blisters popped. She hoped her hands healed before their first competition on Saturday. She knew Hamlet had it in him, but she was finding it hard to get her groove again and the more she struggled, the harder Klaus worked her. She was aware she should be thankful. Every day there were messages from people trying to get on a waiting list for his tuition or to have him work with their horses and here she was cursing him. It hadn't taken him long to proposition her again in a rather formal way, inviting her to share his room rather than the bedsit, but she had politely declined. She preferred to spend her nights with Gonzo the stable cat curled up at her feet, occasionally reading the tattered horse magazines found lying in the tack room, but she was usually so exhausted she couldn't keep her eyes open for long.

The days went by, announced only by the countdown toward their first dressage test together. Remarkably Klaus was letting her ride Hamlet, rather than just assist with the training, so he could concentrate on his own horses. She knew if Hamlet placed highly, Klaus would turn his eye toward him and things would change. She was damned if she did and damned if she didn't. The knowledge did nothing to ease the pressure.

The morning of the dressage test was cold and foggy, but Gloria was used to getting up early to begin working all the horses she had to get through. Lanah, the cheerful groom who came every morning before school and all day on weekends to muck out the horses, was already toiling away with her wheelbarrow. Gloria hoped Klaus didn't have designs on her, but there was an inordinately high amount of good-looking female staff at the stables. Lanah stopped to pat Hamlet and kiss his nose.

"He's my favorite. He's such a cutie!" she lisped through the teal brackets of her braces.

"He is a good boy," Gloria agreed, pausing with her mane comb to watch Lanah fussing over Hamlet. She smiled and reflected on how different it was here to the ranch with all its masculine energy and open spaces. Here everything was so manicured and each item, horse, and person had an exact spot where it was meant to be at any given time, including herself. Everything was done to strict routine and procedures and there was no room for error. Hamlet ate his breakfast while she plaited his mane and sewed it into place. The first thing Klaus had made her do was pull Hamlet's mane and trim his tail, which he said gave him away as a mule from the Wild West. Remembering it now, Gloria hugged Hamlet's silky neck and said, "You're not a mule, you're a well-traveled gentlemen." She tucked the needle back into the thread and put it in her pocket where it wouldn't get lost. "Do you miss her, Hammy? I sure do." Hamlet carried on eating, unmoved by her questions, and she hopped down from the upturned bucket she'd been standing on and went around to begin on his tail.

The truck ride to the show seemed to take an age with all the horses in the back. Klaus drove, venting his nerves by making impatient comments about other drivers on the road, running his hands repeatedly trough his blond forelock, which he did when he was irritated. Monica, the head groom, sat between them, her face down in a women's magazine until she looked up and pronounced herself carsick, driving Klaus to new levels of distraction. Lanah was in the back with the horses, no doubt having much better conversation.

"Monica, what I tell you about reading in vehicle?" Klaus snapped, his accent becoming more pronounced.

Monica shut the magazine, located a mint in her handbag, and looked out of the window in a high sulk, rolling the mint against her teeth until Klaus was tooting at the traffic and Gloria was leaning so far against her side that if the door opened she would fall out. Monica had not taken to Gloria's presence kindly. When they finally got there, Monica was tasked with tending to the horses, while Gloria and Klaus went to register and get their numbers. The air was crisp and a thin mist hung over the green fields. There was already a line at the coffee van, and people were eating jam donuts as they strode about in gumboots and big coats. Excitement and nerves clawed at Gloria's stomach. She had to prove that Hamlet would be worth Klaus's investment or he would be sold on. She liked Hamlet way too much and couldn't bear the thought of Lo's horse going to some unworthy spoiled brat. The image of Lo cantering across the summery Wyoming fields with her chestnut ponytail bouncing in the wind crossed Gloria's mind, a treasure from the memory vault. She tucked it back where it belonged, it was her secret, and went to check the competitor running order. She was competing against Klaus on one of his youngsters, a black mare called Zig Zag X, and she knew he would expect to beat her. She went to prepare Hamlet and begin to warm up, away from Klaus who was liable to be snappy and expected a certain amount of warm-up space in the arena to be allocated to him just because he was a big name.

The mist began to dissipate as the sun broke through the clouds. Unlike a lot of horses who needed focusing and calming down to be ready to work, Hamlet was prone to being lazy and becoming bored, so Gloria knew not to overdo his warm-up. Instead, she took him for a long walk around to familiarize him with the environment. He was looking so longingly at a child eating a gelato that she gave in and bought him one and let him eat it while Klaus wasn't watching. "Don't tell anyone and don't get colic, or we'll both be in trouble." Hamlet curled his lip in disgust. "Now that's a telltale sign so don't do that." She startled as Lanah came flying around the side of the food truck and motioned for them to come.

"Your section has started. Klaus is in a mood!" She looked at Hamlet and went to flick some strawberry foam from his chest.

"Don't ask," Gloria said.

Before she went into the indoor arena, she watched the second rider perform the end of the test, running through it in her own mind. The arena was marked with letters to give the rider a reference as to where they needed to perform certain movements during the test. She knew Hamlet could do it all standing on his head, it was just a matter of keeping him active and engaged and on task. She watched Klaus go in and perform a revoltingly perfect test to a crowd which had gathered in the stands just to watch him. There were appreciative murmurs and claps. Gloria decided she had seen enough and went to set Hamlet on task.

As she walked a circle, waiting for the bell to indicate she could begin, she realized she'd never seen Hamlet in front of a crowd. Lo had mentioned that he enjoyed it, and as the bell went he seemed to lift another few inches off the ground. Gloria took a deep breath and let it all fall away as she felt Hamlet collect himself, lifting his hocks and rounding his back, his ears like two sharp arrows. He trotted boldly into the ring, showing off the hard work he had been doing. The test seemed to pass in a dream, Hamlet tuned in to Gloria's every request, leaving her to focus on timing and accuracy. As she halted and saluted the judge, she let out a breath she didn't know she had been holding. Hamlet swaggered out of the arena to a round of well-earned applause. Gloria had no idea how well others had done, all she knew is that she had been privileged to ride such a wonderful horse. Lanah was pink with excitement.

"I think it'll be between you and Klaus!"

Monica was leading Zig Zag X, but she stopped to say, "You actually weren't terrible. I wouldn't be surprised if you come second or third."

Gloria shrugged and moved off to walk Hamlet around away from the crowds to await the results. It was busy now, groups of competitors and their families milling around, pony club girls eating from buckets of hot chips and spectators up in the stands waiting to see the young horse classes and then the Grand Prix. Hamlet still wasn't in peak condition, but he was a fine-looking horse that people hadn't seen before, and anything from Klaus's yard drew interest. As Gloria stood in the shade of a gum tree, she was approached by a man inquiring after Hamlet's breeding and whether he was for sale.

"I'm not sure yet," Gloria said, feeling some of her enthusiasm for the day wane. "His owner lives overseas. Klaus is the best person to speak to."

It wasn't long until a woman approached with a similar inquiry, which Gloria fielded in the same way. "I'm sorry, I have to go and check results now."

"Of course you do, good luck," the woman called as Gloria began to walk away. She knew she was being rude, but she didn't care. The thought of anyone else owning Hamlet made her jealous and depressed.

"Look!" Lanah shrieked across the crowd of people and horses. "You're second! Hurry up!"

Gloria threw Hamlet's reins over his neck and scrambled up in an undignified way, eliciting a dirty look from a woman with a Highland terrier on a lead. She urged Hamlet into a trot, and they made it just in time for Hamlet to slot easily in behind Klaus on the black mare.

"Well done," he said over his shoulder, generous in his victory.

The crowd was all abuzz as the places were called and they each stepped forward to be presented with their rosette. Hamlet stood while Gloria dipped down so the judge could place a medal around her neck and congratulate her, then they were off trotting around the arena for a victory lap behind Zig Zag's gleaming rump. Music played and the crowd clapped in time. Hamlet was living it up, flicking his polished hooves out and arching his neck, pretending to be scared of the arena markers. As Gloria left the arena, well-wishers patted Hamlet and offered warm words, but Gloria felt hollow. She'd achieved better than what she had hoped to in such a short space of time, but she still didn't feel happy. She slid off Hamlet and gave him another pat. "You can have all the gelati you want now. I might even have one too."

"Hey!"

Gloria pretended not to hear and kept walking. She felt someone touch her shoulder. "He's not for sale!" she snapped, regretting it even as she turned to see who she'd been so rude to.

"I sure hope not."

Gloria stopped in her tracks, her mouth hanging half open. Hamlet had no such reserve. He bustled forward to greet his mistress by nuzzling her stomach. Lo laughed and rubbed his face. "You did good, Hammy, but you'll have to wait. I need to see my sweetheart." She looked at Gloria with her familiar gold-flecked eyes. "Hey, baby. You sure know how to ride a horse!"

Gloria stood stupidly, letting Hamlet's reins run through her hand. After a moment she whipped her hat off and patted her hair, which was parted in the middle and slicked into a bun. "What? But you...How?"

Lo's hair had been trimmed and her face was tanned. She wore a puffy green parka over Gloria's blue floral dress with cowboy boots. Gloria had never seen anything more beautiful in her life.

"But..."

"Oh, shut up and come here." Lo opened her arms and Gloria fell into them. Strong, capable arms that had been working on a ranch for weeks. Hamlet stood dopily, his reins trailing on the ground as Lanah leaped to retrieve them and people cast curious looks in their direction. Gloria had forgotten the crowd as she breathed in the scent of Lo that she didn't realize she knew so well. Her face pressed against the silky fall of hair, her arms around the familiar breadth of ribcage beneath the jacket. Her arms felt almost glued, like she couldn't let go even if she wanted to, but eventually Lo pulled back and they stood there, looking at each other, holding both hands together in between their bodies. Gloria drank Lo in, only then realizing how messy she must look herself.

"Oh, you're bleeding," Lo said, looking up from Gloria's hand to meet her eyes. "Your white breeches!"

"Stupid blisters. I'm sorry!" She looked around for something to wipe Lo's hand that had her blood on it, but she had nothing.

"Here. I brought tissues because I knew I would cry." Lo reached into her pocket and then gently pressed a tissue to Gloria's palm. "I'm not sure there's much we can do about your breeches. Can we go somewhere for five minutes? Have you got time?"

"Lola, angel." Gloria took a shuddering breath, still struggling to come to terms with this reality. "I missed you. Let's find somewhere private." She turned to Lanah. "Would you mind taking Ham back to the truck?"

Lanah nodded and began to lead Hamlet away. Gloria took Lo's hand in her least blistered one, holding it tight as though she might float away like a balloon, an angel back to heaven. She knew that Klaus or at least Monica would be around the truck getting ready for the next test, so they found a quiet bench away from the crowds. They sat, Gloria's hand shaking as it held Lo's. She put her hat on the bench beside them.

"So you're not angry at me?" she said as they sat down.

"Why on earth would I be angry at you?"

"I assumed you were angry at me because of what Peter said at the dinner table after we went out on a ride. I was worried that you thought I'd only spent time with you for money or out of a sense of duty."

"Did you?"

"No!" Gloria gave her hand a wriggle. "I might be good at what I do, but I'm not that good!"

Lo laughed. "I know. I was so full of self-doubt though. I didn't know why anyone would want to be around me, but you just sorta stuck around. I must admit that I was a bit upset when Peter said he would pay you for taking me out riding, like I was a child on a pony ride or something. Still, you need to earn a living, I understand that."

Gloria raised her eyebrows. "Are you serious? That check is still pinned to the fridge. I can't take that money, it was stupid of him to try. Perhaps you could take it back? I did ask him to let you know."

"We're not exactly speaking to each other at the moment," Lo said, starting to fiddle with the zip of her parka.

Gloria looked down at those restless fingers and noticed a white band of skin where her wedding ring had been. "What happened?"

"I guess I fell apart a bit after you left. Peter was at me about the ranch, telling me there was no point and if we moved soon we could begin a new life in town without the stresses it was bringing. He's keen to start trying again for babies"—she smiled wryly—"seeing as I'm so ancient and my years are limited. It was too much for me. I put my foot down and said I'm hanging on to the ranch. It was my uncle's and it means something to me. We've agreed to split our assets, he can keep the office and apartment in town and Brewster can buy the parcel of land near him. Peter can take the finances from that sale, then I'll keep the rest of the ranch. I've been working hard out there ever since, getting the guesthouses ready again. I don't want Sue-Anne or the boys to lose their jobs, they're really the only family I have. It'll just be me, all alone on the ranch."

Gloria pictured Lo alone on the ranch as winter fell like a gray blanket, and she squeezed her hand. "You should take the horses back with you. The three months isn't up yet, and seriously, when you see Sonnet you'll be surprised. She's come a long way. Klaus can be a prick, but he knows how to train horses."

"So she's under saddle again? She actually was a sweet horse to ride."

Gloria tensed her back muscles, which were still sore from hitting the ground. "I'm not sure if I'd say sweet exactly, but I did manage twenty minutes before I was bucked off the other day."

Lo's mouth formed a surprised circle and she laughed. Oh, how Gloria had missed that deep, throaty laugh.

"Thanks!" Gloria smiled. "I look like a piebald pony under these clothes. I'm covered in purple bruises."

"Oh, baby." Lo let go of her hand and gently rubbed her back. "I must say you do look, how will I put it? Professional, in those clothes."

Gloria looked down at her white breeches, spattered with blood, and her black leather top boots. She had felt good that morning in her white stock and black tailcoat, but now she was sporting blood, brown horse hairs, and dust. No doubt her hat had given her a red line across her forehead. Her medal hung stiffly around her neck in attempt to redeem her. "Thanks, I think?"

"You do. I couldn't take my eyes off you in the ring, and look at this." Lo lifted the medal and examined its inscription before placing it gently back against the buttons of Gloria's coat. "You make it look so effortless. I think you have a big future, with the right horse." She looked out across the green striped turf, toward the parked horse trucks and floats. "So," she said, a little too casually. "How's Mike?"

Gloria's face flushed with pleasure. It all felt so dreamlike, here at the equestrian park with Lo beside her. She had just completed a successful round on a dream horse and now here she was with Lo, who had seemingly fallen from the clouds. "I'm not sure. Probably angry. We've gone our separate ways too." She touched a finger to a blister, pressing it to feel its taut bubble.

Lo lifted her hand away and held it between hers again. "Are you okay?"

Gloria looked up and smiled. "Yes, Lola Angel, I've never been better."

Lo's pink lips pressed into a smile and Gloria thought she could see tears shining in her eyes. "I know things have been messy but I was wondering, if perhaps, I know you might not…"

"Spit it out, woman," Gloria said.

"Well, I was thinking that if the horses were to come back with me, you might consider coming back too."

Gloria's hands began to shake again. "To settle the horses?"

"To settle me!" Lo laughed and a man walking by with a takeaway coffee cup smiled to himself at the sight. Gloria knew she'd seen that radiant smile before. "Plus, I have a horse that needs a rider. His name's Hamlet, you may have heard of him after his successful test today."

She remembered that smile. Lo in the photo on her living room wall. Carefree and happy. "Beautiful horse. I've heard the owner's not bad either." She leaned playfully on Lo's shoulder. "But will Peter care?"

"Frankly, I don't care. He's living in town. He hasn't been to the ranch in ages. Don't worry, he's handling it all right, throwing himself into the legal preparations. It'll be the fastest divorce in history!"

Gloria looked off toward a marked-off arena on the grass where a rider on a large gray horse was cantering a circle. "You know, there's an interested party in our house. Once the sale goes through, what do you say we buy Peter out of the side near Brewster's? I don't want you to lose any part of the ranch—it's yours."

Lo smiled again. "I think it's definitely something we could talk about. Now, should we go and see our horse-baby?" Lo stood and helped Gloria to her feet.

"I think so. I told him I'd buy him an ice cream."

Lo put her arm around Gloria's waist. "We'd better not disappoint him, then."

Bella Books, Inc.

Women. Books. Even Better Together.

P.O. Box 10543
Tallahassee, FL 32302

Phone: 800-729-4992
www.bellabooks.com